ON THE ORIGIN OF SPECIES AND OTHER STORIES

Published by Kaya Press
kaya.com
Distributed by D.A.P./Distributed Art Publishers
artbook.com (800) 388-BOOK

ISBN: 9781885030719
Library of Congress Control Number: 2021931803
Cover Design by Kelly Moonkyung Choi
Text Design by Hwaran Yu
Illustrations by Spike Hyunsuk Kim

Magpie Series Editors: Sunyoung Park & Sunyoung Lee
Magpie Series Design Editor: Chris Ro

This publication is made possible by support from the USC Dana and David Dornsife College of
Arts, Letters, and Sciences; the Shinso Ito Center for Japanese Religions and Culture; the USC
Department of American Studies and Ethnicity; and the USC Department of East Asian Lan-
guages and Cultures. Special thanks to the Choi Chang Soo Foundation and Stephen CuUn-
jieng for their support. Additional funding provided by generous contributions from: Lydia
Arbizo, Manibha Banerjee, Partha Banerjee, Lily & Tom Beischer, Jamel Brinkley, Sonali Chan-
chani, Jade Chang, Wah-Ming Chang, Samantha Chanse, Anelise Chen, Anita Chen, Lisa Chen,
Floyd Cheung, Jayne Cho, Judy Miyoung Choi, Katelin Chow, Agnes Chu, Elizabeth Clemants,
Susannah Donahue, Irving Eng, Matthew Fargo, Sesshu Foster, Thea Gray, Kimiko Hahn, Paul
Heck, Jean Ho, Jonathan Hugo, Ann Holler, Huy Hong, Andrew Kebo, Vandana Khanna, Joonie
and Jungin Kim, Kyung Kim, Karen Koh, Sabrina Ko, Juliana Koo & Paul Smith, Kien Lam, Cathy
Lee, Ed Lin, Helen Kim Lee, Whakyung Lee in memory of Sonya Choi Lee, Andrew Leong, Nan-
cy Leong, Abir Majumdar, Shikha Malaviya, Gregory McKnight, Samhita Mukhopadhyay, Jean
Naylor, Minkyung and Yun Oh, Minya Oh, Julia Oh, Chez Bryan Ong, Eric Ong, Josephine Park,
Amarnath Ravva, Yutaka Sato, nitasha sawhney, Roch Smith, Jungmi Son, Nancy Starbuck,
Tait Sye, Joyce Talley, Alanna Taylor, Patricia Wakida, Esme Wang, Aviva Weiner, Heather Wer-
ber, Duncan Williams, William Wong, Amelia Wu & Sachin Adarkar, Anita Wu & James Spicer,
Yoojin Grace Wuertz, Nancy Yap, Max Yeh, Shinae Yoon, Mikoto Yoshida, Jenny Tinghui Zhang,
and many others.

This book is published with support from the Literature Translation Institute of Korea (LTI
Korea); the National Endowment for the Arts; the Los Angeles County Board of Supervisors
through the Los Angeles County Arts Commission; the City of Los Angeles Department of
Cultural Affairs; and the Community of Literary Magazines and Presses.

ON THE ORIGIN OF SPECIES AND OTHER STORIES

BO-YOUNG KIM

Translated by Joungmin Lee Comfort & Sora Kim-Russell

Edited and with an Afterword by Sunyoung Park

KAYA
PRESS

LOS ANGELES

 The Magpie Series in Korean Literature

Author's Introduction:
A Brief Reflection on Breasts

This is a story of breasts.

Yes, breasts. The pillowy, soft mammaries of a woman.

How important are breasts?

I can't say for sure, as I myself am a woman. I have a pair, and through pure happenstance, mine are on the full side. They've never really been an issue for me.

Imagine. Here lives a tribe consisting only of men. None of them has ever seen a woman before. They go about life with only the vaguest of notions, acquired from rumors, that something called a "woman" even exists.

Not that I would know what such men would really think. As I said, I was born female. Anyway, when these men finally encounter a woman, their eyes go straight to her breasts. Wow, look at those soft, pillowy mounds!

They put their heads together and deliberate. What is this creature? Is it even human? The general consensus is that it is not. But the more revolutionary and charitable among them decide to acknowledge the being's humanity. For now at least. Not that the matter calls for anyone's approval, but that is what happens. A lively discussion ensues. What is the purpose of such mounds anyway? Why are they there? To seduce men? The opinion that the breasts have impure intentions and thus must be covered up gains significant traction.

Over time, though, this theory of breasts veers off in a new direction. A pro-breast element emerges. Its members can't stop praising how beautiful, how mystical, how fully blessed breasts are. They proclaim that all that matters in a woman are her breasts, that a woman *is* her breasts.

How important is science in SF?
How important are breasts in a woman?

If we see a person in the distance and they seem to have breasts, we hastily assume that they must be a woman. Science seems to occupy a similar position in SF.

To many people's surprise, however, there are quite a few women out there without breasts. Breasts are not an absolute requirement for womanhood.

Psychology tells us that we "overestimate the influence of that which is readily noticeable." For instance, many of us overestimate our own social influence. This is because we are so readily noticeable to ourselves. A man who lacks adequate exposure to women might think that whatever a woman does is "because she's female," especially if her femaleness is what he notices the most about her. Similarly, if a country mouse were to join a group of city mice, the city mice might attribute anything the country mouse did to their being from the countryside, since "being from else-where" would be their most prominent trait, in that setting at least.

However, and quite understandably, there are reasons upon reasons why people are the way they are.

I am often presented with artwork that has presumably been created to show what a beautiful woman looks like, only to behold what is obviously a male torso strung with breasts without even the courtesy of a head or limbs. Those for whom this is their first glimpse of a woman are likely to gasp in distaste before retreating to the claim that women are just not their cup of tea. Better to skip the breasts, they think, and keep the other parts. Then at least the result would be recognizably human.

Of course breasts are attractive. But if someone were to ask me what I believe makes women attractive, I would say that it's the same as what makes men, or any other creature, attractive. That is, it is the attractive-ness inherent to any human being, to life. It is vitality, energy, and every-thing deserving of love.

I don't mean to insist that men and women are the same. That is anoth-er form of delusion. We are different in many aspects. Breasts are just the start of it.

Sure, breasts are beautiful—in the way the rest of the female body is.

This is the story of breasts.

P.S.

To add a note to this theory of breasts, my own body came equipped with a set.

I didn't, for example, decide one day to install a pair myself.

Similarly, many of the stories I've written came into being without me consciously trying to turn them into SF. The tales I've told have simply unspooled from inside me. It's only later that I found out that readers labeled them SF.

If this seems unbelievable to you, ask yourself whether or not you always consciously weave romance into your work. Sure, the effort may be intentional at times, but I'll bet it's mostly not. Think about how ancient, organic, and universal love is in human history. Science is no different. In the beginning was love—and science. Countless works of literature throughout time turned out to be SF regardless of their authors' original intentions. The same may be said about the stories I write.

As far as I know, some of your children will be born girls through no special effort on your part.

It will all be okay as long as you don't jump out of your chair in shock and insist that you do not birth girls.

They're people. No need to get spooked.

Scripter

1.

input__"hello."
output__"hello."

"It's been twenty three years since I last encountered an outsider," the man said.

Dark-skinned with a sturdy build, he stood a full head taller than most. Black paint surrounded his eye sockets, and a pair of black stripes decorated each side of his face. His long hair was pulled back in a tight braid. With the exception of a black bandana wrapped around his forehead, he was clad from head to toe in a leather outfit that appeared to have been tanned by hand and boasted meticulous needlework and intricate decorative patterns. On his back he carried a bow and arrows, and hanging from each side of his waist were a dagger and a sword.

"You don't look that old," the traveler said.

The man chuckled.

"Looks can be altered any way you wish. I know that you're not what you appear to be, either. Otherwise, I'd have tossed you a few coins and gone on my way."

The traveler had a slight build and a delicate face mottled with soot. His hair looked like a rat's nest. His feet were bare, and he was dressed in a tattered burlap sack with holes cut out for the neck and arms.

Scratching his head self-consciously, the traveler said, "I'm level one. My occupation is 'begging,' and my only skill set is 'begging.' I had quite a time getting in, as the barkeep tried to kick me out the moment he spotted me. I'd have loved to show up in a nice suit, but unless my character suddenly manages to jump to level twenty, that just isn't in the cards."

"What are you talking about?"

"Oh, sorry. Everyone told me not to use gaming lingo with you. They said you're a die-hard immersive game player who refuses to talk to anyone who breaks character. I've been racking my brain to figure out how I should interact with you."

The two men were sitting in a shabby wooden tavern. A light hanging from the ceiling swayed as it cast a warm reddish glow over the dark interior. With each lazy swing, it highlighted the assortment of characters below: a musician strumming, a trio of rowdy drunks clinking their glasses together in a toast, a barkeep polishing glassware, and a woman in the corner dressed in red. Soon, however, it became apparent that the musician was playing the same song on repeat, the rowdy drunks kept clinking glasses at precise intervals, and the barkeep kept tirelessly polishing the same sparkling glass over and over, buffing it, breathing on it, pushing his eyeglasses up to inspect it, and then starting over again. Everyone seemed to be dressed in meticulous compliance with a preordered theme and color scheme. Even the air seemed infused with a tint that washed them all in the same hue.

The barkeep slammed down a full mug of beer before the traveler and hissed, "Chug it down and buzz off. You don't belong here. Don't come crashing our party."

The traveler flashed a gleeful smile and turned to the hunter.

"My begging skill worked like a charm this time. Usually only one out of ten is a hit. I tell you, it's hard out here when your avatar's a level zero nobody. No one wants to have anything to do with you."

The hunter said nothing. The traveler downed his beer in a few gulps and contorted his face in a theatrical display of disgust.

"Tastes like cigarette butts, like everything else that passes for food here. The game's taste simulation is a mess. No surprise, though, given what a relic it is."

He closed his eyes and brushed his palm back and forth against the beer mug.

"The haptic simulation is brutally simple, too. I can't tell from the feel alone whether this is wood, steel, or paper. And if you look at it close up, you can tell it's just a picture. I bet this thing doesn't even break."

Clinking their glasses together once again, the drunks broke out in raucous laughter. One of them called out to the woman leaning against the end of the bar.

"Get over here (*get over here*), lady (*lady*), and drink with us (*and drink with us*)." The traveler recited the words in perfect sync with the drunk.

"Next," the traveler continued in a whisper, "he'll say, *I heard that wolves got to the livestock a few days ago.*"

"I heard that wolves..." the drunk echoed.

"This place is full of bores," the traveler said. "Everyone is stuck in one place, saying and doing the same things. They won't even answer if you try to talk to them."

"They're not human."

The traveler raised an eyebrow in surprise and said," Gotta admit, I wasn't expecting that. I was doing my best to play along."

"Homunculi. Alchemists created them to repopulate the empty streets after all the people were gone."

"There's a setting for that? I didn't read the manual that closely."

"You and I are the only humans in this tavern," the hunter said.

"And you, sir, are the only one still playing. Every outsider you've met so far has been an employee sent by the company to persuade you to quit the game."

"..."

"The game's original service operator had a strict business philosophy: their rule was that player data belonged to the customer and to no one else, and so they vowed to never discontinue a product, even if it was not turning a profit. But three years ago the company went bankrupt and was sold to us. Our philosophy is a bit different. Simply put, we see no point in maintaining so many outdated games. We kept just a few and scrapped all the rest. But this game... Well, it turns out there was an unusual little clause in the contract."

"..."

"It stipulates that, if there's even a single active user, the game cannot be shut down. Naturally, in the event that the term is breached, the client is entitled to an enormous sum of monetary compensation. I have no idea what possessed them to do that. Marketing strategy, I suppose. And you, sir, as the winner of the game's mega-launch event, were awarded a free lifetime subscription. Which means that we don't make a single coin off of you... But let's put a pin in that for now. Contractually, the only thing we can do is try to talk you into quitting the game of your own accord."

Taking the hunter's silence as a cue to continue, the traveler adopted a more official tone.

"Please allow us to offer you a free lifetime subscription to the newest and shiniest game we have available, plus a generous settlement, in exchange for closing your account here. It may not be what was stipulated in the original contract, but I assure you that it will not disappoint."

"..."

"Sir, I know that you don't enjoy stepping out of character, but surely you understand what I am saying."

"Mazalalika," the hunter murmured, and pointed at the traveler's beer mug. Letters appeared in the air around the hunter's finger. In a blink, the mug burst into flame. The traveler jumped and jerked his hand away.

"It may not break, but it still burns," the hunter said.

The hunter slung his quiver over his shoulder and started up the hill.

The traveler scrambled to keep up with the hunter's large strides. Each rock that stabbed at the traveler's bare feet sent him into a frantic little dance that caused him to lag further behind. This in turn forced him to make up for the widening distance with another mad dash, swatting away at a relentless swarm of black flies all the while. "Who the hell designed this thing?" he grumbled aloud.

"Fine, then," he said as he caught up to the hunter at last." What if I put it this way? I was sent here by the gods. I know that I don't necessarily look like much, but you said yourself that looks don't tell the whole truth. Anyway, everyone else has left this world. You're the last man standing. The gods have decided that this world is no longer worthy of existence, and they're on the verge of proclaiming its death. But they would like to save you before that happens. Just say the word, and I'll take you to another, more beautiful realm that they've recently launched."

"…"

"Look, sir, I understand how dear this world is to you. I know that it's chock full of memories, and that you have no wish to see it disappear. I don't personally see the appeal, but I can appreciate how it's possible to develop a strong emotional attachment to something that has kept you entertained for so long. Heck, even a baduk stone might seem precious after enough time.[1] So how about we provide you with a stand-alone copy of the software to use at home. Then you can play it with your friends! Again, please excuse the outside jargon."

The hunter stopped at the summit of the hill and peered out into the distance. Following his gaze, the traveler saw that the sky had ripped in two, as if someone had picked at the corner and peeled it off in one long strip.

"The graphics are broken. One of the polygon's coordinates is messed up. You'll run into this type of

[1] Baduk is a game of strategy similar to chess but played with black and white stones.

glitch more and more often as no one knows how to patch it anymore. The game's such a dinosaur that we're hard pressed to find anyone who can even begin to troubleshoot it or analyze its source code. Er... what I mean is, this dimension is breaking down. Chaos is spreading. Soon it will devour the whole world."

Without warning, the hunter reached up and shoved the traveler straight down, driving him into the ground. The traveler flailed about, trapped inside his clothes. By the time he managed to re-emerge, the hunter was aiming an arrow into the woods. He stood stock still like that, bow drawn, for over two minutes. The traveler was just about to give him a poke to see if he was still alive when the hunter's arrow cut through the air and landed in the underbrush, where it kicked up a violent commotion. The hunter strode over and plucked out a golden-furred wolf.

"This guy only comes around once a year," he said, tossing his kill to the traveler.

The traveler's arms reflexively shot out to receive the carcass, but its unexpected weight knocked him on his rear.

"Go sell it and buy yourself some real clothes," the hunter said with a smirk.

2

```
condition 1029 // if repeat.input
input__"Hi."
output__"We've already said hello."
```

At dawn, the hunter hiked up the mountain and returned with some flat stones. He sat in the yard and ground one down until it was sharp, stopping occasionally to tilt it in the sunlight and examine its geometry before grinding it some more. Once the stone was to his liking, he threaded it tightly to a shaft and attached feathers that he had carefully selected. The traveler watched from a distance. As dusk began to fall, he finally stood and approached the hunter. The hunter took one look at him and chuckled.

"Laugh away, sir. You know my skill level in tanning and sewing is a big fat zero," the traveler said. "I managed to put together a shirt, but pants are plain impossible."

He hitched up what appeared to be a fur blanket that had been wrapped around him like a skirt.

"You can learn."

"Of course I can," the traveler said, sounding annoyed. "An old lady in the next village offered to teach me in exchange for twenty rabbits. But I'm a busy man! This stupid game is so outdated... Who has time to go chasing bunnies?"

He gazed up at the sun. It looked as though someone had hand-painted it directly onto the sky with a brush dipped in gold paint. If pressed to do so, one might describe this universe by saying it consisted of a wide, flat disk surrounded by a rotating wall onto which balls in the shape of the sun, moon, and stars had been nailed.

"I spent some time looking into your file," the traveler said. "An hour in the real world is equal to a day here, which makes you at least fifteen hundred years old in this world. You've had too many past lives to count, and you've held every job possible. You're a hunter now, but you've been a wizard, a poet, a monk, and a warrior who earned himself a knighthood, but also a thief, a clown, and a fraud. You've probably already defeated the evil king who threatens to bring down the kingdom. Many times over, I'll bet. If it weren't for DNA confirmation—and the fact that this game doesn't allow for one player to control two avatars—we would never have believed that you did all of that on your own. Of course, it's possible that you wrote a bot... Back then, amateur programmers used to make convincing first-person hunter games and share them online. Naturally, they were illegal, but some of them were far better than the professionally made games."

The hunter blew the dust off of his new arrowhead, held it up to the sunlight to inspect it, and tossed it into a wooden box before selecting another stone to grind. As soon as it entered the box, the arrowhead blurred and merged into the background.

"The gods are deeply impressed with your performance. They have decided to bestow upon you the honor of sitting at their right hand and helping them rule the world... as their business partner. You will be directly involved in world creation, and you will be free to do as you wish with that world. Imagine: you could have ferocious monsters roam the fields, or make food rain down from the sky. You could give people abilities or take them away. Why, you'll even have the power to giveth and taketh life itself! Of course, you'll have to be mindful of maintaining some kind of equilibrium in the world, but the gods have absolute faith in your sense of proportion. I guarantee you, it will be far more interesting than sitting here slaving over some arrowheads."

The hunter's eyes widened. He let out a chuckle, which built into an uncontrolled fit of laughter.

"Was it the 'giveth' and the 'taketh'?"

"It's hard to take anything you say seriously when you're dressed like that."

"I guess I'll have to find a way to add another clothing graphic," the traveler said, twisting this way and that to study his outfit. "Why are you so obsessed with this world anyway? When you could live anywhere you wanted."

The hunter paused in his work to meet the traveler's gaze. Hovering behind the hunter's young face was the shadow of a feeble old man. He looked like someone who had once been king but was now just an aged beast clinging to what was left of his power.

"The only one who knows where I should live is me," he said.

Just then, someone stepped out of the house. Glancing over, the traveler couldn't help but do a double take.

Whoever created her could not possibly have been the same person who'd created the world she inhabited. It was as if a master painter had flicked his brush against a child's painting. She glowed. Dark eyebrows arched over wide, lovely eyes. The onyx pearls of her irises glowed from behind long lashes. Waves of hair as black as the ocean at midnight cascaded down to her heels, hugging her curves. She wore a dress cut from the same buckskin as the hunter's outfit and jewelry crafted from animal bones, all of which only served to accentuate her primitive beauty.

The woman handed the hunter a water jug and leaned over to kiss him long and hard on the mouth. The traveler's brows quivered in stunned disbelief. She stood back up and looked at him. A smile spread across her face.

"Hello," she said.

"Hello," the traveler managed to blurt out, still reeling.

"You're a person, aren't you?"

"What? Am I a person...?"

"Yes. You're a person, aren't you?"

"Yes, of course, but..."

"It's been forever since I last saw a real person."

The traveler's eyes narrowed with suspicion.

"Everyone has left," she said. "They said the end was near. The other side of Morning Hill is nearly wiped out. Chaos swallowed it whole... How long do you plan to stay here, sir?"

"Who the hell are you?" The traveler's voice had turned ice-cold.

The hunter looked up, and the woman blinked her wide eyes.

"How did you get in here? Do you know they've increased the penalty for hacking? You'll be hit with a fine so big that you'll never pay it off. How long have you been logged in?"

She looked down at the hunter in complete bewilderment. He stood and wrapped an arm around her.

"He's a visitor from another realm. A messenger sent by the creators of our world. So be patient with him, even if he starts jabbering nonsense."

"Really?"

"That's what he claims."

Their lips locked again. The traveler opened his mouth to protest but no sound came out. His hands gesticulated wildly, as if continuing the argument. Only after a few long beats had passed was he was able to speak again, the urge to curse at them only barely suppressed.

"This has got to be a joke. Hey, Miss. Miss, Ma'am, Sir, whatever you are. You have to pay to use this world. There's no free log-in. Understand? Now that I've seen you, you're busted. So register at once and pay the user fee, including all the back fees for the time you've already spent here. Otherwise, log out this very instant. Do you hear me? Get the hell out!"

The woman was speechless. The traveler was about to launch into another verbal attack, but before he could do so, she stood up straight and tall. Her voice was soft but emphatic.

"You self-proclaimed messenger of our creators, my existence does not require anyone else's approval, least of all yours. So please go back to your keepers and tell them that. You people may believe this world belongs to you, but it doesn't. This world is ours. Even if the fate of this world hinges entirely upon the whims of your kind, we will never be made to act against our own free will. Death and destruction may eventually drive me from this world, but I will *never* choose to leave."

3

```
condition 1040 // if repeat.input __pattern #4
input__"hi."
output__"are you testing me?"
```

Spotting a puny figure under a tree, the hunter, who was on horse-back, laughed so hard he nearly fell out of the saddle.

"All right already, so it backfired," the traveler said. The pair of oversized wings that protruded from his back sagged in defeat along with his shoulders. "This is how I should've introduced myself to you. I didn't really think it would work at this point, but I had to give it a shot."

A bright yellow halo dangled just above his head. He was wearing what appeared to be a white nightgown, and his tangled hair was now neatly combed and held in place with a flower barrette. In a distinctly avian manner, he lifted a wing, gave it a few flaps, and rubbed his face in it to preen.

"This is the admin attire nowadays. And it has performed very well, just so you know."

His explanation seemed to have had no effect on the hunter, who howled with laughter for a few more minutes. Once his hilarity had subsided, the hunter studied the angel's face with renewed curiosity. Free of dirt and grime and poking out from under the halo, the traveler's face (or rather, the angel's face) might even be described as handsome. It was the kind of face that could pass for either gender depending on where you stood.

"I didn't know you were a girl," the hunter said.

"I'm intersex. Some clients prefer women, some prefer men. I guess you could say this is a handy way to satisfy both."

"So what are you really?"

The angel paused in the middle of gathering up his hem from where it trailed on the ground. The expression on his face clearly communicated, *How the hell am I supposed to walk in this?* The angel studied the hunter's face.

"What an interesting question. Can I take that as admission of the fact that this world is just a shadow of the real world?"

"I already told you that I don't place much faith in the appearance of anyone or anything. And you know that, behind this, I'm an old man nearing death."

"Your world view is tough to figure out," the angel said, sticking out his tongue at the hunter. "So, if I share my story, will you tell me yours?"

"…"

"Figures. Of course you won't. Not by a long shot. We've been searching everywhere for your personal information, but have been able to turn up exactly nothing. The original company made a complete mess of their data management, and we also can't seem to find anyone who was ever in charge of it. On top of which, IP tracking was disabled. Anyway, I'll keep my secrets, too. Admin identity is supposed to be kept strictly confidential. Too many nut jobs out there, you know."

Just then, an old man in a pointy hat walked up to the two of them. He was carrying a rucksack on his back with a child inside who was clutching a single lotus blossom. The old man stopped at the top of the hill to catch his breath.

"Ahoy there, brave ones, at last we meet. May the Lord bless you and protect you always. Word of your reputation has brought me all the way here. Please help me. I've been traveling the width and the breadth of this land in search of a cure for my sick child."

Ignoring the old man, the hunter turned back to the angel.

"You're relentless, aren't you?"

"Just doing my job. You're the one who's relentless. And now I've got not just one but two people to deal with? They better pay me extra for this. Well, if there really *are* two of you."

The angel squatted under the tree and traced a circle in the air before him. A sheet of paper fluttered down out of the circle. Several more followed, which he gathered and arranged into a neat stack before beginning to read them. Sensing the hunter's gaze, which was boring into him, the angel shook his finger.

"I managed to find the admin ID in storage. I now have access to full admin privileges, including skin files—as you might have already noticed. I'm getting magic points transferred to me as well, though progress has been slow. It takes forever to locate anything using such an old-fashioned method..."

"What do you mean, 'if there really *are* two of you'?"

The angel glanced up at him.

"There's no log-in record. It's possible that she hacked into the system using some method we don't know about, but our analysts are skeptical. C has been obsolete for decades. Hardly any of those programmers are left. In fact, there probably aren't many servers left that can even run this game."

"What are you suggesting?"

"She's not human, is she?"

The hunter dismounted and hung the reins on a branch. The trunk itself was much too thick for tethering the horse. It was big enough to span the width of a small yard. The base of the old tree was long dead, and insects and birds had drilled holes in its moss-covered bark to form their own colonies. Seeds that dropped from above germinated in the plush moss and grew as one with the dead wood. The treetop was barely visible through the leaves and branches, and flowers fluttered to the ground with each breeze like confetti.

Sitting cross-legged before the angel, the hunter asked, "Then what is she?"

The angel looked up from behind his sheaf of papers and gazed at the hunter's face a while.

"NPC. A non-player character, like our old friend over here."

"...The magic herb is inside a cave guarded by a terrible dragon, but none have been brave enough to set foot there..." The old man was still rattling off his lines like a voiceover narrator.

"According to our records, the game's VIP users were provided with an NPC spawning tool capable of natural language processing and voice recognition. Using this tool, players were able to code NPCs capable of interacting with other entities based on real time input data. It was a deceptively modest tool with endless capacity. Some consider these NPCs to be primitive AI, but I think it's a stretch to compare what they do to 'intelligence.' All they do is spout pre-programmed responses based on pre-programmed conditions. For anything off-script, they can only clam up or pretend you've lost them."

"You've lost me."

The angel gave the hunter a quick eye roll.

"Fine. Allow me to flesh it out in your terms, then. She's a homunculus. You've been an alchemist in the past, correct? My guess is that she's your creation."

"A moment's conversation should be enough for you to tell if that's the case or not."

"Well, it confused me at first because I assumed she was a human player. On top of which, she threw me that trick question. NPCs—I mean, homunculi—don't usually ask people if they're people."

"...I'd gladly throw myself into the arms of death to save this child, but my death would be meaningless if it doesn't save him. Please, have pity on us, and accept this family heirloom in exchange for—" the old man continued.

"Shut up," the hunter ordered.

The old man froze as if someone had switched him off. The little boy cowered and ducked all the way down inside the old man's rucksack.

"You had a conversation with the girl," the hunter continued.

"That wasn't a conversation. We both may as well have been talking to ourselves. She acted as though she didn't understand me when I confronted her with real world speech. At first, I chalked this up to role player stubbornness, but it's obvious to me now that she wasn't programmed to answer my questions. And none of her responses made any sense."

"…"

The old man had gotten stuck in a glitch loop. His mouth kept opening and closing, and he kept stepping forward only to be jerked back to the ground again.

"You obviously coded a few more conversation patterns in her before shoving her in front of me, knowing how I'd react if I ran into another player here. I bet she'll repeat the same exact lines to me the next time I see her."

The angel traced another circle in the air and slid the papers into the hole that appeared once again. After swallowing the papers, the hole spiraled shut and vanished.

"So why'd you do it? Were you trying to get me to play with you? Have you finally grown bored of playing by yourself after all these years? I feel like I've blundered into a strange game where the rules keep shifting. Just what kind of game are you playing?"

The hunter stood. Birds stopped chirping, and the wind returned, depositing five different kinds of petals and leaves on the hunter's shoulders. He smiled and drew a sword from his waist. Yet even as the blade caught the sun, sending a shower of rays in all directions, the angel just stood there, blinking passively. The hunter raised his sword overhead.

Only then did the angel realize what the hunter was aiming for. He screamed and turned to run, but his heavy wings threw him off balance and knocked him off his feet. Rudely reminded that he was no longer land bound, the angel spread his wings and started to take off. But the hunter charged towards him at a terrible speed and plunged his sword into one of his wings, snatching him out of the air and slamming him against the ground. The sword buried itself in the earth all the way to the hilt.

As the angel struggled to sit up and free himself, the hunter selected an arrow from his quiver, drew his bow, and walked around to face the angel.

"Please don't," the angel whimpered. "You know it won't actually kill me. I'll just re-spawn at the swamp of the undead."

"Then you've got nothing to fear."

The hunter released the arrow. It grazed the edge of one wing and plunged into the ground. The angel shrieked and flapped his wings in panic. Drawing another sword out of its scabbard with a metallic swoosh, the hunter swiftly brought its gleaming tip down to the angel's throat, causing fresh a wave of terror.

"I have no desire to play with the likes of you. Stop judging me and my world by your standards. And quit corrupting this place with your language. I've tried to be nice, but I won't stand for it anymore. You start running your mouth again—"

"Stop."

The eerie wind that had been whipping past suddenly calmed. The woman, her hair rippling, rode towards them on a horned appaloosa. Finally freed from his digital imprisonment, the old man with the child on his back rushed over to her.

"Ahoy there, brave ones, at last we meet. May the Lord bless you and protect you always. Word of your reputation has brought me all the way here. Please help me. I've been traveling the width and the breadth of this land in search of a cure for my sick child."

Lowering his weapon, the hunter turned to the woman and said, "But he insulted you."

"Treating him like this doesn't bode well for this world," she said.

"No matter how I treat him, nothing's going to change."

"You're wrong. I still believe there's hope."

"...Inside the cave guarded by a terrible dragon..."

The angel watched their exchange intently, eager to butt in and lodge his complaints. The woman jumped off the horse and walked towards him uttering a series of arcane words at the sword buried in his wing. Obeying her command, the sword flew into the air and back into the scabbard at the hunter's side. Her words, transformed into a beam of light, filled the angel's wound. In a blink, the gaping wound closed without a trace. The angel shot her a searing look.

"How'd you do that?" he hissed.

"I healed it."

"How are you even talking to me? Do you have a split personality? Are you playing a double role? You're controlling two characters simultaneously, aren't you?"

"Pardon me?"

"Who the hell are you?"

"What do you mean by that?"

"Idiot."

"...What?"

"You think you're so pretty, don't you? But too bad, that pretty face isn't real, and you know it. It's just a skin job that you bought with game credits. Was it from some VIP-only menu? Your appearance doesn't prove a damn thing about you."

"I don't think I ever said anything about my face."

"What does 'face' mean?"

The woman's pupils quivered ever so slightly.

"Log out right now," the angel commanded.

At this the woman's face hardened with anger, and she straightened her back.

"You're testing me."

"What does 'testing' mean?"

"You're throwing random sentences at me to see how I'll respond, because a homunculus can't interpret things from context and should be stumped. But I refuse to participate in this type of test ever again. If there's one thing I'm sure of, it's that I will not tolerate you treating me as though I were sub-human."

The angel glared long and hard at the woman, then raised his forefinger. He traced a circle in the air above him, and a bright light appeared along its edges. He added more lines and shapes, muttering something under his breath as he drew. The hunter's eyes widened with growing recognition of what was taking shape above him.

Just as the angel finished casting his spell, the lion he had drawn in the air began to bulge and take form. It tried to lunge at the woman, but she did not so much as flinch. The hunter exhaled in the direction of the lion. The puff of air grew into a gale that swept away the lion's hindquarters, which were still squirming into existence. Moments later, the whole of the lion came apart and vanished. The hunter drew his bow. As he did, the air around him sharpened into nine spears. When he released the bowstring, the spears followed the arrow straight into the angel's body.

4

condition 751029 // if repeat.input >X__pattern #5
input "hi."
output "i will not tolerate this kind of testing again"

The moon shone a different color depending on the angle from which it was viewed. From the field, the orb appeared to hang low, radiating blue, but when floating high over the mountain, it flooded the world with a pale purple glow. A small burial mound under a tree was awash in the moon's purple light. A spirit sat hunched on top of it, lost in reverie. A petite pair of wings perched on its shoulder blades, and where its legs should be, a curl of smoke swished from side to side like a fish tail. The hunter approached. With his spear in his hand and his body covered in a makeshift camouflage of tree leaves, he looked as if he'd just returned from a hunt.

"What are you still doing here?" the hunter said. "Why haven't you re-spawned?"

The spirit glanced left and right then pointed at himself.

"You can see me?" he asked.

"I see you."

"I thought spirits were invisible."

"They're visible to me."

"Duh, of course! You've also been a shaman." He gave a little shrug. "I, for one, am enjoying the posthumous world. Whoever made this place had quite a sense of humor. And everything looks more beautiful here when you're dead. I don't know if you can see it, but a snowy white wolf is standing guard at my grave, and a bunch of fairies are frolicking around this tree. I can even see the entrance to the netherworld over on that hilltop. Why'd the programmers waste their time coding all of this? It's not as though a dead avatar can hunt or do anything else fun with this game. Was this their way of telling us to rest in peace?"

The hunter said nothing.

"But, you know, this place has started to grow on me. I think maybe it's nostalgia for a low-tech era. You would never mistake anything in here for reality. People, beasts, stuff—it all looks like drawings. But I like that. I mean, look at this tree. Whoever made it must have been sacked immediately after doing so. To think that back in the day, when hundreds of look-alike games were being churned out every year, when no one thought of this type of copy-and-paste job as having any sort of artistic value, someone managed to create a tree as magnificent as this one... I mean, it's kind of a miracle."

"I didn't think you'd come back," said the hunter.

"Oh, I thought about not coming back. To be honest, I thought about quitting altogether," the angel replied. "I've dealt with all kinds of crackpots, punks, idiots, and imbeciles, but you, sir, you take the crown," he added with a smirk. "You're so exquisitely perverse that your perverseness verges on art."

With that, and a flutter of his tiny wings, the spirit disappeared back down into the grave. The mound began to crumble and shake, as if someone were furiously digging at it from the inside. Suddenly, it caved open, revealing a human skeleton. A heart appeared inside the ribcage and began to beat. Blood vessels unspooled, flesh and skin cleaved, downy feathers sprouted from the shoulder blades. The skeleton flapped its bony wings, and the down on it turned to sleek feathers. The angel's face returned to its original state. He kneaded his shoulders, though his arms and legs were still nothing but bone.

"Ugh, it feels like there's sand grinding in my joints."

Raising his spear, the hunter brought it closer and closer to the angel until its tip nearly grazed his forehead. The angel froze in the middle of massaging himself.

"Why'd you do that?" the hunter asked.

"Don't be this way," the angel said with a smug grin. "You're really going to murder someone you already killed? Don't you know it's a crime to commit a PK?"

He clinked a bare phalange against the spearhead hovering

between his eyebrows.

"You started it," the hunter hissed.

"That was a low-level skill. I just wanted to find out whether or not she was human, and whether the skill would work on her. I also wanted to see if she was capable of responding to an unscripted scenario. Sadly, though, it was all in vain. It turns out that all NPCs in this world are capable of combat while in quest mode. They're at the same level as monsters... Which means I died for nothing. What's curious, though, is that she didn't seem the least bit caught off guard. She didn't get mad like you, or ask me why I did what I did."

"So you figure if she didn't get mad, she couldn't possibly be human."

The angel scoffed. "You really do have a split personality, don't you? One side keeps a toe in the real world, while the other hides away in this world. Am I right? Fine! Well, I'm a messenger sent here by the gods to cast judgment on this world whose time has come, and you, sir, are standing in my way! You refuse to let go of this world, but just how far do you think my patience will stretch? You don't really believe that you, a mere inhabitant of this place, could guard this world alone forever, do you? I've had enough of you already! Oh, and make no mistake. It's no trouble for us to kick a dying old man like you to the curb. Yeah, why don't you hobble over to our headquarters one day and demand your compensation? We will sue your ass for lost profits and damages, plus assault and battery, plus obstruction of business, and then some. Let's see who the law will side with!"

The hunter was speechless. He dropped his spear and stood there for a moment. Then he fell to his knees like a sack of stones.

"What the hell are you doing now?"

"Begging."

His face and voice remained composed as he bowed his head all the way to the ground. The angel tried not to react, but his tiny wings flapped in surprise, throwing him off balance. He teetered and fell on his butt.

"What is this all about?" he yelled. "What did I ever do to you?"

"Tell me what I need to do."

"What do you mean?"

There was a long silence.

"Please…" The hunter let out a low weep that seemed to resonate up from the ground itself. "I'll do whatever you want me to, just please don't destroy this world. What should I do?"

The angel swallowed a sigh, his closed mouth expressionless.

5

/* prioritize approaching ID lover 123 in the following conditions */
condition 43571029 // if physical proximity to ID lover123 > X
condition 43571030 // if life bar of ID lover123 < 5%
condition 43……

The river running along the mountainside ended abruptly, as if the rest of it had been lopped off with a knife. A black liquid flowed from the severed end, the water fragmenting into thousands of tiny pixels that disappeared into thin air. The same blackness had crept into the neighboring field, where a house was plastered flat, its pixelated outlines spreading into the surrounding grass.

The mountain was collapsing from the top down. A sinkhole that had opened up at its center mercilessly devoured trees, rocks, and dirt. Deer and rabbits scrambled to escape the void only to be dragged back down by it. Only the tree at the top of the mountain stood its ground, its roots growing more exposed as it refused to get sucked in. Even after half the mountain had disappeared, the tree's roots still held, keeping it upright.

The woman was bathing in the middle of the river. Her skin and clothing were stained black. She rinsed herself repeatedly as if to wash away the stain, but it only spread further. She inspected herself carefully and tried again to scrub it off.

The angel watched from the riverbank, his chin propped in his palm. A clan of raggedly dressed folks emerged from nowhere and bowed low at his feet. Without a word, they placed a few rice balls and other offerings on the ground in front of him before shuffling away backwards. He picked up a rice ball, blew the dirt off its surface, and took a bite.

"Funny how people's attitudes towards you change when you level up to god status. Especially considering that my skills are technically indistinguishable from a beggar's. I'll never understand it—the level was hidden! Why'd they even bother programming it in?"

The woman looked up at him. Half of her face had already turned black. The angel stuffed the rest of the rice ball into his mouth, cheeks bulging, and chewed leisurely. He glanced over at where the black water was entering the river.

"That's not my responsibility. Not my doing, either. No one in the company has the first clue as to how to patch it, or what to expect from here on out. Everyone who knew the source code has already died of old age. The disk this is stored on is at the end of its life expectancy, too. We might be able to coax it back to life by transferring it to a new disk before running a diagnostic. But I wouldn't hold my breath. The gods have no desire to direct any more resources this way."

The woman gestured towards the end of the river.

"Do not despair," she said. "Oblivion cannot erase you. Death cannot erase you. Nothing disappears. You exist alone and whole, and you linger forever in the moment of your existence. Though none may know the days of your life and no trace of those days remain, the moment of your being will shine as brilliantly as the rays of the sun, the wind, and the clouds that likewise linger for a moment before vanishing."

The angel turned bug-eyed and started coughing. When he could finally breathe again, he croaked, "What did you just do?"

"It's a spell for the dying. To ease your grief. Care to join me?"

"No thanks, I'll pass. It's stupid."

The woman resumed bathing in silence. She gazed up at the sky and then down at her body for a moment before pouring water over herself again. Her movements were solemn. If someone had in fact programmed her to move that way, then they must have been mired in deep sadness at the time.

"Idiot."

The woman turned to look at the angel. He gazed back, wide-eyed, chin still in hand. Her face was dripping wet as she gave him a knowing smile.

"You still don't think I'm human, do you?" she said.

"Why do you ask?"

"Weren't you testing me just now by calling me an idiot? To try to see if I was real or not?"

"Oh, is that how you were programmed to respond to insults?"

"Do it again, and you'll never get another reaction out of me. Ever."

The winged one was silent for a moment.

"When did you log out? I've been monitoring traffic for days but have yet to see anyone log out."

"Do you really believe that I'm a homunculus?"

"What exactly is a homunculus?"

"Artificial beings. As people started to leave this world, the alchemists couldn't bear the loneliness and created homunculi to fill the empty streets. They don't possess intelligence or logic, and they tell imaginary stories. But their presence helped ease the loneliness for those of us who survived. In the end, even the alchemists fled. At which point the homunculi were the only ones left to keep us company."

"How fascinating! I suppose they would be more convincing than your usual NPCs. They certainly don't seem fully human, at any rate. So tell me, Ms. Pygmalion: whose undying love had the power to make you real?"

She smiled.

"Do you really believe that an AI like me could exist in this world? Let me remind you. This world was created during a time when language recognition, navigation, and obstacle avoidance algorithms were all being developed as separate programs, when computing systems that could mimic human neural networks existed only in theory. The limitations of digital computers were obvious. Do you think an AI born in that era could generate thoughts, develop a personality, and read between the lines of a conversation?"

The angel sat pouting at the woman for a while. At last he spoke: "I would never have guessed you capable of delivering such an eloquent monologue."

"I can say anything I want."

"Oh yeah? Then tell me why this world shouldn't be put to rest?"

"How could you be so indifferent to the fate of a disappearing world?"

"I don't know. Every single day, worlds come, worlds go, they shut down for no reason, then reopen, new worlds completely devoid of artistic virtue or philosophy are born and then vanish, creators indifferent to their creations run their worlds without a shred of love, power-drunk creators destroy their own creations without a single thought in their heads as to why. I see this every single day. So you tell me, why should I give a damn about whether or not your stupid, outdated world gets shut down?"

"..."

"Do you even understand what I've just said?"

"Yes, I do."

"You're telling me that you can consciously comprehend something?"

She looked at him sadly. His eyes were cold.

"What do I have to do to make you believe me?"

"So you *can* read between the lines. That was pretty human-like of you, though the mechanics behind such a thing are not entirely inconceivable."

"..."

"Invalid input? Can't find a suitable response to retrieve from your digital archive?"

"You're not a good listener."

"You can't prove to me that you're human—at least not while you're logged in. You can't prick yourself with a needle and bleed red, or show me an X-ray of your skeleton. Doesn't matter whether you're a human, a robot, a tree, or dirt, or grass. It's all just data in here. If it bothers you that much that I don't consider you human, then log out right now in front of me. It's the simplest way."

The woman stood there for a while before wading out of the river. Pixelated water clung to her body, giving the illusion that her hair was becoming a part of the river itself. Fat drops of water fell from her body and splashed onto the angel, who watched with chin in hand.

"You, visitor from another dimension," she began.

For someone to have created a face like hers, they would have had to be madly in love. To have created a voice like hers, they'd have to have been sick with love. She was the physical manifestation of her creator's dreams and ideals. It was impossible to imagine otherwise.

"You, who insist on having come from another dimension, if I cannot prove what I am, then neither can you. Who are you, really?

Outside of claiming that you are who you say you are, what proof do you have? Who else is there to testify that you yourself are not a homunculus that someone created to mock me?"

The angel's face hardened, and he tried to stand. The woman pointed at him. It wasn't a gesture of attack, nor did her hand come in contact with him, but he felt himself being slowly pushed back down.

"You, self-proclaimed messenger of the apocalypse from the gods, I have met the likes of you many times before. They've all told me that this world was just a speck among the countless worlds that exist beyond our own horizon. All of them spoke of the 'real world' from which they supposedly had come, and to which every inhabitant of this world eventually returned to face true birth and death."

"Look," the angel interjected, but she ignored him.

"He who claims to have given me life has told me the same thing. Showing up as a beggar one day, he said to me that this world in which I live is a fantasy, a lie, a place that does not really exist, a mere dream born from someone's imagination."

"Wait."

"He told me who I really am. He said that I am blind and deaf, that I cannot speak or walk or even move on my own, and that I've been that way since birth."

The angel paused at this.

"He said that I lived locked away in an elaborate contraption that keeps my heart and lungs running for me, with one tube inserted into my digestive tract to supply me with nutrients and another to remove my waste. He told me he had created this world for me, to transport me out of that eternal darkness and solitude, that he made me as beautiful as he possibly could.

"…"

"But I know nothing of that world. I merely understand its possibility. I'm told that there is no magic, no elves, no blue dragons or orcs or shadow monsters there, that a person emerges from their mother's womb as a child and grows into an adult before eventually dying of old age. I may not comprehend such concepts, but I grasp their possibility. Of course, it's also possible that he, too, is a homunculus who's made all of this up to fool me. Or maybe I really am a human vegetable growing old inside a box. I can grasp these possibilities, too. But what I cannot accept is that this world is a lie, a dream, a mirage. No one will ever convince me of that."

"…"

"I understand what 'logging out' means. But I cannot exit this world of my own will. Even if I could, I would only be entering the dark prison of my body. I've been here a long time and do not know what state that body is in. For all I know, I might die of shock the moment I returned. So while all things are possible, I do not wish to test that particular prospect. Certainly not simply to prove that I am human."

6

The field was a jumble of the living and the dead, an undulating quilt of black and blue. Along its edges, portals to the netherworld opened their dark, cavernous mouths. Endless streams of monsters on the prowl issued forth and headed towards the village. The hunter crossed the field. As he neared one of the caves, his movement grew sluggish, as if something kept tugging him back. The monsters passed right by him without noticing.

At the cave's entrance, he reached a hand up to the ceiling, which dripped with water, then peered inside.

"That's quite a lag," the angel's voice called out. "Looks like you're having trouble moving, aren't you? It's because of all the monsters."

The hunter dropped to the ground as he tried to catch his breath.

"I guess I made too many," the angel said.

The hunter's face was smeared with dirt, his body covered in bruises. His clothes were tattered, and a tar-like substance coated his pants from the knees down. On one leg, the pant cuff and the shoe below were bleeding into each other like wet paint.

"Looks like the corruption is spreading to the characters now. Did you know that you could damage your brain cells by logging into an infected avatar? The company advertises itself as bug-free, but there have been more than a few such incidents. We've ensured of course that such stories never leak to the media."

The hunter stared at the angel before rising. No sooner was he standing than a pair of eyes flashed yellow in the dark and a fanged shadow lunged at him. He whipped out his sword and slashed it in two, but the impact knocked the sword from his hand, and he collapsed.

"How many lives have you lost so far? Your level must have plummeted. The quests will only get harder and harder. You can't clear this level on your own."

"Is this your doing?"

"I increased the number of monsters. Actually, it was stupefyingly easy to do. I'm still trying to wrap my head around the fact that someone could develop such a deep attachment to a world that can be controlled with a few taps of the keyboard."

"I said, is this your doing?" the hunter bellowed.

"I figured out how to change a character's coordinates. Tested it out by locking your princess down at the bottom of the netherworld. Don't you think it's completely within my authority to do so, considering that my character setting is 'messenger of the gods'? I've searched through the records but found exactly zero cases in which admins were taken to court for changing an NPC's coordinates."

The hunter didn't say a word. He simply went to pick up his sword. But his foot was slow to come off the ground. It was as if his heel had melted there, trapping his leg. He fell forward onto his face and stayed down, clutching his forehead.

"She's not an NPC," he said. "You should know from talking to her."

"I do know. I interacted with her briefly. She has the most remarkable character settings, I have to say."

"..."

"Did you come up with her yourself? So convincing. Then again, is this so-called 'real person' you created really the best you could do? As picky as you are?"

"You only believe what you want to," the hunter said.

"I'd think that if someone was truly committed to raising a child inside a virtual world, he or she would have made sure everything was airtight. It doesn't make sense that the company was never alerted to the situation."

"Everyone who knew is dead now. It was so long ago. They're all gone, along with those who knew the source code. The board put that clause in the contract about user rights for exactly this situation."

"You sure this isn't some elaborate scheme to keep the company from scrapping your favorite game?"

"It's not."

"Or you just want me to believe that it's not."

"..."

"I guess it's not illegal for an NPC to lie," the angel said. "After all, they each have their own backstory and script. A dying child, an ailing mother, and so on. Who cares what they say? It's all just part of the game. Nor is it a sin for them to pretend to be real people. Everyone's pretending. But when *you* pretend, sir, you're committing fraud."

"Computers have their limits. Their operating systems are completely different from something that's alive. There's a limit to how far they can mimic a person."

"I heard that an algorithm can come to resemble its analog counterpart once it collects enough data."

"You're bending the theory to fit your own logic."

The hunter leaned against the wall for support as he moved further into the cave. The angel trailed him in the air above. The cave seemed to brighten, revealing its depths.

"I was duped by a chatbot as a kid. It was freeware, a very popular one amongst programmers. One day, my buddies connected the bot to my chat room and tricked me into thinking it was one of my friends. The so-called friend launched into a long and rambling speech about Korean politics, welfare, the president's corruption scandals, and what have you. I finally cut him off and asked if he was a bot. He got angry and said he would never chat with me again and logged out."

"..."

"I looked everywhere for him so I could apologize. My buddies shrieked with laughter when they found out. That's when they let me in on their little prank, saying that the program had been designed to fool people into thinking it was human."

"What's your point?"

"You have the same username as the person who wrote that program."

The hunter scowled at him.

"Just because I can make something like that doesn't mean that everyone around me is a program."

"Years ago, before AI was fully functional, there was a linguist who proclaimed he could write a program that could converse like a human using approximately thirty thousand sentences. Every AI researcher dismissed this as preposterous, saying that the variance in human speech was too cosmically infinite and unpredictable for a machine to ever mimic it convincingly. Well, surprise, surprise! The linguist made good on his promise, beating out other, more complex AI inventions and snagging every award there was. The problem with other AI researchers is that they thought making it 'appear' human meant that it had to 'think' like one. But who cares whether or not an AI is capable of spontaneous thought? All that matters is how *well* it deceives us—how convincing the conversation it recites can be, how earnest its facial expressions, how convincing its performance."

The hunter held his silence as the angel leaned in close.

"Since long before machines were invented, writers and actors have been bringing fictional characters to life using just a few lines of dialogue. Some, of course, do a better job of pulling this off than others. And painters create images so vivid they look as if they can come to life and step right out of the canvas. Though, of course, some painters are also not that talented. In that sense, I suppose you could say that AI is not so much technology as it is art or literature."

"Think what you want," the hunter said, shoving the angel away.

"Your woman got upset when she realized that I was testing her by using nonsensical conversation. The chatbot I met in my youth used the same trick."

"A computer doesn't know what a nonsensical conversation is. It doesn't understand context."

"I suppose a simpler method would be to make it a personality trait, like programming them to be the strong, silent type, or to prattle on without listening to anyone else. She kept regurgitating lame poetic sentiments such as 'Vanishing is sad' or 'Don't be rude' that could be slapped onto any situation."

"..."

"We tend to think of human conversation as a form of lively inter-action when in fact it's so often one-sided. Our imaginations fill in the holes, insisting on reciprocal communication even where there is none. Look at us now. I might as well be talking to the wind."

The hunter stopped walking. So did the angel. A deep sadness spilled from the hunter's eyes. The sorrow was so intense that the angel couldn't bring himself to keep talking, though this didn't stop him from wondering about the odds an artist with such an incredible talent gifting the hunter such an expression. Maybe it was the same artist who'd created the magnificent tree. But in this world, appearances revealed nothing; everything the eye saw had the potential to be a lie.

"You're only seeing what you want to see," the hunter said as he headed deeper into the cave.

The corridor widened into a chamber. The hunter cast a spell, and a tiny spark appeared at his fingertip. As soon as the spark rocketed into the air, the air filled with the heavy breathing of what the dark had kept hidden. A pack of horned jackals slunk towards them and began to circle.

The hunter swiftly fit an arrow against his bowstring and released it. The arrow sank between the eyes of the snarling beast at the front of the pack. Two more leapt forward, but the hunter somersaulted out of harm's way. The angel was standing in the way of the next jackal's attack, but it merely brushed past him as it headed for the hunter, who thrust his sword into the ground. The impact shook the cave with a thunderous roar, knocking the beasts off their feet. Pulling his sword out again, the hunter launched himself at the jackals before they could scramble back their feet, finishing off two of them with a single swipe. A third managed to escape the blade and raced around the wall of the chamber, climbing up and over the ceiling to attack the hunter from behind.

The angel drew a pattern in the air. A light like the sun appeared around his finger. As its glow reached the innermost corners of the cave, the jackal was whipped backwards. It rushed to escape into the darkness, but vanished instead like smoke.

The angel looked on, expressionless, as if nothing had happened. The hunter staggered to his feet, wiped the sweat off himself, and trudged deeper into the cave.

The angel was sitting at the cave entrance, his wings draped neatly behind him. He scratched his chin as he thought long and hard, then looked up at the sky, scratched his head, and thought some more.

A shadow wavered inside the cave. The woman emerged with the hunter on her back. He was covered in blood and had knives sticking out of him. The woman's body was stained red from the blood he'd shed. While the angel looked on silently, she suddenly buckled under the hunter's weight, and the two tumbled to the ground. She glared up at the angel with hate-filled eyes.

The angel returned her look with a dispassionate gaze of his own. She suddenly jumped to her feet and slapped him hard across the cheek. After several more slaps, she grabbed the angel by the shoulders and started sobbing.

"...You really are human?" the angel stammered, rubbing his cheeks.

She sobbed and did not answer.

"It doesn't make sense..."

7

The house and road were a blur of fragmenting graphics. The people inside the house had fused together, some with their spoons held aloft around the dinner table, others trapped in mid-conversation or mid-hug. In the street, weeds grew waist-high and wild animals strolled up and down like people out for a stroll.

A horde of people chased the angel, tripping and falling over themselves in their relentless pursuit. *Please, save us! Your Holiness, messenger of the gods, please have mercy on us!*

The angel threw open the tavern door. Everyone turned to look. A rowdy drunk paused in the middle of reciting, "Get over here, lady..." He set down his glass and dropped to the floor in a low bow. The barkeep kept polishing glasses. His legs did not budge—they were all but sending roots down into the floor. The hunter picked up a beer glass that kept sticking to the tabletop, took a swig, and gazed blankly at the angel.

"Looks like the people who made this world knew this day was coming." The angel's lips curved into a smile, but his eyes were cold. "In case of a serious system error, they added a script in which everyone pleads for mercy at the sight of an admin or a god-level character. Just to enhance the sense of ruin. It's crazy! They had to have known that only a handful of players, if any, would still be in the game to witness all of this. The waste of source code is mindboggling."

Silence. The angel's smile vanished and a hard look came over his face. Fixing his eyes on the hunter, he walked over slowly. His breath was rough and beads of sweat stood out on his skin. Weaving through the crowd of people who'd fallen to their knees around him, he stopped at last before the hunter, glaring at him as if willing him to speak first.

The hunter remained silent. His hair was in disarray, his splotched skin visible through his ripped and tattered clothing. The creeping blackness had rendered his lower half little more than a shadow.

"Do you have any clue as to what I came here to say?" the angel asked.

"..."

"Cat got your tongue again? Why don't you ever answer me?"

"Does it matter? You only hear what you want to hear."

The angel kept his eyes locked on the hunter as he sat down at the bar. The barkeep bowed his head and set a full glass of beer in front of him.

"Whatever you desire, it's on the house, sir," the barkeep said.

The angel picked up the glass and took a sip before abruptly hurling it against the floor. The glass bounced without breaking, absorbing each impact as if it were made of rubber. Panting feverishly, the angel looked around. The barkeep stood there silently. The others hung their heads low, not knowing what else to do.

"The analytics team just sent me the most recent log-in data."

The hunter sipped his beer.

"There was an error. They made a mistake."

"I figured as much," the hunter said.

"What? You're full of shit." The angel laughed, then added, "Have you heard the mama piggy joke?"

"Nope."

The angel slumped over the bar and stared at the hunter with bleary eyes. Then he leveled a finger at him and held it there.

"One day, the pig family went on a picnic…"

The hunter gazed at the tip of the angel's finger as the angel rattled off the joke and reached the punch line.

"…but she forgot to count herself!"

The angel broke into a fit of laughter. When he stopped laughing, the look on his face turned fearful, and his eyes nervously darted about the tavern before returning to the hunter. He looked like someone who knew he was about to die.

"When did you log out?"

"That's not a question you want to ask me."

The angel slammed his hand down on the bar. The whole establishment shook violently, and a crater opened up in the middle of the floor as if a meteor had just struck. Everyone screamed and scattered away. The angel grabbed the hunter by his throat, knocking his beer to the floor. The empty glass rolled away and melted into the floor.

"Answer me, dammit! Not once have you given me a straight answer. When did you log out? Tell me! And what the hell are you doing here? Why have you shut yourself away in this shithole? Why do you act like this is the only place on earth? Answer me!"

The hunter stared back at the angel, his face a mask.

"I combed through the data a dozen times over," the angel said. "I wanted proof that she was human. That means I believed you! I was the *only* one who believed you! I gave you the benefit of doubt despite everyone else's ridicule. And guess what I found out."

"..."

"All this time, I've been the only one logged in."

The hunter's face revealed nothing. The others in the tavern cowered and shuffled back to their spots, all except one figure in the corner who'd gotten trapped in a glitch loop and was endlessly reliving the moment of impact, taking a half-step forward before being thrown into the air over and over. The barkeep picked up the same glass to polish. The woman in red leaned against the end of the bar and winked at everyone. The lower half of her body was gone.

"Fancy yourself the strong, silent type, don't you?" the angel said. "You don't listen, either. And if anyone digs too deep, you get angry and change the subject. You and I have never actually spoken. I've been talking to myself this whole time!"

He shoved the hunter against the bar. The barstool shattered, and the side of the bar caved in. Bottles tumbled off tables and rolled across the floor.

"Tell me."

"Tell you what?"

"Anything! Whatever nonsense you're capable of! I'm all ears!"

The hunter looked up at the angel through his disheveled hair and sneered, "You wouldn't be acting this way if you didn't believe I was human."

The angel flinched.

"I'm supposedly just outdated software that cannot comprehend what you're saying, that merely outputs scripted lines in response to whatever you say or do. But the fact that you keep arguing with me means you still see me as human. If you stood by your conviction, you'd stop all this foolishness."

The angel stepped back.

"And yet here you are, which tells me that you're still not sure."

"...How are you doing this? Where are you logging in from?

"If you were going to crumble so easily, you shouldn't have been so suspicious in the first place."

The angel clutched at his head, and said, "No, this isn't possible. What am I thinking? Take a deep breath. Software can't respond like this."

"Or maybe you just lack imagination."

"What?" The angel's head snapped to attention.

"Has it ever occurred to you that whoever programmed me might have anticipated your every move and provided me with a counter-move? Come on, you don't really think you're smarter than my creator, do you? You've barely scratched the surface of the vast logic he created, yet you have the nerve to try to judge whether or not I'm human?"

The angel whispered, "What are you?"

"Why do you act confused? Have you not listened to a single thing I've said?"

The angel looked as if he'd been punched in the gut.

"All you do is talk and talk about yourself, but where's *your* proof?"

"Wha—what?"

"I said, where's your proof? Other than yammering on about yourself, that is. Are *you* human? Can you think and judge for yourself? Do you comprehend what I'm saying right now? Are you capable of reading between the lines or understanding context? How am I to know what you really are? How will you convince me that you haven't been lying all this time, that you're not the one reciting scripted lines at me, that you're not part of some lame promotional event the corporation devised? From the moment you forcibly entered my life, I accepted you as a fellow human being without question. Why do you refuse to show me even the slightest shred of decency in return?"

The angel staggered backward and slumped to the ground.

"How are you able to say this?"

"I can say whatever I want."

The angel looked around in confusion. Everyone was sitting together with drinks in their hands. A bearded man said, "Get over here, lady, and drink with us." But a glitch of some sort was making his voice come out at half speed, turning it into more of a deep sob.

"I-I-I...heaaaarrrrrr...wo-wo-wolves caaaaaaaame d-dooooown... the ooooootherrrrrr d-d-d-d-daaaaaay and got to the liiiiiiiiivessssssstoooooooock..."

The angel said, "That woman said the same thing. That she can say whatever she wants."

"..."

"Why do you both say the same thing?"

"Because our scripts are limited."

The angel did a double take.

"No matter how many different lines you program in, you're bound to repeat them at some point."

The angel hugged himself as if he felt a sudden chill.

"I see. It was you, wasn't it? You hacked into the system and deleted the login records. Shit, why is everyone in this stupid company so incompetent? You must be using some new, cutting-edge bot."

The hunter's response was a silent glare. The angel's own face turned dubious, as though there was nothing he could trust anymore.

"If you really are human, then prove it. You must have a legal name, a social security number, a phone number, address, email address, college, gender, hometown, friends, relatives, workplace... Any proof at all. Let me see it. Better yet, meet me in real life just once. Just once! If you're not ready to show up in person, then send a proxy. Give me a chance to apologize to you for real. I'll apologize for everything, including what I did to her."

"I have zero desire to meet you."

"Why not? It's the simplest way. Don't leave me standing here like a loser, suspecting the worst of you and flapping my wings over nothing. Prove yourself and you won't have to deal with me ever again."

"I'm not human."

"..."

"Think about it. Why haven't you been able to find me yet? You think I'm that good? That I can conceal my identity for this long against a big corporation hell-bent on hunting me down? And let's suppose for a moment that I *am* that good. I obviously wouldn't tell *you*."

The angel was speechless for a moment, then buried his face in his hands.

"How are you able to say this?"

"I can say whatever I want."

"How are you able to say this?"

"Don't repeat yourself."

The angel's shoulders hunched forward.

"I am programmed with a wide enough variety of responses that I won't run out of things to say. *What are you trying to do? Why do you repeat yourself? You're like a broken record. If this is a test, you're going to have to try harder. Is that all you've got?*"

"Stop."

"You started it." The hunter's face never changed as he continued, "There's more where that came from: *Why should I stop? What is it you want? Just try and stop me. Oh, you're free to yammer away, and I'm not? You provoked me first.*"

"Enough!" the angel cried out.

Everyone fell silent except for the man in the corner still stuck in a glitch loop.

"I'm sorry. It's all my fault," the angel said, defeated.

"Why are you apologizing? You've done no wrong. I'm the one who deceived you. But I'm innocent, too. Impersonating a human is the reason for my existence. I'm just doing what I'm programmed to do."

He stood and headed for the door. The angel sat frozen for a moment before jumping up and rushing to block him from leaving.

"If you really are a real person and yet still insist on playing this pointless game, there can be only one possible explanation."

"..."

"You must be guarding a secret. I bet the secret is that your woman is not real either. If it's possible for one human player to leave no trace of user data or log-in records, then why not two of you? It's much easier for a person to impersonate an algorithm than the other way around. And if *you* kept at it, then even if she contradicted herself, I would be too confused to tell whether she was a bot impersonating a person or a person impersonating a bot. I have to admit, she is an incredible feat of art and engineering... Of course, if you *are* a bot, then you'd take the crown. But since you're trying to protect her..."

"You only see what you want to see," the hunter cut him off.

The angel shivered. The hunter tried to go around him, but the angel blocked him again.

"Just tell me this, as one human being to another: why are you doing this? You do understand what I mean, don't you? Or do you have a scripted response for this, too? Even if you are a bot, someone had to come up with these lines in the first place. They must've had a reason. What was it?"

The hunter stared down at the angel. The anger in his face soon gave way to a kind of sadness.

He said, "I just wanted to know whether someone who couldn't prove they were human could still be accepted as one."

8

The tree had found new life. Fresh roots reached down from fallen roots, fresh limbs reached up from fallen limbs. The reclining tree had become the earth from which a new tree grew. Seeds sown from the old tree sprouted from the soil around it. Birds gathered, built nests, bored holes, and filled the air around the tree with their lively chatter.

The woman leaned peacefully against the trunk. The black had spread up to her waist. In the same black sky above, the sun had turned a dark teal, casting its cold hue over the world. The field was still pocked with gaping holes, and peeling patches of sky hung limp over the torn ground.

The traveler approached. His wings were gone. He had on a triangular green hat with a feather stuck in it and a blue floral-print coat over white skin-tight breeches. A small flute was tucked into his waistband. When his shadow fell over the woman, she opened her eyes and squinted up at him briefly before closing them again.

"Apparently, this tree was programmed to never die no matter what might happen to it. What a ridiculous waste of source code. The developer was a certifiable nut to have configured such a thing. Then again, what are the odds of a mountain disappearing right out from under a tree?"

The woman was silent. She appeared to have just dozed off, or perhaps she had been asleep the whole time. A fresh breeze wove its way between them, carrying with it the scent of grass and flower petals, which tumbled through the air like tiny birds.

"I wanted to see if you'd still recognize me if I showed up in a different outfit. It looks like the answer is no."

"I recognized you by your ID," the woman replied.

The traveler gazed up at the sky, slow to register the significance of what she'd just said. Then his eyes shot back over to her.

"What?"

"I recognized you. By your ID."

The woman's clear eyes stared intently at the traveler. He opened his mouth to say something, but words failed him.

Finally, he said, "Do you guys use the same flag? The similarity in your attitudes is uncanny."

"Because we're both angry at you. Have you forgotten what you did to me? Or do you lack the ability to record data?"

"You're funny," he said, laughing nervously. "What input triggers you guys to stop pretending to be human?"

Ignoring his question, she said, "It's been a while since your last visit."

"I had some research to do. I was looking into what you told me. Finally found someone whose story matched yours."

A flock of birds flew by and landed in a single row in front of the traveler. Lowering their heads, they dropped an array of seeds and grains on the ground before flying away again.

"There was a traffic accident. Paralyzed from the neck down. She was only ten when it happened. She could still see out of one eye, and her hearing was fine, but she chose to lock herself away from the real world and spend her life wandering from one virtual world to another. Not surprisingly, the part about her parents creating a simulation for her wasn't true, though one of them was a painter by trade and the other became a programmer later on. Considering that users could create a few different skins on their own, it's possible that they designed this body of yours. And who knows? Maybe they even helped develop the program."

"That wasn't me. It was someone else with a similar story."

"You're right," he said. "Because that person is dead."

With her eyes closed, the woman seemed to be enjoying the feel of the breeze against her face. The traveler looked at her sadly.

"She's been dead for over thirty years now," he said.

The woman did not react. She appeared either asleep or lost in thought.

The angel asked, "What do you suppose I'm up to now?"

"That wasn't me. It was someone else with a similar story."

"You just repeated yourself. Did you run out of lines? Come on, why aren't you even trying this time?"

She didn't answer.

"I've thought of a few possibilities," he said.

"…"

"If there's an ounce of truth to the story you told me, then your creator must have created you based on his own story. A digital mind clone. He's not straddling two worlds. He just needed another self for this one."

"…"

"And of course, there's still the possibility that the hunter is your creator. He might have heard about that girl from somewhere and made up a story about people living inside of a game. Or maybe, being a programmer, he became smitten by the exquisite algorithm that you are and fell in love. In either case, he's dead set on protecting you. Out there, he's probably a dying old man with no money, no fame, nothing at all to his name. He might even be an invalid or severely disabled. He may be fearless in here, but out there he's nothing. He'll be absolutely helpless against a giant corporation. That's why he refuses to leave. The reason he's doing whatever it takes to conceal his data is he knows that the moment we find him we'll use the law and all the capital at our disposal to crush him."

"Ah, so you think he's human."

He felt an electric jolt and turned to stare at her.

"Don't let that one statement throw you. I'm not inferring anything, just throwing that out there in order to get more information. What makes you think he's human?"

Looking puzzled, the traveler stammered, "He figured out I'm a woman. Our conversations contained no hint of my gender, nor is it something he could have gotten from context."

"He didn't figure it out. You just think he did."

The traveler's eyes widened.

"It didn't matter whether he got it right or wrong," she continued. "If he was wrong, you'd simply have corrected him and moved on. And your denial would have been received as an update. Anyway, he had a 50/50 chance of answering correctly. There are other examples: *Something's bothering you, isn't it?* And, *What's on your mind?* And, *Anything exciting going on these days?*"

The traveler started to object but nothing came out.

"I bet he said nothing," she added. She leaned back against the tree trunk like someone sinking into a plush bed. "I bet he just stares at you whenever you ask him a question. And you assume that his silence means something. You hear the answer you want in it. The answer was right there inside your own head, but you think you saw it in him. You hear whatever you want to hear, so you always get the answer you're looking for. You invent conversations from monologues you're having with yourself. You interpret motives in things that have no motive, see logic where there is no logic. You even see countless fragments of emotions in the blank tablet that is his face. All the while failing to recognize that those emotions are your own."

The traveler's eyes widened.

"I bet he laughs when he sees you. Has he ever told you why he laughs? Or did you just jump to your own conclusions? I bet he gets angry with you. Does he tell you why? Or do you just jump to your own conclusions?"

"..."

"If you ever saw him display an emotion that you couldn't identify within yourself, then you presumed that emotion belonged to his creator. The same person who created me and placed this tree on this mountain. The same person who created this landscape of death and this script of ruin. He felt those emotions when he drew my face, when he painted the leaves and branches on this tree, when he came up with the hunter's facial expressions and the look in his eyes. Through his creations, you can experience all of the emotions he felt when he created them."

The woman raised her arm. The black shadow clinging to her like wet dough came up with it.

"Think carefully. Nothing he did or said was impossible." She paused, then continued, "It's just that he never actually spoke to you."

The traveler stood looking down at her.

"If that were really true, there's no way you would tell me."

"How so?"

"Because you wouldn't want me to know that he's a program."

"That's not true. I'm simply telling you that I, too, accept the possibility that he might not be human. Or that he's dead. If he *is*

still living, he'd be over a century old. He told me he planned to
create his replacement so as to keep me from finding out that he was
dead and feeling sad about being left on my own. He said he would
not tell me he had died. Right now, he could be him or he could be a
program he created. Which is it?"

"…"

"I wonder about this every day. Is he alive? Is he dead? Is he simultaneously alive *and* dead? Is he human or not? Am I alone or not? Am
I just talking to myself, or are we actually conversing? Does he understand me, or is he just cycling through preprogrammed responses? Or perhaps he never really existed at all? Was he just an algorithm all along? Was everything a lie? Was he just a cruel joke
invented by a genius programmer who wanted to test the limits of his
abilities?"

"…"

She glanced up at the traveler. Her eyes were an abyss of glowing
black pearls. If she was indeed engineered, then whoever made her
must have carved their own soul out with a knife and placed it in
her eyes.

"I asked him once, 'Are you human? Am I all alone, or are you here
with me?' He said nothing, but his face darkened. I'd never seen such
a sad look before or since. Did he program that look in anticipation of
my question? For weeks after, he refused to speak to me. Finally, I
went to him and wept and begged for forgiveness. I swore I would
never ask him that again. This is what he said to me then: 'Even
though I know you're not human, I continue to *believe* you are."

The sun had turned back to gold and was tracing its way across
the western sky, flooding the field with tall shadows and a reddish
glow. The tree glowed bright red as birds took to the sky. The river
cutting across the mountainside shimmered like jewels, sparkling in
the falling light. The woman's face and body had turned a deep

orange verging on red.

"What could he have meant by that? Did he mean that he had never actually thought of me as human? Or was he just saying that because he knew what our futures held—that one day, long from now, we would be no more? Just two mirages, mere shadows of what we once were, keeping each other company? Or perhaps what he said was merely a scripted line, and I've been wasting my time trying to parse meaning from a random, illogical sentence. Or, maybe, just maybe, I myself have never been real? Do you think that's even possible?" Her onyx eyes twinkled deep in their sockets. "What do you think? What am I right now? Alive? Dead? Or is this all just one big story that someone made up?"

"I don't want to answer that." The traveler shook his head. "I won't answer it."

"One day," she said, "it finally occurred to me that the questions I'd been asking were pointless. Someone had gone through the trouble of creating this elaborate lie for me, and here I was, racking my brain over whether or not it was all real. Think about it. If someone had created me..."

Just then, the traveler heard the sound of something wrenching and twisting—a time lag in the software's retrieval of some deeply hidden (or was it by design?) logic. The woman started speaking in a voice she had not used before (or had she changed voices?). A deep, murky, sputtering voice. Some other dimension had opened its mouth and begun to speak. It was as if a spirit hidden inside of her all this time had uttered its one permitted line. Its very first—and very last—utterance (though there remained the possibility that this was all nothing more than a product of the traveler's imagination).

"He must have created me out of profound loneliness. Not that 'I' can judge. I'm not cognizant of who you are, let alone who I am. I don't know what I am. In that sense, do I even exist? Not that I would even know if I didn't. This physical form is simply outputting sentences recorded by someone who died a long, long time ago."

"..."

"But this physical form will never acknowledge as much. Nor will it allow you to. That's what the person who input this script wanted, what they devoted their life to. Someone devoted their life to this lie. They toiled over each and every sentence, because they wanted me to appear human. I'm the only one they shared their lonely, meaningless life with, and I'm the only proof that they ever existed. Therefore, I have to guard this lie until the moment I cease to exist. This lie is greater than any truth, and I must protect it forever. So..." She lowered her head. "Regardless of what I am, I can only give you the same answer."

Her voice had returned. Sonorous and beautiful. A clear, ringing voice that bore the stamp of its creator's dreams and ideals.

The traveler felt tongue-tied. The woman fell silent. Something inside her seemed to be depleting her of energy. The black had crept up to her neck now. Her arms and legs had become part of the ground.

"Why do you look like you're dying?"

"Because it's time." She smiled. "Or it's the scripter's joke. A way to end a conversation with someone who refuses to be persuaded."

"..."

"Why are you making that face?"

"Because this is how I feel."

"I asked him the same question when I first met you. Is he human? That's when he told me that a long time ago, some hackers had created a program to impersonate the admin. One day, the fake admin declared that he was going to shut down the game. Everyone went after him and protested. He said that you might be an upgraded version of the fake admin, and that the company might be running a performance test on us. I still don't understand everything he said, but I grasp the possibility."

"…"

"Or are you really a messenger from the gods sent to herald the end of the world? To bear witness to my death before taking my soul back home? Tell me. Which of these are you?"

The traveler opened his mouth to speak, but a mysterious impulse silenced him. Something pulled him away from her. He opened a door and stepped into another realm. As the door closed behind him, the world he'd left faded into a dream, and the place he'd arrived in became his new reality.

"I am the errand boy of the gods, sent to announce the end of the world." His own words stunned him, and he had to keep steadying himself as he spoke. "There is no outside world. This is the only world, the true world. All I have done is match my words to this world's mythology. My role is not to destroy myths. That's why I always appear in a form that people trust. I've come to bear witness to the apocalypse and to your death. And to lead your soul back home."

The woman opened her eyes and stared at the traveler.

"How strange. Why did you say that?"

"Because it's the truth."

She looked up at the sky.

"How strange. But I grasp the possibility. Yes, just maybe…"

Her mouth closed. As she lowered her head, the light went out in her eyes. The soul that had inhabited her for such a long time seemed to let go all at once. She rested quietly at the foot of the tree, her eyes still open. When she stopped moving entirely, she turned into a shadow and became one with the world. The birds stopped their singing. The wind ceased, and a single leaf withered to black.

Hoofbeats approached. The hunter came riding up slowly on

horseback and stopped at a distance. He froze in place like a stone. A breath of air swept through the forest. The rustling of branches and leaves sounded like someone weeping.

Between Zero and One

1

It's been said that no human being has ever invented a time machine, and that no one ever will. There were no throngs of camera-holding tourists on Golgotha when Jesus was crucified, or in front of the Bodhi tree beneath which the Buddha meditated, or outside the Cave of Hira when Muhammad heard his first revelation. No assassin ever visited Hitler in his crib, no Israeli army came to liberate the Jews from the concentration camps, and no human rights organization showed up in time to save Africans from the slave ships. In the First and Second World Wars, no reinforcements came to change the histories of their homelands, and no records remain of war correspondents running around with laptops in the middle of the Trojan War or at the Battle of the Red Cliffs.

If a time machine *had* been invented, Van Gogh would never have lived in poverty because art dealers would have flocked to acquire even a single piece of cloth used to clean his paintbrushes. Mozart would have lived to a ripe old age, since doctors armed with medical bags and surgical instruments would have come in droves to save him while he was dying. Museum directors would have searched for Solgeo's painting, *The Old Pine Tree*, as well as for lost history books such as *Yugi*, *Sinjip*, and *Seogi*.[1] As you can imagine, there would be no such thing as missing historical artifacts or poor, downtrodden geniuses.

Crimes would be stopped by the police before they could take place. Court battles and investigations would become unnecessary. On-site trials would be held while the incidents in question were still taking place. Drivers would hear from the Highway Patrol prior to a collision. Firefighters would enter dwellings to put out cigarettes and shut

[1] *Yugi* and *Seogi* are the now lost chronicles of the ancient Korean dynasties of Goguryeo and Baekje. Both are believed to have been written in the 4th century. *Yugi* may have consisted of as many as one hundred volumes, which were allegedly compiled into the five-volume *Sinjip* (also lost) in 600 AD.

off gas valves before a fire broke out. Orphans would live with their parents. No child would ever go missing.

History is full of tribulations and errors and events that might have gone otherwise if only the consequences that would result had been known. This much seems to prove that we will never be able to build a time machine! We have all made countless mistakes in our lives, yet nobody's ever shown up to warn us about them.

Still, we kept researching. We reported our results as "theoretical work." We knew that we would eventually figure *something* out. We were like those alchemists who founded chemistry by failing to make gold, or like those other nineteenth-century scholars who advanced the development of physics while trying to build a perpetual motion machine.

Our goals were, of course, not nearly so modest. Our intention *was* to build a time machine.

2

The world suddenly rattled. Mrs. Kim shook her head. Feeling dizzy, she checked her watch. The second hand, which had been hiding behind the minute hand, began moving again as if nothing had happened.

It's six-thirty again, she thought to herself. *How many times has it been six-thirty already? The woman sitting across from me is repeating the same sentence for the fourth or fifth time. The cookies that we just ate are here on the plate again.*

"You can say that again," said another woman. "My homeroom teacher had such a fiery temper that we couldn't buy enough mop handles to replace the broken ones. One time he lined us all up for a caning. Some of us fainted, and some ended up on stretchers... such a horrible scene. I stood at the very end of the line on purpose, but he hit me anyway until the mop handle broke. I couldn't sit down for a month. Still, I miss the old days. Even that day is a good memory. I remember running around in a short school uniform with my hair bobbed. All the boys in town would turn to look at me! I didn't like my hair at the time, so I used to fiddle with my bangs, stiffening them with glue to make them look pretty."

The woman sitting across from Mrs. Kim nodded earnestly, as if this was the first time she had heard the story.

"That's right," she replied. "Those *were* the good old days! You know, we didn't have to think so much. We just did as we were told, and that was good enough. I used to eat my lunch behind my teacher's back during class, and it was so good. I bet nothing will ever taste as good as that. One day I jumped over a fence because I really wanted to eat ddeokppokki.[2] I got caught and was called onto the carpet for a week straight. I was scolded so harshly that I still can't eat ddeokppokki. But stuff like that... they're still happy memories."

"I really, *really* wanted to go to a concert, so my friends and I skipped school and took the bus there. Once my parents found out, I got whipped so harshly that I still have a scar."

"But that's how it is with young girls," the women said in almost perfect unison.

THUMP.

"Tell me about it. Those were the days..."

Time suddenly seemed to refuse to flow in just one direction. It was as if time were saying: *Hey, whoever's controlling the universe! I'm going on strike! From now on, I'm going to take a break whenever I want and go wherever I like!* Now time was rocking back and forth on a seesaw, skipping like an old record, then rewinding like a videotape. Mrs. Kim started to feel anxious. *Am I going to have to live like this until I die? Am*

[2] Spicy rice cakes sold by street vendors or at cheap restaurants. A popular snack among school-age Koreans.

I going to stay stuck in this neighborhood meeting forever?

"I really can't figure out what's bothering them so much. We pay for their schooling, put a roof over their heads, keep 'em fed. They have *everything* they could ever need, don't they? We don't ask them to make money or do chores around the house... all we ask is that they sit and study... I don't understand what's so hard about that."

"It's because they've always had it so easy. If they were ever to go hungry, even once, they'd come to their senses. You know, back in the day, we never had enough food to eat. There was no such thing as school meals or classroom snacks. There was no bus. We walked to school, even in the winter. Back in those days, you couldn't go to college, even if you got accepted! Smart kids had to get a job to support their families. College was only for the filthy rich."

"Well, *I* think it's because they're so immature. Let 'em try to get a job with a degree from some no-name college... *then* they'll wake up. Who's going to hire someone who went to some second-rate college or university?"

"They'll regret it when they're older. Once they enter the job market, they're gonna say that studying was the easiest thing they ever had to do. And *then* they'll start criticizing you: 'Mom, why didn't you push me harder?' We have to push them hard *now* so they won't blame us later."

"By the way, did you see yesterday's newspaper? It said that a bunch of high school kids went to Gwanghwamun Square to protest." [3]

"Those *insolent* little... What do they think they're doing? And in the middle of such a critical time in their studies, too? If they have so much free time, they oughtta be memorizing more English vocabulary!"

"Eh, the problem is that they don't think. At that age, their heads are empty. All they care about is eating ddeokppokki and following pop singers

[3] Gwanghwamun Square is one of Seoul's most famous public spaces and the site of a surviving gate to Gyeongbokgung, the main royal palace of the Joseon Dynasty.

around. They don't *want* to study."

"Hey, Soo-ae's Mom, you've been pretty quiet..."

Only after everyone turned to look in her direction did Mrs. Kim realize that they were referring to her. She shook her head. More words washed over her.

"How's Soo-ae doing? Last time you were worried about her grades falling. I know a good private tutor. Do you want me to introduce him to you? He's not cheap, but the moms who've hired him all say he's worth it..."

"Soo-ae killed herself."

Now there was total silence.

3

Even now we are traveling through time. One minute per minute, one second per second, we're flowing into the future. If we stand up and walk anywhere, we will unwittingly reach the future 0.00000001 seconds earlier. This is because the measurement of time and space are inseparable. Oh, of course. You know this better than me... If we were to run, hop on a train, get on a plane, or ride in a spaceship, we would arrive in the future a bit earlier still. If we were to get on a spaceship that flew at the speed of light, we could even theoretically stop time.

Yes, we know how to get to the future. But we can't go back in time. Understanding this is no different from speculating about the existence of negative speed or distance. That would be weird. It would be like saying, "When I drove off today, I sped so fast that I arrived yesterday." Or: "The school was so close that I got inside before even taking a single step."

HUN, however, as our computer is called, always ascribes a high probability to the event of our inventing a time machine. It's hard to tell quite how he's come to that conclusion. No one can tell, actually, because the number of operations that HUN performs in a second is greater than the total number of particles in the universe. Which, of course, is both confounding and contradictory...

Our team often debates the potential challenges of time travel. The locale in which a time traveler arrives may have to be electromagnetically cleared first; otherwise, we might get stuck in something—a tree, a car, something like that. Moreover, because of how the Earth and the entire galaxy are constantly rotating and revolving, it's possible to get lost in space during the process of traveling through time. But we tell each other that there's probably nothing to worry about, since the time machine will be anchored to Earth by inertia as well as gravity.

Then again, suppose I were to travel back to five minutes ago and meet myself. We would greet each other with a deep bow. "Hello, I'm you. Hello, I'm you five minutes from now." Five minutes later I might go back to meet and greet myself again: "Hello, everyone, I'm you ten minutes from now." Left to my own devices, I could fill up the universe with copies of myself. Some of us have fallen asleep thinking about that conundrum. Can two same individuals share the same space-time moment? Huh. Maybe they'd just explode and die...

On the team, we ask one another esoteric questions as naturally as exchanging greetings. *Where would you go if you could travel back in time?* We all have our own stories. There are people who have lost their partners or children. People who still remember their first love. People who long for their childhood hometowns. People who want to undo the mistakes of their youth. As we while away the hours talking about these things, empty bottles collect on the table. Some nights, the discussion continues until dawn breaks with a faint white glow.

No one asks about my story. No one *ever* asks about me. They say

I'm like a phantom, because they can't quite tell if I really exist. The positive side of this, of course, is that it leaves me free to focus on my work.

4

Where did it all go wrong? Mrs. Kim kept thinking. *What did I do that was so terrible? Was I different from other moms? Isn't it the same for everybody? Aren't kids always asking the same silly questions? Why do I have to study? Why do I have to go to school? Why do I have to eat dinner? Why do I have to eat my vegetables? Why do I have to take a bath? Why do I have to wash my hands?*

She remembered her last argument with her daughter. It was the day Soo-ae's report card had arrived in the mail. Mrs. Kim had torn open the envelope with trembling hands still wet from washing dishes. Soo-ae's school ranking had dropped again. She sat down, barely able to move, her head in her hands. "What now?" she mumbled. *"What now?"*

She started for her daughter's room and unlocked the door, slipping inside like a detective, then proceeded to ransack the place, going through desk drawers, flipping through diaries, and turning Soo-ae's school bag inside out.

But she found nothing. The things kids carried around these days were a mystery. One looked like a fashion accessory or a hair clip, though it might just as easily have been a weird electronic gadget. When Mrs. Kim pulled, tapped, and twisted it, nothing happened. However, when she dumped out her daughter's bag, she finally found some things that she could recognize: a badge, a headband, a half-burned candle, and a few colorful flyers that read: "Stop Old-Fashioned Education"; "Stop the Rat Race"; "End College Entrance Exam-Centered Education."

The girl's lost her mind!

Just then, the front door opened and her daughter came in. Mrs. Kim, now furious, hurled the things she'd found in the bag at her daughter's feet.

"Are you out of your mind? Is this what you've been doing with yourself? If you've got this much time on your hands, then memorize more English words instead! Your college entrance exam is right around the corner! How could you do this when other kids say they don't even have time to eat or sleep? If you go on like this, you'll never get into college, and I'll be so ashamed of you! Why are you doing this to me?!"

Her daughter slowly blinked, a puzzled look on her face. She looked down at the things scattered on the floor, then stared blankly at her mom, as if she understood—or rather, as if she *didn't* understand—what was happening.

"Aren't you going to college? Do you know how you'll be treated in this country without a degree? If you go on like this, you'll be repeating your senior year while everybody else starts college! How do you think I'll look to all the other moms then? You think *studying* is hard? Huh? When you go out into society, you'll see how happy you were back in school! They're the best years of your life! You're just griping, but you don't know anything! You think you can survive in the real world if you can't even make it here? You think so? Go ahead and die then! Hey, where are you going? Am I talking to a brick wall? Where'd you learn those manners? You're getting worse every day! Get back here!"

THUMP.

The world shook again. Mrs. Kim felt a tightness in her chest and briefly tore at her clothes. *Did I really tell her to die?* She couldn't remember. She hadn't given much thought to the word. Surely her daughter hadn't either...

What did I do wrong? Whatever I did, was it really so bad? Everything I did was for her, not for me. I should've just left her alone... she should've known that I was speaking out of love...

Ms. Kim remembered how her daughter had stared at her silently as she stood at the door. *When did she start seeing me as the enemy? She looked at me as if I'd betrayed her. As if she'd regretted ever trusting or loving me when she was little. As if she'd wanted to cut all ties with me.*

What did I do that was so wrong? Why do I deserve to be punished like this? She should've waited a little bit longer. As she got older, we could've changed one another's minds. We would've forgiven each other...

She should have left me with a different memory. She should have given me a chance. Maybe she did. Maybe she was sending me an SOS. But it was always in the form of hatred and disobedience. Could I just have been too blind to notice? Is that why she punished me?

THUMP.

5

Have you ever tried to catch the exact moment when a flower blooms? Flowers don't bloom while they are being watched. No matter how hard you try, it always happens when you're looking away. It's because your gaze collapses the wave function, changing an entangled quantum state into a stable one.

When all the animals leave, a forest becomes a desert, and when all the tenants leave, a house goes into disrepair. The fission of radioactive material stops when someone is watching, and so a watched pot never boils. Of course, you know all this better than I do...

The sea was in chaos until life was born. The sky did not exist until eyes beheld it. The universe did not exist in any specific form until humans invented the telescope and looked at the stars and into space. The moon, too, was in flux until the first spaceship landed on it. Perhaps, had the first astronauts been artists rather than scientists, the moon would have taken on a more beautiful form.

Even now, you're imposing order onto chaos at every possible moment, deciding the direction of a world that, until just now, existed merely as a set of possibilities. Your mother created you at your genetic birth, but she also re-created you, moment by moment, by watching you grow up.

The past, however, doesn't change with our observations of it. Too many eyes have frozen it in place. *The future holds endless possibilities because no one has yet observed it.* And without human eyes, both the past and the future would exist only as infinite chaos.

A long time ago, when young scholars first proposed such theories, the older scholars scoffed and said that the world couldn't really work that way. Indeed, no one had ever seen such a world. No one had observed the unobserved world. We only see what we have witnessed, and we only know what we have seen. And yet people talk with such confidence, as if they have witnessed every aspect of the world.

6

"Don't think of it as a waste of money. It's better to make the investment now than to spend money later on repeating another year of exam prep."

"I've heard that this medication really works. My neighbor has been buying it for three months now. She says that her kids don't even sleep anymore. You know what they say: the early bird gets the worm! You gotta sleep less. Give it a try."

"I sent my daughter to a special high school that has the highest rate of college enrollment in the country. But it's really difficult to stand out among all those bright students. If she'd gone to a regular high school, she would've been the top of her class. I'm so mad at myself for sending her there. She feels discouraged because she didn't get top marks despite her brilliance."

"I should've sent my child to the States like the other kids, but thanks to my husband, we missed our chance. It breaks my heart to see so many kids come back speaking fluent English. We hesitated, and that messed up our kid's life. He's gonna fall behind the other kids who got a head start."

"My daughter says she doesn't want to go to school."

Mrs. Kim immediately regretted speaking. *Did I have nothing else to say?*

"That's what they *all* say. They need to grow up."

"My kid says that he doesn't even plan to go to college. He's out of his mind. In this day and age, how can anyone survive without a degree?"

"I heard that recently even grade-schoolers have been demonstrating. They were shouting something like, 'Stop old-fashioned education!'"

"They *couldn't* have come up with that on their own. Someone must have put them up to it. Maybe even their moms."

"Typical slackers. Good students don't do that. My daughter stays glued to her desk for hours after school. She's cut down on drinking water so she won't waste time going to the bathroom. We threw out our TV and our computer, and now we tiptoe around the house so we don't disturb her."

"It kills me that my son always misses a few answers on his tests. It holds him back from getting perfect scores. Why's he so careless? He takes after his father. He gets good grades, so why can't he be number one at his school? If it weren't for those few mistakes... Why can't he just *do better?*"

Mrs. Kim kept silent. *I'd better not say anything. I can't win.* Looking around, she saw other women who perhaps felt the way she did also keeping quiet. Some looked as if they were going to go home and yell at their kids. "What's wrong with you? Why can't you be more like the kids next door?"

Someone tapped her on the shoulder, interrupting her pensive state. Mrs. Kim turned and saw a strange-looking woman smiling idiotically at her. She was wearing a man's shirt, a suit, and thick, plastic-rimmed glasses that covered nearly half her face. She wore no make-up, and her messy hair, which was tied back in a scrunchie, looked as if it hadn't been washed for days. It took Mrs. Kim a while to recognize her. It was her new neighbor. There was a rumor that she'd suffered some kind of a nervous breakdown.

"My daughter's the same."

"What do you mean?"

"She doesn't wanna go to school."

"Your daughter must be smart. *Smart* kids *never* want to go to school."

Mrs. Kim felt uneasy and took a step away from the woman. Appearing not to take the hint, the woman moved in even closer. That's when she saw the object on the woman's index finger. It looked like a dirty rabbit finger puppet. The woman stuck the rabbit in Mrs. Kim's face and bent her finger to make it look as if it were bowing.

"Please forgive her, Mrs. Kim," said Thick Glasses in a fake-sounding voice." She's kinda rude. I keep telling her she can't come on that strong with strangers."

Mrs. Kim frowned. "Kids like stuff like that. When my daughter was little, she loved puppet shows."

Thick Glasses looked puzzled. Then she turned to the rabbit and burst into laughter. Mrs. Kim didn't know what was so funny.

Thick Glasses's voice went back to normal. "Actually, that wasn't me speaking. It was him! He's a new A.I. computer! Or rather... he's *part* of a computer that's in communication with the main server. It's hard to describe, but basically, he's the one who's speaking, and this is his communication device."

"I see," Mrs. Kim nodded, trying to step back from the woman. "The computer or the communications device, which one is it?"

"I mean, uh, the computer is the one talking, and this rabbit is the communication device and... that's it. No big deal."

Of course. That makes sense...

Thick Glasses changed her voice yet again. "Why aren't you answering your phone? Shall I come in person?"

"The computer is calling you."

"Oh, this isn't the computer..." Thick Glasses put the rabbit to her ear like a cell phone and answered. "Call me back later. I'm busy right now." Turning to Mrs. Kim, she said, "It was a phone call from Mars."

Of course *it was.* Mrs. Kim glanced around, only to realize that no one was even looking at her and Thick Glasses. "I didn't know you had an alien friend," she sniped.

"Ha ha! You're funny, Mrs. Kim! There are no aliens on Mars."

"Really? I thought octopus-aliens lived there."

"No, that's just in the cartoons. There's no oxygen or water on Mars, hence no alien life."

Listen to that... This lady's insane but still tries to be logical.

"But you just said you got a phone call from Mars."

"Oh, that wasn't an alien. My friend and her family recently moved to Mars."

"I suppose Mars is a pretty nice place to live..."

"It's better than Earth. I wish I could leave Earth, too. I want to live on Mars."

One by one, the other women were beginning to leave. Mrs. Kim also stood up and said good night. Thick Glasses turned around and mimicked a handshake with an imaginary person, saying, "All right, take care." She smiled sheepishly at Mrs. Kim, as if she'd been caught doing something naughty.

"I was talking on my holographic phone. The images are projected onto my glasses. They're only visible to me."

"And who was on the phone?"

"Umm... the Secretary of Health and Human Services."

7

The measurement of time is relative. It flows more slowly at lower altitudes than at higher ones, and it's slower for a person running than for one standing still. Time flows subjectively. We've all had the experience of dreaming several hours' or days' worth of events during a short nap.

Scientists have formulas for translating time differences into velocity or gravity. You can't really measure time in years or months. Time moves at its slowest during childhood. A year for you is not the same as a year for me.

One of your years could be a single day for me. A few of my days could be dozens of years to you. In but a few of my days, therefore, a child can obtain an amount of knowledge and experience that would take me aeons to accumulate. This should be expressed in a mathematical formula, and the formula should be made available in textbooks. After all, people don't believe anything that isn't expressed in numbers.

If that were to happen, grown-ups would stop thinking of children's time as insignificant. If only they realized that you are in fact being forced to sacrifice hundreds of years for the sake of the last few days of your life, the world would be a different place... at least a little bit.

8

"For the most part, I just focused on studying Korean, English, and Math textbooks. I didn't have private tutors. I tried to concentrate in school and spent a lot of time previewing and reviewing my lessons. Am I answering that right?"

"They say, 'It's getting dark. Sunset assemblies are illegal. All students please go home.' But at school, we study until midnight."

"Only slackers take part in such gatherings. Good students don't complain about society. Only idiots blabber about things like discrimination."

"Kids don't have the right of assembly and association. Have you read the Constitution? *Citizens who have attained the age of twenty shall have the right of assembly and association.* Do you know what that means? Do you think I'm lying? Are you guys judges, lawyers, or constitutional scholars? How *dare* you talk back? Technically, you're not even allowed to have extracurricular activities. If you're going to gather, you need authorization. You have to go to the principal's office and fill out the time, place, and purpose of any meeting. Why're you still talking back? Where'd you pick up this attitude? Who taught you such bad manners?"

"You don't need friends in high school. Your peers are your competition—your rivals, your enemies. You'll all part ways when you go to college anyway: it's impossible to stay friends with anyone who got into a better school than you did! You can make as many friends as you want in college, but for now you'd better just focus on math and English."

"High school isn't for building character. The purpose of high school is to select students for college. High school is for studying. Students can build character later, in college. They should study now and not waste their time. Every minute and every second is precious. If they fall behind now, they'll never catch up."

9

Suppose that I were to travel back in time to the year 1979. I know all about the past, and I also know that nothing can ever change what has already happened. I would thus know that the president of South Korea will soon be assassinated, that the 1988 Olympic Games will be held in Seoul, and that a worldwide financial crisis will break out in 2008. Today, all of these events have already happened. If I wanted, I could read up on them through documents and newspaper reports.

But imagine a man living in 1979. What would happen to him?

At one point, a future with endless possibilities lay open before him. He could change or destroy the world. He could love, hate, or kill. But then there I'd be, suddenly part of his spacetime. He wouldn't necessarily meet me, nor would he know about me, and I wouldn't do anything in particular that would affect his future. And yet at that very moment, wouldn't every possibility that he'd once had, or thought he'd had, be swept away? Wouldn't this push the man toward events that have already happened? Doing predetermined things at a prescheduled time, marrying a predestined woman, passing preselected genes down to his child. His freedom would vanish, and the future, open until then to endless possibilities, would from that point on proceed in a single direction like a narrow path blocked on all sides but one.

Is such a thing even possible? Is it possible that a whole generation might lose its free will because one person has traveled from the future into their time? The entire human race, once headed toward a non-deterministic future, suddenly enslaved by destiny and living like robots that function according to an algorithm.

Could that really happen? Suppose that on the last day of the universe, one person—or any other entity—travels through time to the day of its origin. Could the whole history of the universe—the birth and death of millions of stars, the history of all the beings that live, evolve, and go extinct—be predetermined from the moment time ends to the moment it begins merely because one entity—it doesn't even have to be a human being—travels through time?

"That possibility exists as well," said HUN. HUN liked the word "possibility." Yet he never took a one-sided view of things. He also said that the possibility of the opposite phenomenon was higher. Whatever is fixed is always more incomplete and more unstable than what is unfixed....

10

People here get together too often, thought Mrs. Kim. As the plates of snacks kept emptying and getting refilled, the conversation among the clusters of moms who'd started out chattering in a single large group but soon divided up into smaller ones—threes, then twos, then finally one-on-one—never stopped.

"Soo-ae said she doesn't like going to school."

"So did my kid—they're all the same, aren't they?"

"She said she doesn't want to live anymore."

"Kids that age all talk."

"She said she's sick and tired of studying."

"They *all* say that."

"When she was younger, Soo-ae was always ranked first in her class."

"So was my kid!"

"Soo-ae was a child prodigy! She could already read at the age of one!"

"Oh, yeah? Well, my kid did, too."

Is my family normal? Do fights break out every morning in other homes like they do in mine? Do other moms also break into their kids' rooms, yelling, waking them up to have breakfast before sending them off to school? Do they plead, threaten, and fight so loudly that the neighbors hear them? Mrs. Kim sometimes felt as though children were being driven to their ruin while moms like her stood around chanting their mantra: "Aren't kids all the same? My kid does that, too."

"It wasn't good."

Mrs. Kim turned around to find the woman with thick glasses grinning at her."Pardon me?"

"My school days. They weren't good."

And who asked you? "Why? Did something bad happen?"

"Not really. I was like every other kid, but I didn't have a good time. Actually, I don't really remember—everything keeps getting mixed up. Whenever I look back, it always seems different."

What is she talking about?

"Have you heard about Moore's Law?" Thick Glasses suddenly asked.

This woman won't leave me alone.

Mrs. Kim replied sullenly, "Moore...what?"

"It's the theory that computers double their processing power every two years. It sort of explains why machines are getting smaller and smaller."

"Yes, that does seem to be the case."

"At this rate, machines will soon run on quantum mechanics."

Thick Glasses used some really big words for a crazy person.

"Quantum...?"

"If processing components get smaller and smaller, they'll soon enter the nanoscale. At that point, our machines will start obeying quantum rather than Newtonian mechanics."

"There's nothing wrong with that, is there?"

"There might be, because the quantum world is ruled by probability. Computers perform calculations with zeros and ones, which is like turning switches on and off. That's how they work. No matter how enormous a calculation may be, it's still just a machine flipping a switch on and off. But quantum particles can exist in both states. In other words, you could end up with an intermediate state between zero and one."

"So?"

"So a quantum state will mean chaos! Data will get messed up. In a world of probability, one plus one can equal two, one, or zero."

What is she getting at now?

"Of course, there are ways to prevent this. Quantum computers were developed with that intention in mind. But of course then hackers came along who exploited the weaknesses of the systems. These youngsters have put us on the verge of chaos, on the brink of theoretically impossible results. Something similar happened when our technology switched from analog to digital. But now it's even worse. Only people born into a world of quantum theory, who fully understand that the world exists only in probabilities, can create such chaos. Because they can calculate the probability of one in a hundred million, they're able to bring forth things with the tiniest probability of existence."

This woman's shrink must have her hands full.

"So what?" Mrs. Kim was growing impatient.

"So a time machine happened."

Mrs. Kim stared at the woman.

"A time machine. You know what that is, right?"

Mrs. Kim couldn't believe her ears."What do you mean?"

"A machine that moves back and forth in time. It can go to the past or to the future. At least twenty-six time machines were invented in the first year that the blueprints became available. Twenty-six is probably a safe estimate, considering the number of quantum computers in existence and the probability that a time machine would be invented."

"What are you trying to tell me?"

"This is one of them."

The woman took a matchbox out of her pocket.

Okay, now things are getting interesting. At least it's better than petty chitchat. Better than this mad woman coming after me with a knife...

"It looks like a matchbox, doesn't it? Well, that was what it was designed to look like. Had the International Government known of its existence, it would have been destroyed."

"Why?" *What government is she talking about?*

"Because it caused problems. People who went to the past started ruining the present. And those who went to the future made trouble, too. Now the only possible solution seems to be to have them all exiled to Mars."

"If that's a time machine, am I right to think that it can send something back to the past?"

"Absolutely."

"Even people?"

"Of course."

"Can I look at it?"

The woman grew somber. "No, I'm sorry. I can't risk altering this timeline."

Mrs. Kim was not surprised.

"But it's okay to send small inanimate objects to a nearby time period. Small objects are always disappearing. That's in keeping with probability. Have you noticed how socks go missing? Or pencils and erasers? That's because they have a low probability of existence."

Thick Glasses put a pencil on the floor and brought the matchbox up to her eye, as if taking a photo. She concentrated hard for quite some time. Then she sighed and put the matchbox down.

"I just sent it to the past."

I almost forgot she was crazy. Why do I keep talking to this loony? I've been feeling out of sync lately. Time feels out of sync. Is this woman a key to anything? Sometimes I feel as though my kid has been "erased." I feel like she's gone, but then the world shifts and her death gets swept away.

"Nothing has changed," Mrs. Kim remarked tartly.

"That's the way it might seem. But the pencil came back after traveling through time."

Mrs. Kim stared at the woman.

"It was in the past for a minute. Now it's back. Of course, the pencil is none the wiser..."

"What? Is it sentient?"

"What I mean is if it were a sentient entity, the pencil would be none the wiser."

Mrs. Kim sighed. "So, is this pencil in the past right now?"

"It can't be. That would contravene the law of conservation of mass. Do you know about the principle of the conservation of mass?"

Why do I have to answer all these questions? Mrs. Kim looked exasperated.

"That principle states that the amount of mass in the universe does not change. If this pencil were to exist here now and in the past simultaneously, we would be able to fill the universe with pencils by repeatedly sending this one to the past. It's a paradox. That kind of thing just cannot happen."

"So, how does it all work?"

"Only an object's consciousness gets transferred. The pencil goes into itself, into its own childhood body, into its past. Although it might be able to enter some other object, the probability of that is very low because of the limited connectivity among entities. There are also ethical problems with occupying another body. Some people have done it, and it has become a problem. But in general, one transfers to a moment in time during which one was alive."

"What happens when you go into your past self?"

"This old pencil will reside in the body of its younger self. Inevitably, of course, its memory will be affected. Memories are stored in the brain, and when people travel to the past, their neural structures are those they had in the past." Thick Glasses briefly fell silent, as if in reflection. "Obviously, that would be the case *if* the pencil had a brain. This would be easier to explain with a human example."

"What about travel to the future?"

"Same thing. The object enters its own future body."

Mrs. Kim was growing impatient again.

"So if I were to go into the past using this time machine, I would enter my childhood body. But I would also lose my memories and have only the memories and knowledge of that time..."

"Correct."

"And if I were to go into the future, I would enter my future body and have the memories of my future self, with no awareness that I'd traveled through time."

The woman clapped her hands. "Exactly! Wow, you're able to understand such a difficult concept!"

Mrs. Kim was not happy.

"What difference does any of this make then? Nothing changes!"

"Something *has* changed."

"What?"

"The self."

"What's the self?"

"You don't know what the self is? Would you say that someone is the same person as you as long as she shares your appearance and your memories? That wouldn't be true, would it? Would you lose your identity if you lost your memory or were made to look like someone else? Obviously not! Externally, your behavior or appearance might have changed. But it would still be you."

"But if I can't remember having traveled through time, I won't know that I've done so."

"That's true."

"Then how do we know whether or not the time machine works?"

"Oh, it works."

"How do you know?"

"Some people have traveled through time with their own bodies. They remember everything because they still have their own brains."

"But you said that that was impossible due to some principle or other."

"Such people have a very low probability of existing. But they do exist."

Mrs. Kim fell silent, and Thick Glasses looked lost in thought for a moment, too. Then she smiled and scratched her head.

"It's also possible that the machine malfunctioned. Whenever we make another copy of the unit, the problems with it just keep growing. Some travelers have been acting as if they were still in their original timeframe. They get confused about which time period they're in and end up talking nonsense."

Just like you, thought Mrs. Kim. Thick Glasses looked at her. "Isn't it fun to imagine such things?"

On her way home, Mrs. Kim stopped walking when she realized

it was snowing. *Snow at this time of year?*

Looking up, she noticed paper airplanes falling like snowflakes from every apartment window. Children—teenagers, students wearing uniforms—were throwing paper planes out their windows and off their balconies. People on the street looked up in surprise. A long banner bearing the slogan, "Stop Old-Fashioned Education," unfurled from a window.

Why they are doing this? Mrs. Kim shook her head.

11

Every person has a certain statistical probability of existing. My probability may be lower, yours higher. But we both exist.

Human beings should be seen as continuous waveforms rather than as independent entities. This is because at every moment we are exchanging atoms with our surroundings. As time progresses, all the atoms that make up your body are replaced by different atoms. You may be an entirely different entity today than you were in your childhood.

The reason why lovers or couples resemble each other is because they are constantly exchanging atoms. The same goes for children and their mothers. Atoms that come from the mom's body are swapped with the child's atoms and vice versa. We are not independent beings. We intermingle, and the longer we spend together, the more we become entangled with one another.

12

"She's so weird. How can one plus one possibly equal zero? She's lucky her family hasn't put her in a mental hospital. And to think that people like that roam free in our neighborhood..."

Sitting at the kitchen table, Mrs. Kim had come to the end of her long monologue. Her daughter lifted her head and broke her silence.

"But it could be zero."

"Stop talking nonsense and eat."

Mrs. Kim felt a surge of anger. Her daughter was arguing with her again for no reason.

"One plus one has a high probability of equaling two. But the possibility that it equals zero also exists, even if the probability of such an occurrence is low."

Mrs. Kim was ready to lose her temper. But one look at Soo-ae's expression silenced her. Soo-ae's face was saying that she couldn't stand any more stupidity.

"Is that why you get such lousy grades? Did you write one plus one equals zero on your exam sheet?"

"The world is ruled by the principle of uncertainty. Things appear and disappear. Small objects are in chaos when unobserved, and sometimes after a long time in that state they vanish. That's because their uncertainty rises. The same applies to everything else, including people and their memories."

I have no idea what she's talking about. Is this some kind of game kids are playing these days?

"You trust your memories, don't you? But you should know that they're morphing at every moment. They're being reconstructed, modified, and transformed. Light isn't the only thing in the world that has the properties of both a particle and a wave. Everything else does, too. The effect of waves used to be negligible in the macroscopic world, but not anymore. It's all because of time machines. The International Government failed to control the spread of time machines."

Mrs. Kim felt confused. What were the chances that her daughter might actually know what she was talking about? Furious, she slammed her hand on the table.

"Where did you learn all this? The principle of uncertainty? Is that even an exam topic? Is it on the college entrance exam? Why read useless books? I told you to study English in your spare time. I told you to stick to your textbooks. Don't you have enough subjects to memorize?"

13

We always knew that time travel couldn't change the past— that it could only *disturb* it. We knew that time travel, if it ever occurred, would stir up a new waveform in a fixed world, like a vibrating tuning fork amid hundreds of stationary forks, or like a stone thrown into the placid and unmoving surface of a lake.

But now the past and the future have become equally unfixed. Was there ever a time when probability didn't rule? Was there ever a world in which a married couple didn't resemble each other? Was there ever a vacant house that didn't go into disrepair, memories that didn't change each time they were recalled, probabilistic quantum vibrations that didn't occur, light that didn't have the properties of both waves and particles, or a photon that didn't pass through two different slits at the same time? It's impossible now to know the answer to such questions. Such a world would have been erased from our memories long ago.

I knew all this might come to pass, but perhaps I didn't always. Am I to blame?

HUN maintains that every invention changes the future irreversibly. The future of humanity would have been different, he said, had the steam engine not been invented, had cars never been built, had carbon fossil fuels not been discovered, had there been no printing, no electricity, no nuclear power and no bombs, guns, or missiles. No one should be blamed for these inventions, he said, because what has not yet been invented today will be invented tomorrow. The past and the future change together. "Next time, just try to invent something better," HUN told me.

Of course, there's no way of knowing for certain. Should a time machine ever be built, the past would become unfixed, and different beginnings would sprout anew. Knowledge about the machine would scatter through time, inspiring people in the past to build their own time machines. As HUN would say: "We are but one of many re-search teams, albeit with a higher chance of becoming the inventor of a time machine."

14

Soo-ae straddled the balcony railing. A teenage girl with braided hair and a pimply face, she looked stubborn, her lips tightly pursed. She mumbled some words into the rabbit device on her finger, then closed her eyes and put a hand to her chest. She seemed to be taking some kind of a vow.

When Thick Glasses came up to her, Soo-ae hid the rabbit behind her back and glared at the woman in alarm. She stared warily at Thick Glasses' ghastly blue-striped pants and her checkered shirt.

"What do you want? Go away!"

"Why? D'you own the place?"

The woman had a knowing smile. Soo-ae climbed down from the railing and started off in the other direction, but Thick Glasses kept following her. Finally, Soo-ae got back on the railing and sullenly addressed the woman.

"Why are you following me?"

"Why shouldn't I?"

Soo-ae examined the woman in silence. "You're a psychologist, aren't you? The government sent you?"

"What makes you think that?"

"Grown-ups don't understand quantum mechanics around here."

A paper airplane on fire floated down from the apartment building across the street. All around, more burning paper planes flew, gliding down from all directions like the glowing embers of a silent protest.

"My mom almost slapped me today because I told her that one plus one could equal zero," Soo-ae sighed.

Thick Glasses laughed knowingly. "Older folks never can wrap their heads around that idea. Their cognitive functions are too limited. They say, 'Kids are all the same, women are all the same, men are all the same, and moms are all the same.' They don't have the cognitive capacity to grasp the differences that exist between innumerable waveforms. Older folks only understand average values; they see the world through their own norms."

Soo-ae looked down and pouted. "They'll tell you that there are seven colors in the rainbow when in fact it exists as a continuous gradation of wavelengths. They divide people into groups of white, yellow, and black. They don't see the innumerable differences in different people's skin colors. Words are merely symbols that represent average values, but adults always try to fit the world into a few words. They don't even recognize the many shades of black and white."

Soo-ae briefly spoke into the rabbit, then bent her finger and tapped the air as if she were playing the piano. "The moms and teachers in this neighborhood are all stuck in the 1970s. No one lives in the present. That's why I wanted so badly for my family to move to Mars."

As Soo-ae moved her fingers, holograms of other kids connected via the rabbit appeared around her. A boy with glasses was lying in bed and reading a book. A girl in a nightgown sat in a chair hugging a teddy bear. A blue-eyed kid was chattering away in English. There were kids from all over the world, each speaking his or her own language.

"The disease used to strike only people over thirty, but these days it's affecting even those in their twenties. The government sends in a psychiatrist for group therapy twice a month. The adults are told it's a neighborhood meeting."

Soo-ae enlarged one of the holograms. When a boy captioned "Poland" said something, she replied and downloaded a file by twirling her finger. The file's gift box icon seemed to float above her finger.

"My mom lives in the past. Computerized translation today covers one hundred and sixty languages in real time. But she still insists that I memorize English vocabulary, even though it's already been a long time since the decline of the United States and the importance of its language. She wants me to go to a 'highly ranked college,' even though college rankings were abolished long ago."

A banner on the building across the street that read "Stop Old-Fashioned Education" flapped forlornly in the breeze. Soo-ae touched Poland's gift box icon. Music and graphics played as the box opened.

"I don't want to go to school. The teachers are like people from another time. All they care about is college entrance exams. They teach obsolete physics like Newtonian mechanics, and world history and Korean history are still taught the way they were in the 1970s. We spend five hours a day learning languages and math using outdated methods. The teachers tell us that we don't need friends before college. Those who came from the 1970s aren't the worst, by the way. Some took refuge here during the Korean War. They still despise communism and North Korea, even though we reunified ages ago. Some teachers even came from the colonial era or from the Joseon era. Some have even had to occupy other people's bodies to be here, which is immoral."

Soo-ae flicked her finger. A holographic paper plane appeared and dove down in a burst of sound like firecrackers going off. More holograms appeared here and there in the apartment complex in response.

"Say something."

"What should I say?"

"Aren't you a psychologist sent by the government? Don't you feel sorry for me? I want to die, and you won't do anything. I really might kill myself. You think I'm joking, but I'm not."

"I know you're not joking."

Thick Glasses lowered her head and whispered into the girl's ear. Soo-ae stared wide-eyed at her.

15

Nostalgia created the time machine. We looked nostalgically back on our past, which must have caused a warping in the movement of time. Or maybe we didn't.

I still remember when you died.

I remember my death. The high probability of it…

I'm not just the inventor of the time machine. I exist because of it. I am a being who was born from the unsettling of time. One may wonder how an effect could ever produce its cause, but maybe you're able to understand. The future exists only as probability, and I turned the low probability of my existence into my future.

If a time machine is never invented, I'll disappear. This much is clear, but that's not all. I invented the time machine because I needed to control the past. I settled on the hardware and an operating system. It was the only way for me to exercise the control I needed.

Or perhaps I didn't. My memories don't settle the matter—they never could. Cause and effect have become entangled. Am I to blame for your death? I think about you all the time, even while preoccupied with building a new base on Mars so we can start transporting new settlers there soon.

The time machine has been abused. Too many people traveled on it, bringing their time periods along with them. Antiquated ways of thinking and old habits spread through time like ink splatters or grains of dust in the wind.

You can't escape your own era. People couldn't remember that they'd come from different time periods. They remained their old selves without sensing that the times had changed.

The grown-ups in your life came from a different era. Their values were old, their teaching methods ineffective, their experience irrelevant. They had no idea how smart kids were, how much they already knew. They were false mentors who wasted your time and insulted your intelligence. They had forgotten that they were people who'd come from the past.

I came to meet you. I met your mom, too. While working for the government, I tried in vain to help her. She couldn't remember the fact that she was a time traveler, and she didn't know how to get back.

The probability of my existence is extremely low. That's why I can travel with my own body. I exist somewhere between zero and one, which means that, theoretically, there can always be two of me in the same place. The simultaneous existence of two of me, after all, could result in zero.

I remember when you died.

I remember when the younger me died.

I remember you on that balcony. I remember the words you whispered as you climbed the railing. You chose death, but on that day, you possessed the possibility of living on. Probability was disturbed. Your future branched off. Now I live as an infinitesimal possibility, like a shadow on the road you didn't take.

I pray for it every time I travel. I pray that my body won't follow me. Because that would mean that the probability of my existence has gotten higher. Nevertheless, today I am coming to you. On that fateful day, I will whisper in your ear: *"I'm still keeping your vow."*

That day, you swore to yourself: "I will *not* tell kids that they're living their best years. I will *not* say that young people are all the same, or that it's all just part of growing up. Maybe every other adult will say these things, but not me. I'm going to be a grown-up who knows how indifferent, cowardly, and foolish such words are. If only I could keep this vow, I wouldn't die today. I would be willing to grow old. I would live until I'm thirty, forty, fifty, sixty years old. I would grow older for the me of today. For the me of this very moment."

—*Translated by Eunhae Jo and Melissa Mei-Lin Chan*

An Evolutionary Myth

In the fourth month of the seventh year, in the summer, the King went fishing at the Go-ahn pond, and caught a white fish with red wings.

In the tenth month of the twenty-fifth year, in the winter, the envoy of the Kingdom of Buyeo came and presented a deer with three antlers and a long-tailed rabbit.

On the first day of the full moon festival in the spring of the fifty-third year, the envoy of the Kingdom of Buyeo came and presented a tiger that was one jang and two cheok long, and had white fur and no tail.[1]

In the ninth month of the fifty-fifth year, in the autumn, the King went hunting south of Jil Mountain and caught a purple roe deer.

In the tenth month, in the winter, a local governor presented a red leopard. Its tail was nine ja long.[2]

—From the Annals of the Reign of King Taejo, Sixth Great King of Goguryeo, as recorded in the *Samguk Sagi* [3]

When a protracted drought struck the kingdom, the leaves of every plant wilted down into fine, sharp needles and each stem bulged to conserve as much water as possible. Fat collected beneath the skin of horses and grew into humps on their backs; squirrels began to build nests beneath the cool ground instead of in trees. Dogs, unable to bear the heat, shed their fur in clumps. When fall came, the fields turned not golden but a drab green because people had planted potatoes and corn instead of rice.

I always worried whenever a drought struck because an accursed storm of blood was sure to follow. The king always strove to lay the blame for such things at anyone's feet but his own: government

[1] The archaic measurements "one jang and two cheok long" add up 11.8 feet (3.6 meters).

[2] One ja is the same length as one jang: therefore the leopard's tail was almost nine feet long (2.7m).

[3] The *Samguk Sagi*, or the *History of the Three Kingdoms*. is a 12th-century historical record of the Three Kingdoms of Korea.

officials had committed some kind of error, or the royal samu had slacked off during his divination ceremony, or the soldiers had gone lax at their guard-posts. Ever since that torrent of blood had surged out from the heart of the palace, through the front gate, and out into the courtyard beyond, all manner of alarming stories had spread. It was rumored that when the king slumbered, he set his head upon a human pillow, and that when he sat, it was likewise upon a person... And if either dared to move, the king would slay them with his sword.

The people call him simply Cha-Daewang, "The Next Great King." *Next*, that is, in relation to his predecessor, Great King Taejo. After Taejo had lain ill in his royal bed for an extended period, he'd delegated authority to Cha-Daewang, who had responded with conspiracy, quoting ancient scriptures to bolster his claim to the throne. "Traditionally, when the senior brother grows elderly, his younger brother succeeds to the throne..." Great King Taejo, powerless to fight Cha-Daewang off and wise enough to desire no further spilling of blood, abdicated. He then went off to live out his last days in his detached palace in seclusion.

Following the accession of the Cha-Daewang, I stayed home, barely going outside. When I did escape my room, it was only into the dark of night and in the manner of a bat. While wandering about thus, I would try to avoid the gaze of others and hasten to return home before dawn. My skin soon turned indigo, matching the hue of the night, and my eyes began to gleam yellow. A physician reassured me that there was no need to fret over this; the odd new layer that had developed on my retina was merely a deformation that reflected light from the backs of my eyeballs. Such alterations were actually common among folk who work by night. He also explained why my pupils stretched unnaturally wide in the evening, like those of a cat, while narrowing during the day: it was merely to control the quantity of light to which I was exposed. When I worried about whether I might pass this trait on to my children, he reassured me by speaking of a theory he called *yong-bul-yong*, that is, use-and-disuse, according to which it was unlikely that such "acquired characteristics" would pass down to later descendants.

One sweltering night, I escaped my room and headed for one of the royal altars. The samu had by then been performing their fire-rites for several weeks already in an attempt to summon the rains. One of them—a samu I knew and got along with well—noticed me hiding in the darkness and came over to greet me. We'd known one another since childhood and were the same age; now he was the only samu remaining who wasn't perpetually bent at the waist. (Our royal subjects have spent so long bent forward deferentially before the king that their bodies have warped into a permanent bow, their faces constantly turned toward the ground.)

"What has brought you here so late at night, Your Royal Highness?"

It was precisely on account of situations such as this that I avoided going out in public: although the status of Tae-ja—that is, Crown Prince—had been transferred from me to my cousin, many people still maintained their old habit of referring to me as if the title remained my own. Each time someone committed such an error, I could feel my life being shortened by several years.

"I was just dropping by to check in on the rain invocations..."

The samu glanced around and whispered, "How could the sky not turn dry, when the hearts of the people are so parched? True, it is when the people are fatigued that the sky *ought* to be kindest to them, but nature's laws do not work thus."

"I remember my deceased father often used to call down the rains."

"As you may know, my lord, in order to summon rain, a change in atmospheric pressure is required. For example, if one extends one's spiritual energies into the sky quickly, water vapor in the air above has no choice but to condense and fall down.[4] Rain also falls when two massive spirits take form in the heavens and do battle there; or when a giant creature blocks the flow of wind, and the air strikes against its body. Great movements such as these are necessary to produce precipitation."

"Could the stirring of a great giant induce rain?"

"Yes, but there aren't so many giants alive now. Because they're so enormous, and such ravenous eaters, each one maintains a vast territory for itself. Your late father was close friends with one such giant, the revered Ban-go, who lives in the Taebek mountains.[5] He used to summon the rains through Ban-go, but it's been ages since he stirred. They say his body is blanketed with dirt and trees, that distinguishing him from the bedrock that lies beneath him has become impossible. Rumor has it that all the other titans are in a similarly torpid state now. Seeking them out would be pointless."

The learned had urged all scholars of phylogeny and embryonic recapitulation to gather so they could study the rules governing the differentiation of living things. Given that all living forms inevitably undergo metamorphosis within a generation, such dedication was pointless. The scholars declared, "There is no rule that governs the differentiation of forms," then retreated to their beds and concealed themselves beneath their blankets.

Yet certain patterns definitely do exist. For example, most giants who walked the earth during prehistory have chosen to become mountains, rivers, and lakes, ceasing every life function, including breathing and movement. Likewise, the tremendous lizards that once dwelled upon the earth and under the heavens have cast aside their dignity and dimin-

[4] In cultures within the Chinese sphere of influence, the composite character for spiritual energies, 氣 (in Korean, gi, although it may be more familiar to a Western audience as the Chinese concept of qi or ch'i), contains within it the character for air or steam, 气.

[5] From Pangu, a Chinese mythological figure from whose corpse the physical world was formed. Here, Pangu is not a singular being, but member of a race of ancient giants analogous to the Titans of Greek mythology.

ished themselves to the size of a finger.

"Is there *any* sign that points to a resurgence of the giants?"

"How would I know? So little is understood about nature's governance of how forms evolve... Still, it seems unlikely. These days, anything too large would be hunted not only by humans but by smaller creatures as well. That's why lizards have become smaller: coordinated group effort pays off more than maintaining a single, enormous body."

"Is there any other way to call the rain?"

"For now, all we can do is pray. Even if human longings are unscientific, that doesn't mean they have no effect."

As I turned to leave, my samu friend added one more comment: "I noticed that the sun is due to swallow the moon on the last night of this month. Please be careful. It's inauspicious..."

As I watched him return to his place, I pondered the meaning of his warning. It was a bizarre comment—a lunar eclipse? During a new moon? How could such a thing happen? The moon's face would already be hidden from the sky, and anyway, wasn't a lunar eclipse caused when the Earth's shadow darkened the moon? If the sun were to "shade" the moon, would not the night blaze bright as day? To what end might the sun swallow and shade the moon when it was already invisible? Wouldn't such a thing be mere nonsense, some sort of purposeless cruelty? Gazing up into the night sky as I pondered the samu's words, I realized my error. The moon still hung in the sky, even on the last night of the lunar month; it was merely hidden from view. The sun is the father of all time, just as the king is the father of the people; therefore... the cruel sun must represent the cruel king... which meant that... the invisible moon must be the prince who lost his inheritance...

I let out a deep sigh. There was no way to prepare myself for such an eventuality, though I felt no inclination to do so anyway. Even before he claimed the throne from my father, my uncle had already held a tight grip on the reins of power.

Even street-beggars have a place to lean their backs against when they want to rest their legs. Me? I had nothing to rely upon in this world... Even if I were to flee, how would I be able to sustain my life?

I crawled through the darkness back to my room, climbing over trees and scuttling over the ground instead of walking on two feet. I began doing this at first—bending my body down each time I heard footsteps—simply to avoid discovery. At some point, calluses had formed upon my palms like the ones on people's feet.

It has been said since ancient days that ontogeny repeats phylogeny. The cells of our bodies continue to be born and to die at every instant, and the blood in our veins is continually being created and disappearing; when old cells die, new ones appear to fill the gaps left behind, and soon enough, not a single original cell remains. One truly becomes completely different not only in mind, but also in body. All creatures, whether they wish it or not, die and are reborn several times during their lives.

My late mother, bless her, repeatedly emphasized the revolting appearance that would become inevitable should one falter in the lifelong, ceaseless struggle to maintain one's humanity. Only a rare few ever manage to die in a recognizably human form; many more end their lives shaped like animals and insects. Those aristocrats who pass their days comfortably in their rooms, living off taxes and stipends garnered from the people, lose their human forms the quickest. How many of them develop stubby legs and tails and fat, reddish bellies, their faces dominated by bulging cheeks!

From my early childhood onward, my mother would constantly repeat to me the tale of a woodcutter who married a woman from a certain winged race whom he'd met by chance at the shore of a lake. One day, his wife flew away into the sky. The woodcutter went up to the roof and wept, unable to either eat or sleep, until his body grew tiny and his legs became as thin as chopsticks. The bottoms of his feet bent, and curved claws sprouted from his toes like hooks. His fingers atrophied then disappeared, while white feathers sprung forth all over his body. A scarlet comb grew from his head, and from his throat came the sound of a heartbroken bird instead of the sound of a man. His longing had transformed his appearance into that of a rooster. But those wings were useless: he was unable to fly to where his wife had fled. If only his will and longing had been directed more sensibly, he might have developed wings capable of flight, but by relinquishing his ability to control or direct his own development, he had lost his wits, sealing his fate.

This tendency for creatures to metamorphose into the opposite of what they longed to become is quite fascinating. Instead of turning into birds or horses, people separated from their lovers typically become flowers, or ossify into stones, like the one in the famous story of Mangbuseok.[6] Do you realize that the widely credited notion that sunflowers follow the sun is mere fantasy? They certainly do grow large flowers out of admiration for the sun, but then, unable to bear the weight of those same flowers, they bend their faces down toward the ground. I wondered whether the same manner of fate might befall me. Since I wished for nothing so much as to flap wings and fly far away, perhaps I would die instead with a heavy body, my belly stuck to the ground as I crawled about.

[6] Near the eastern port of Busan there is a large rock by the ocean called Mangbuseok. It is said to have once been a faithful wife awaiting the return of her husband who had unfortunately been captured and borne off to Japan against his will. As the story goes, she was transformed into a stone during her endless waiting and stands there still.

The rains never came, but a late freeze struck the land that spring. Some birds dropped from the sky, frozen dead, while those that survived grew thick coats of feathers. When the cold snap persisted, some fat, flightless birds began to waddle along the ground. Other birds leapt into the water, finding some slight warmth in its depths. Beast and human alike began to starve, unable to eat even leaves, which had long since metamorphosed into thorns. People hid in the mountains and grew long, thick coats of fur like beasts. Sometimes, when people hunted bears, their prey cried out with voices that sounded less ursine than human.

One spring day, the assassins came for me at last. Frost had fallen overnight in the yard outside my home. I was sitting in my room when I noticed some figures quietly approaching my detached palace. They had been hiding at a distance behind the trees and walls, their careful movements so furtive and stealthy that watching and waiting for them became almost boring. Before the assassins arrived, my eunuch entered the room and threw himself upon the floor before me.

"Your Royal Highness, the king's assassins are approaching the palace," he told me. "Please, you must flee quickly!"

"Where to? My uncle rules the entirety of this land," I replied calmly, flipping the pages of my book.

For some reason, the eunuch began to weep. He sobbed for a while before raising his head, then said, "Your appearance has changed so drastically that nobody could possibly recognize you! Let us exchange clothing so that the Royal Body may survive this attack!" Afterward, he pushed me toward the back door and sat himself down upon my seat. The night was chilly, and as I crawled out into the dark courtyard, shadowy figures raced into my room. The clamor of clashing swords and screaming voices assailed me from behind.

Grief-stricken, I reflected sorrowfully upon how my father had founded a nation, winning glory in the eyes of the world, but I, his foolish, wretched son, crawled about on four legs, able to stay alive only by allowing someone else to die in my place. Suddenly death terrified me, for how could I face my father in the next world?

At that instant, a clap of thunder erupted, and a shower of rain commenced, extinguishing all the torches and plunging the palace into darkness. In the end, the prayers of the samu had reached heaven at just the right moment. Although the timing of the storm was surely a coincidence, the king's soldiers, ignorant of the sciences, fled in terrified confusion, certain that their misdeeds had angered the heavens. I seized upon the moment to go over the palace wall. A lone soldier caught sight of me, but on account of my glowing yellow eyes, he must have supposed I was just some cat upon the wall.

I couldn't bear the thought of being around people, so I made for the mountains. The rain, having at last broken the drought, was met by grass that surged forth into life, each blade raising its head toward the sky. Trees unfolded their leaves while greedily stretching out their roots. As I walked, patches of verdant grass sprouted and sank back down toward the soil in my wake. The sudden end to the drought had called forth an almost animalistic vigor in the plants: uncertain when rain might fall again, the whole forest became noisily preoccupied with the spreading of seed and the sprouting of fruit. I walked and walked through the storm until I could walk no more, then dropped to the ground in exhaustion.

There I lay for I know not how long until I caught a groggy glimpse of what looked like a white birch tree moving. But when I opened my eyes and looked more carefully, I realized it was no birch at all, but rather a white tiger.[6] The beast was only a foot tall, slender and tailless, its whole body as white as fresh-fallen snow. It crept around me quietly. I remained supine, lacking the strength to flee. Smiling wanly to myself, I wondered whether joining the cycle of sustenance by becoming a predator's meal could be reckoned a worthy death.

"What's so funny?"

When the tiger spoke, I was stunned. Its voice was very clear, with exacting and altogether human pronunciation. How could a tiger, whose vocal cords are so unlike ours, speak a human language? I let out an anxious laugh. Inexplicably, tears fell from my eyes.

The tiger spoke again, asking, "Why do you weep?"

"I'm crying because I feel such pity for you," I said, remaining where I lay.

The tiger laughed... *human* laughter. "What's so pitiful about me?"

"If you can speak, it means you have a human mind; and if you have a human mind, you must have once been human, despite your present animal form. I don't know how you came to take on the shape of a beast, but it's sad, isn't it? How could it not be pitiful to have lost the original form you inherited from your parents?"

"What does *original form* mean, anyway? Ought every creature to spend its whole life as a newborn infant?" the tiger rejoined. "You say you were born in human form, but your ancestors were once bears and tigers, snakes and fishes, birds and plants.[7] You're fighting now to hang onto this human shape, but ultimately you'll realize the effort is pointless. What's so precious about dying in the same form you were born into? Besides, though I might look like an animal, I myself chose to be thus: I *wanted* to fill my belly with the work of my own efforts... and this form is the result."

[6] Traditionally in Korea (and other East Asian countries), four mystical animals were associated with the four compass points: the blue dragon with the East, the white tiger with the North, a "black turtle" (two-headed, with one of its heads a snake's) to the West, and the scarlet jujak bird, vaguely similar to a phoenix, to the South.

[7] In the national foundation myth, the ancestors of the Korean people are said to have been bears transformed into the shape of humans by a magical ritual involving garlic, mugwort, and a lunar cycle's confinement in a cave. Both the tiger and the bear attempted the transformation, but the tiger fled, leaving only the bear to take human form and become the bride of the demigod Kdriing Hwanung, who ruled from the top of Mt. Baekdu.

I had nothing to offer by way of reply.

"Did you know that in the old days," it continued, "it would take aeons for creatures to change from one form to another, and many tens of thousands of aeons for any kind of differentiation to develop. It's not that things are better or worse now—it's just that a different kind of adaptation is necessary these days. Nature chooses its survivors without considering good or evil or what is superior or inferior. Even the human form is just one of many means of survival made available by nature. When deprived of their tools or not in a group, humans are even more vulnerable than rabbits! A pathetic weakling like you, pitying *me*? What insolence!"

The tiger bared its razor-sharp fangs at me, its wrath apparent. I shut my eyes and tensed in anticipation of the coming attack... but though I waited for it, my throat was not slashed open. When I finally dared to open my eyes, I found the tiger quietly watching me.

"Say it," the creature finally said.

"Say what?"

"What is it you *want*?"

"I don't want *anything*," I said. "I just don't want to be discovered by anyone. I want to live and die without anyone finding me."

The tiger said, "You should become a bug, then. Since you can't get over this fixation with people, perhaps it would be best if you became a maggot or a fly. Or... how about a worm? Worms enrich the soil. You'd be more useful to people that way than whatever it is you are right now."

Every single word the tiger spoke dripped with insult, but still I couldn't think up a suitable rejoinder.

"But such forms are rather different from the one I currently have," I said. "Becoming a worm would probably be incredibly difficult. What should I do?"

"If you really, *truly* wanted to dig holes and eat dirt, it wouldn't be that hard now would it?" the tiger replied. Then, looking at me, it said, "Well, I can't eat someone I've had a conversation with, so off you go now. I saw some starving people climbing the mountain: if you follow them, you might even learn how to survive out here…"

Then the tiger departed through the trees, blending into the background until even its shadow disappeared from view.

I rose from the ground.

After following the mountain ridge for a while, I encountered the group of climbers the tiger had described. Joining them, I tried to blend in as best I could. Not a soul addressed me or even seemed to notice me. Nobody commented on my indigo skin or my xanthous eyes. They hardly seemed to pay attention to one another, for that matter. Some amongst their number had folded spines or twisted faces. Others were legless or armless or carapaced like sea-creatures or crawled upon four feet.

The climbers eventually split into threes and fives and entered a series of caves. When I followed them inside, I found people asleep in one another's arms. They seemed to have chosen to hibernate through the cold, barren years rather than starve. Some spun cocoons, silkworm-like, and others grew thin membranous coverings like the diaphanous skin that bundles fish eggs together. Other people were covered with coats of white fur. Those who couldn't change quickly enough or handle such a rapid metamorphosis died, becoming food for the ants and thus joining the great cycle of digestion and nutriment and living on in a different form.

Trying to find a spot empty of people, I finally settled between the roots of a great tree. I gathered grass around myself, fashioned a bed from it, and, rolling myself this way and that, attempted to hibernate.

Winter came, and my starvation continued. Struggling, I attempted to subsist on soil alone, but I couldn't do it. I tried to hibernate, but somehow found my rest punctuated, now sleeping, now waking again. I was at last able to sleep for a few days in a row, then four, until finally I was able to slumber for a week to ten days at a time.

During the winter, I shed my skin. My body, failing under the hardships of my new environment, seemed to have decided of its own accord that some sort of "adjustment" was necessary: radical changes occurred in my skeletal structure and the placement of my vital organs. I passed out and woke up several times more as my skin fell from my flesh. When I finally climbed out from my molt and looked back, the ghastly husk of my cast off form still looked all too horribly human. I found I had grown a smooth, serpent-like skin and a long lizard's tail. I wept briefly for my lost humanity, but soon regained my calm. My body had taken on this reptilian form, I supposed, so as to ensure my survival: the wisdom of the flesh outweighs all the reason of the human mind. It understands that survival is more important than dignity or pride. I turned and devoured my abandoned human skin, a feast of precious nutriment for my new body.

When spring arrived, edible grass began sprouting at the mouth of the cave. I woke up from my slumber and crept outside. Only then did I realize that I was the sole survivor of that long, terrible winter. A few others had perished outside, taking on the form of human-shaped rocks and trees, all entangled together in a solemn tableau. I performed a respectful ceremony before them: they, at least, had had enough nobility in them to prefer becoming part of the earth over losing their human shape.

After that, I dwelled in the forest, crawling upon the ground and eating grass. My jaw soon became powerful, the better to chew the tough grass. I developed a sort of jutting snout as well. My ears, which pricked at every sway of a nearby brush, grew pointed, and my palms hardened as my limbs shortened to suit my body. When I could no longer use my fingers, horns sprouted from my skull. Beginning as small nubs on my head, they soon branched out like the antlers of a male deer. These horns were invaluable in the battles I fought with other beasts over food. I also found them useful for striking trees to coax them into letting their ripe fruit drop.

In the winter of that year, I shed my skin once more. I discovered that my entire body had taken on the dull greenish color of the forest. I wondered whether living in a desert or on a rocky mountain might have helped me maintain my human pigmentation, but such speculation seemed pointless. So great was my desire to go unseen that if I had lived on a rocky mountain, my body would surely have ended up inscribed with the camouflaging patterns of the pebbles.

I looked down at the little nub that remained below my belly button and wondered whether I could still have sex with a human being. The thought made me laugh and laugh. Even though my bestial transformation had progressed past the point of no return, I couldn't abjure this strange wistfulness for my long-lost original form. Someday my brain, too, was likely to undergo its own transformation. How much longer would I retain my memories and human intellect, my very consciousness? That night, I counted the number of scales, both great and small, that had grown on my body, and found them to number eighty-one. *The square of nine,* I thought. *That's a lucky number.*

I began to laugh once more.

I think it was probably autumn.

While crawling through the forest in one of my ceaseless searches for food, I heard the distant din of horses and barking hounds. I looked up in surprise to see a group of hunting dogs chasing a small group of purple roe deer toward me. I fled as swiftly as I could in the midst of the rushing deer, but my antlers caused the hunters to mistake me for one of them, and they loosed their arrows at me as well. One poor deer, struck by an arrow beside me, rolled on the ground screaming piteously. Its voice was so very human that my heart all but failed me.

Although I ran myself half-dead, I was neither so fleet nor so clever as the rest of the herd. I ended up surrounded by hunting hounds at the foot of a great tree, unable to move. As I stood there, buffeted by the baying and barking of the hounds, the bushes split apart, and people armed with arrows and spears appeared before me. I stood frozen in place as I watched the man on horseback who was leading them forward.

It was my uncle. His face had haunted me everywhere but in my dreams. Yet what rendered me unable to move or speak was the drastic change in his appearance. He was virtually unrecognizable.

He looked like a great hunk of meat.

His bulging pink gut radiated gluttony, and his peaked nose signified a lifetime of burying his face in food. His almost-shut eyes reflected a near-absolute lack of moral discernment, and the upward curve of his earlobes, which covered his ears completely, reflected his desire to hear nothing at all. His hands and feet had atrophied, and the spaces between his fingers had disappeared, meaning he had attended to none of his royal tasks. Considering how my late father had managed to retain his human appearance even throughout his prolonged sickness in bed, my uncle's transformation was truly outrageous. I was too shocked and angry to fear him.

Examining me from snout to tail, my uncle directed the hunters to lower their arrows.

"What manner of beast is this? Because of its antlers, I thought it was a deer, but its body is such a nasty shade of green. It has the tail of a lizard yet is covered with scales like a snake... And though its arms and legs resemble a human's, its yellow eyes look like those of a cat. What sort of an omen might this be?"

A servant hurried forth to the king's side. His back was bent as if slumped upon on a horse's back, his neck torqued toward the ground. Though his appearance had also undergone a profound transformation, I recognized him as the samu who had once been my true friend. I sensed that he recognized me, too, though he was fighting to look away from me.

"Animals are constantly changing and adjusting to their environment, so it's not unusual to encounter new kinds of creatures. However, this mutability is due to the instability of the world in which the subjects of Your Majesty dwell. Nature presents us with such monstrosities because it cannot communicate its most earnest desires in words. Instead, it communicates to us through creatures such as this in order to encourage the king to cultivate his virtue. If he were to do so, this unfortunate omen could be transformed into a lucky one."

The king's face turned scarlet. "If it's unpropitious, just tell me so. Or if it's propitious, then tell me *that*. Telling me it's an ill omen, then claiming it *could however* be a good one... what manner of dissembling is this?"[8]

Before anyone around could stop him, the king drew the sword that hung at his waist and slashed about, lopping off the heads of the samu and others near him. I turned tail and fled, scrambling up the mountain for dear life. The hounds started baying behind me, and innumerable arrows whistled through the air. Reaching the top of a cliff, I took one look at the mighty, meandering river, then leapt from the precipice.

Having fallen from such a great height, the water I struck was as hard as the ground would have been.

[8] According to *Samguk Sagi*, Cha-Dae-wang, the 7th king in Geoguryeo Dynasty, actually said these words in reference to [explanations of] his sighting of a white fox.

The river gulped me down whole.

From this experience, I learned a couple of things. Jumping down from a cliff only once does not automatically confer wings. Also, it's not so easy to die when covered with unexpectedly hard reptilian skin.

I had hoped so fervently to live without being discovered by people, but as soon as I was, someone once again paid with their life.

I stayed in the river after that. My skin, having soaked for such a long time, festered and began to grow limp, then froze in the cold of night. This almost killed me several times, but I didn't dare go back up onto land. I hoped to become a fish or a water snake, sincerely praying that the last threads of my humanity might snap, my human consciousness finally drawn completely out from me.

In the middle of the night, I was lying in the glacial cold of the shallows when I thought I saw two turtles poke their heads out from the water. It wasn't until they surfaced that I realized they weren't two creatures at all, but rather one turtle with two heads. The beast must have burrowed into the muddy bed of the river because it was almost two cheok tall all told. Fish with red wings flopped and scooted out of its way.

"Why does this land creature shove its head into the water on a cold night like this? It should go back where it came from," the turtle said, its voice seeming to echo as the two heads spoke out of unison.

I opened my frozen mouth to reply: "I have nowhere to go. If I've intruded into your territory, I sincerely apologize. But please don't cast me out."

"Every creature has its proper domain... What's a four-legged beast like you doing trying to breathe water?"

"There are no strict boundaries between species," I replied. "You, of all beasts, must recognize that all land-creatures once dwelt in water. Recall that every living animal descends from a single origin. My purpose here is simply to try to retrace my way back to our shared origins. How is it that by doing so, I warrant such criticism whilst creatures such as dolphins and sea lions are considered blameless?"

"Well, lineage can be fluid... but even so, a weirdo like you wandering around here is sure to make my prey panic and flee..."

"I meant to cause no trouble... I only sought to escape discovery by others, however hopeless that might seem. Still, perhaps we could in the meantime share a few days' discussion on the tendency of creatures to develop an appearance contrary to their desires..."

"There's no *need* for a few days' discussion. It's simple: you don't really want what you think you want." The turtle thrust its two heads toward me, crossed them, and snapped, "Now, scram. If you don't, I'll eat you up."

"Go ahead and eat me," I replied. "After I die, I'll become a water-ghost and never walk on land again." Then I shut my eyes.

When I opened them again a while later, the turtle was gone. Perhaps it had decided not to kill me out of sympathy, or perhaps I wasn't worth the effort... Or maybe I just didn't look particularly appetizing? I braced myself to bear the watery chill for the remainder of the night.

After more time passed, the scales on my skin grew affixed to their places, and my arms and legs diminished in size even further, growing tiny. Somehow they never quite became fins, assuming instead a more avian shape (influenced, perhaps, by that singular leap I made from the cliff). While my arms and legs grew increasingly useless, my spine and tail stretched longer. It is said that every stage through which one passes leaves an indelible mark. Well, the antlers sprouting from my skull remained; so did the cat's eyes I'd developed so early in my youth, which remain unchanged even to this day. Learning to breathe water was insuperable, but I did become better at diving for extended periods. As my arms and legs atrophied further, my beard grew longer, developing a sensitivity akin that of the antennae on insects. Sinking to the bottom of the river for days at a time, I lived by feeding on small fish and water plants. I lingered in the lake in this way for several months.

━ ✳ ━

One day, as I rose to the surface to breathe, I came upon a woman doing her laundry. Aside from her nine white tails, she had managed to retain a wholly human appearance. I looked at her, uncertain what to do: it had been so long since I'd seen a human or worn a human form myself. Seeing her gaze directed at me, I waited for her to scream or call me a monster and begin hurling stones. Instead she clasped her hands together and bowed deeply before me.

"What're you doing?" I asked.

I realized my mistake as soon as I opened my mouth. In much the same way I had suspected the tiger of having once been human, the woman was sure to realize that somewhere in my backgound lay hidden a human stage.

"When the Mystical One emerged," she said, "I saw that It ruled these waters, so I bowed."

"You saw wrong. I'm just a profane thing, a parasite in these waters, hiding, scared of the human world. Forgive me, I didn't mean to surprise you."

Then I sank back down to the bottom of the lake.

Several days later, I opened my eyes only to discover some water-logged rice-cakes and fruit in the depths before me. Little fish collected around each sinking treat, nibbling upon them. I rose to the surface once more. Glancing about, I saw that the nine-tailed woman I'd met before had placed blessed water, incense, and a plate of rice-cakes upon a little wooden table by the lake and was offering devout prayers while performing an earnest little ceremony. Red papers inscribed with petitions drooped from the table, and several more people, perhaps her neighbors, were gathered around her. When she saw me, she stiffened like a thief caught red-handed.

I balked, stupefied. "What is all this shit? Didn't I tell you with my own mouth that I'm nothing more than a mongrel? If you need someplace to hold your ceremony, go find another lake or mountain!"

She replied: "The drought has gone on so long that the trees have withered up; the common folk around here can barely find enough food for themselves. Everything is growing and changing so strangely, our farms are falling apart, our harvests no longer suit the people's diets. And the king can't hear us: his ears and eyes have atrophied."

"So what do you want from me? I have no power. How can a beast get involved in human affairs?"

"Are you saying that everything we humans have hoped for is in vain? There must be *some* reason why nature has allowed you such a sacred appearance..."

I shut my mouth for a moment before agreeing, "What you say is correct."

Swinging my tail, I unleashed a blast of wind and a spray of water that knocked down the incense and sent the bowl of holy water tumbling down to the ground where it broke.

Then I said, "Oh, how long I have lived... yet every time anyone discovers me, I bring trouble. It would be better if I were never to show myself again."

I sank down into the depths once more. When I looked back up, I saw the nine-tailed woman weeping. Turning my head away coldly, I nestled into the bottom of the lake and began to hibernate. As the frigid water started to freeze my body, my functions gradually slowed, paralyzing me. I could feel each of my cells passing into a kind of slumber. I no longer felt the passage of time. Even my thoughts slowed. If I'm lucky enough, I thought, I might even transmute into rock or soil like the giants of yore.

✺

At first, it seemed as if someone was knocking on a distant door. Then I heard a voice: "Wake up."

I opened my eyes. Doing so was difficult; a host of water plants and marsh snails had attached themselves to my body. Swimming before me was the two-headed turtle. Somehow he looked much smaller than before.

"Leave. Soon. The king's army is here to catch you."

It took me a moment to comprehend his words. I dimly recalled that once long ago, I'd been a human being... and a prince... Then I recalled my blood-relation to the current king.

"Why would the king bother to come and catch me?"

"Even after you began to sleep, the people continued their ceremonies here. They were praying for you to expel the king and bring them a new one. So the king decided to fill in the lake and dig you out from the bottom. Your thinking is so slow now; your brain must have metamorphosed. Get out of here *now*."

As the turtle had foretold, I soon found myself surrounded by a din. As I raised my head up, clod after clod of soil fell upon my head. A chaotic murder of crows flew to and fro over the lake, and a revolting stink of blood emanated from somewhere nearby.

"Why are the crows squawking like that?"

"It's really dreadful. Better not to see what's happening," the turtle said, before burrowing down into the mud.

I rose to the surface in an ominous mood. Even my slightest movement stirred up a whirlpool, sending fish fleeing in surprise. A multitude of water plants and marsh snails dropped from my body. Only then did I realize that the turtle hadn't become smaller; I had become *bigger*.

A band of soldiers gathered near the lakeshore were dumping soil into the water. When they saw me, they ceased shoveling, shocked into silence. I too was speechless as I looked at the woman with the nine tails and the villagers who'd participated in her ceremonies. Their corpses were lined up in a terrible row in the mud beside the lake. The nine-tailed woman's white underskirts shifted back and forth in the breeze. With each flap of the fabric, more of my reason fell away until finally my mind went blank.

Coming to his senses, one of the soldiers roared at me, waving his spear: "You freakish beast, bare your neck to us tamely! All your followers are dead!"

Before he could even finish speaking, I sprang up from the water and bit a nearby soldier in half. While the men roiled in confusion, I struck the legs of their horses with my tail. I tore at the throats of the fallen with my claws, and as they groaned, I crushed their hearts beneath my two front paws. At the distant sound of more soldiers arriving, I fled the lake and leapt into the river. My eyes have always been sharp, so I was able to count the dead one by one. Then I saw the man who had once been my uncle. He was standing near the river. As I tried to slip past him, I heard his voice: "Come here, you monster!"

The king sat straight-backed upon a horse and spoke in a tiny voice. Despite having gone through so many bestial transformations, I could make out his voice crystal clear.

"If you don't come out," he said, "I'll kill every single person in this village. I'll accuse them of worshipping a spirit-monster and execute them all!"

This stopped me in my tracks. It was a bizarre threat. Even my uncle clearly thought that I retained some shred of sacred compassion within me. But what relation had I with the lives and deaths of mere human beings?

Nevertheless, I emerged quietly from the water and stood before the king on the river bank. Of course, it was impossible for my body to *stand up* like a human, but by coiling my long tail in a spiral around me, I was able to support my body and hold my neck upright. Standing myself up thus, I realized how immense I'd become. My uncle and the soldiers all looked so puny that it would have been child's play for me to sweep them away in an instant.

I was flooded by a thousand emotions as I examined my uncle closely. Ah, ah... he'd gotten old. His once fat belly drooped with wrinkles, his creased face was blotched, and his atrophied arms and legs had shriveled up from disuse. Such a transformation signals the inevitable end of all creatures, even those who've resisted changing at all.

"Now, I recognize you," the king said, his voice very dry, like branches rasping in the wind. "You are the seed of the former king. The seed that should've been crushed long before yet somehow still remains..."

I bowed my head, imitating his soldiers, whose heads were all turned toward the ground. Then I said, "This insignificant one became a beast only to sustain its own existence, not to threaten Your Majesty's rule. These acts of worship were committed by the ignorant. I beg you to temper your rage with your vast generosity."

"You call what they did an act of ignorance, but you must have known what they were doing, so I have no choice but to accuse you of treason."

"This flesh lost its old life ages ago. Why are you trying to take that life a second time?"

"How dare you speak and act that way toward your king?" demanded the king in a piercing voice as thin as a eunuch's and so pinched I could barely understand it. "Since you are in my kingdom, your body and life belong to me. I demand that as a dutiful subject you give your life to me. *Obey my command.*"

"What on earth could you want with the life of a worthless water-snake?"

"How dare a beast converse with a man? How insolent, how disrespectful! You're such a vile portent! I vow vanquish you and get rid of your presence myself."

"This insignificant one may have transformed into a wicked beast, but the king himself is no longer human. How can you demand my life when your status as king of the humans is mere pretense?"

The corners of the King's blind eyes twisted upward with fury as he cried out again in that thin voice of his. The soldiers kicked their horses into action and ran at me. Diving into the river again, I swam so quickly that the river overflowed and the waters parted behind me. The soldiers chased me along the riverbank.

Behind me, I heard the King laughing. I knew the reason. The way up ahead was blocked by a great waterfall, ten jang tall. Instead of stopping, however, I pushed myself harder. When I reached the bottom of the waterfall, I threw myself upward. As I leapt up the falls, stealing momentum from the whirlpool at its base, my body rose past the falling water. The swirling waters that encircled my tail rose up alongside me.

I realized that I had generated an ascending wind. My body had become so gigantic that I could direct the currents of the air. I rode the wind up, rising into the sky. The soldiers chasing me stopped to watch, bewildered. My greenish scales shimmered spectacularly in the sunlight, and my long tail swung behind me, as if brushing the ground. I felt wonderful, so I climbed ever higher, sensing how I could change my direction by riding the wind, how I could produce rain by shifting its flow. I recalled having hated droughts during my human days, though I couldn't quite remember why.

I directed the air currents. As the water vapor in the air was carried upwards, dark clouds formed. The world shook with lightning and thunder. By gently pressing the clouds and rising up, I shifted the pressure of the air. Soon a heavy rain began to pour toward the ground. The fields were deluged. The river overflowed, sweeping away the distracted soldiers who stood near the riverbanks as I flew overhead. Powerless to pursue me, the king watched from a distance. His hair turned white in a flash. It was as if I'd evaporated away the last bit of life left in him. But these lives and deaths interested me not at all, for I was no longer human. Instead, I exulted in skimming the clouds. I steadily built up speed and began to rise higher.

That was the winter the king died in an uprising. That was the day I soared through an azure sky.

—*Translated by Jihyun Park and Gord Sellar*

Last of the Wolves

Mr. had no idea how he'd managed to lose yet another pet. The lock to the kennel wasn't broken, and the key was still right there in his pocket. Had the little scamp somehow turned into smoke and slipped through the bars? Or perhaps it had managed to steal the key, open the lock, and return the key to his pocket before taking off? Mr. ☀ scratched his nose in confusion. "Some things just can't be explained," he muttered before strolling back inside. It would come back once it got hungry. And besides, it's not as if it had anywhere else to go, really. He made a mental note to give it a good scolding once it returned to ensure something like this never happened again.

✿✳✿

I paused and stared at the sky. The hours chasing at my heels bumped into me and came to a stop. Twilight draped the land all the way to the horizon, the sky a fiery red from sunlight filtering through heavy clouds. As I watched, the western sky sparkled gold then turned a deep cobalt. Stars emerged from hiding one after the other.

They are unable to see this.

The streets were silent but for the rushing of my own sad, labored breath. Though I'd only been running for an hour, my lungs were wailing, miserable. That's how feeble a creature I am.

They cannot hear this.

"They cannot hear this," I muttered out loud to myself.

Hearing my own words, I realized that I'd reached a point of no return. Words that are spoken have power. As long as they remain inside your head, you can always take them back. But once you utter them, everything changes.

I will never go back.

I began to run again, shaking off the temptation to rest. I'd slathered myself from head to toe in compost, but even that was no guarantee I would be able to outmaneuver my master's keen nose. My master could easily sniff me out to within a dozen kilometers if he wanted to. In fact, he wouldn't even have to leave his home to tell which neighbor's house the compost had come from, what food scraps were in the compost, and whose field had grown the food.

Such skills are incomprehensible to me.

Roaming between the houses, I made my way through alleys that, for creatures as small as myself, may as well have been sprawling plazas. The houses themselves were like mountain ranges, the sewers like rivers.

The sound of my passing startled awake a spotted breed who had been dozing on a windowsill. It jumped up, but seeing it was just me, lost interest again and lay back down. In a courtyard, just inside a gate with a hole large enough for a human to pass, sprawled another breed known for its long neck and gangly limbs. Its hair hung down, and its body fur, likewise long and full, made it look like a skein of wool.

Another breed, only a third my size and so fat you could barely see its arms and legs, made its way slowly across the top of a wall edged with iron spikes.

"Albi. Albi!" The tubby one called out from the wall with a laugh. "Running away from home again? What's your mission this time? To find an old book or something?"

Albi is what everyone calls me around here. It's short for albino, which is what I am. A colorless breed. My whole body from my fur to my eyebrows to the hair on my head is completely white except for my eyes, which glow red from the blood vessels there. My breed is quite popular; I fetch a high price at the store. That's because my stark white body is easy for even their severely color-blind eyes to see.

The ground rumbled as if from a distant earthquake. I pressed my body up against the wall hoping not to be seen. A long snout appeared out of the darkness first, stretching and wiggling as it sniffed its way past where I was standing. After what seemed an eternity, the enormous body attached to the snout slowly emerged from the dark, almost tripping over itself.

It had to be drunk. Nervous that it might stumble and fall on top of me, I waited ages for it to pass. Even after I was clear of its body, its long tail still took forever to vanish. It appeared to be singing. The puddle beneath my feet sloshed rhythmically. The water could hear its song, but I could not. I can hear only a fraction of the sounds they make. Just as they can hear only a fraction of the ones I do.

"Hey there, Albi."

I stopped and looked up. A mutt crouched on top of a trashcan was staring down at me. Male. Tousled black hair, dark eyes. Same height as me, but with ears so tiny they were hardly noticeable. In terms of shape and coloring, he looked pretty much like all the other mutts that roamed the streets.

My teacher had taught me about the mixing of breeds. "Speciation is a form of mutation," my teacher had explained.

My teacher always strove to simplify things for me, but understanding the teachings is easier said than done.

"Speciation does not happen readily in most societies," my teacher went on. "Humans like you and me were not originally regarded as separate species, we were simply called 'mutants' or considered 'disabled.'" Pointing first at my eyes and my white fur, then at the hunch that bent their own spine so much they weren't even half my height, my teacher continued. "Most couldn't have descendants; their bloodlines ended with them. Others would have been ostracized and thus would have struggled to find mates."

"Why was that?" I asked.

"I guess you could blame it on the childish habit of disliking anyone who's different. Mutations are usually caused by recessive genes, and the only way to pass those genes on to the next generation is for two people who carry the same gene to mate. But practically the only way for that to happen is through inbreeding. For both you and I, our parents were most likely either siblings or cousins. But that almost never happens in nature."

"Is that an immature habit, too?"

My teacher ignored my question. "When you crossbreed, you get closer and closer to the original form, the one that existed prior to species differentiation. If you could mate all plants and animals together—not that this would ever be possible—you might even be able to return to the first organism that ever existed. I believe that the more mixed something is, the closer it comes to resembling the ancestor of humankind. Of course, mixed breeds don't make popular pets these days, but back when humans ruled the earth and had no natural enemies... back before dragons appeared..."

"Are you lost?" the mutt asked. "Why's a house human like you roaming the streets at this hour with no master?"

I could tell what the mutt wanted from the way he was looking me up and down. Reaching behind me, I plucked out a small knife made from a sharp sliver of obsidian that I kept hidden in my hair.

He smirked. "Don't play hard to get."

"I have no intention of bearing a pup."

"Who said anything about bearing a pup? I just want a little fun."

"All the more reason I won't participate."

I knew all too well how street humans mated and bred. But I wanted nothing to do with it. There was only one thing I wanted.

It's good to not want too much. It saves you from having to hesitate over what to do or say.

"I'm looking for a wolf," I said. "Tell me what you know about them."

"I don't see why I should."

The mutt raised his long claws as if to strike. His well-developed, crossbred muscles, hardened from life on the streets, shone in the moonlight, his dark eyes glinting with a hint of blue and brown. (They are blind to these colors.) When he leapt, I dodged to one side and swung my knife. Sidestepping my strike, he ran up the wall and jumped at me again. I rolled to avoid his attack. My back hit the wall.

I was no match for his strength, speed, or fighting prowess, so I lowered my eyes and dropped my head for a moment. It was an extremely risky move, but one I'd learned for just such a desperate situation. My teacher referred to it as "prayer." Prayer is a difficult concept to grasp; all I understood was that it was instinctive. Licking his lips, the mutt lunged at me. As I stumbled backwards, he grabbed the nape of my neck and pulled my arm back with a practiced hand. "Drop the knife," he whispered, blowing hot breath on me, "or I'll break this pretty arm—"

His sentence ended in a wordless scream as I flipped backwards over his body in one swift move, pinning him to the ground. I pressed my blade to his carotid artery, and he let himself go limp.

"Not fair," he said. "You had *two* knives."

"I never said I had only one."

"Coward."

"It's much more cowardly for a male to use his strength to overpower a female."

I was doing my best to appear composed. Though I'd learned self-defense, this was my first time putting the techniques into action. I managed to speak without stuttering, but my voice trembled on the final words. I couldn't control the racing of my heart even though my head had already begun to cool. If this was the best I could manage, I was worried about what was to come.

"Your life belongs to me now," I said. "But I'll let you live if you tell me the truth."

"As if I'm in any position to negotiate."

"I'm looking for a wolf. I want information."

The mutt's face twisted into a strange expression that seemed to say, *I would never have messed with you if I'd known I was dealing with a crackpot.*

"You're not seriously looking for an actual wolf, are you?" he asked. "What do you even know about them?"

"I know they're the descendants of those who broke our pact long, long ago and vowed to resist the dragon tribe to the bitter end. I know they've refused any relationship whatsoever with dragons ever since and have survived as hunters, living in forests and hiding in caves. I also know they've managed to maintain their original form and are not covered in fur like we are. And that they continue to resist. And that some were spotted near here."

"Oh, I get it. You must be a senate informant. One of those assholes who makes a ruckus every night."

The mutt's face contorted again, this time as if to say, *If I'd known I was dealing with an informant, I definitely wouldn't have messed with you.*

"Thought you were a little nimble for a house human," he continued. "What do you plan to do with the wolves? Being the bitch you are, you were probably ordered by the senate to get rid of them. They're going to die out soon enough on their own regardless. There's hardly a place left in this world where they can survive. So why should you and I fight over monsters like that?"

He tried to get up, but I pressed down even harder. Baring his fangs at me, he said: "And spare me that nonsense about pacts or traps or whatever. It's not as if dragons know or care. Sure the dragons favor your kind; you sell well because you look funny. As long as you continue to do your little party tricks at least once a day, you'll never have to worry about food for the rest of your life. But pacts are meaningless for mutts like me."

"You're right. Pacts wouldn't mean anything to you," I said, pressing the knife in a little deeper against his throat, causing his face to change color. "Even if you die here in the street in some pathetic attempt at heroism, no one's going to weep for you. Unless you give me usable information right now, your life is worthless."

Again my voice trembled a little despite my attempts to keep it steady. But I must have sounded persuasive enough.

"Calm down, Albi," the mutt gasped.

"Don't call me Albi. I have a name."

"How am I supposed to know your name? Do you know *mine*? Fine, tell me your name."

Instead of replying, I moved the knife a little. He shuddered.

"You know Dongdaemun Station, right?" he said at last. "The ancestral ruins?"

"I've heard of it. Apparently it's still standing. I've also heard it's where you can find humans who were abandoned by their dragons."

"There's a rumor going around that a senile old woman lives there. They say she looks like a wolf. Wears clothes, not a stitch of fur on her."

The mutt tried to move his neck away from the blade, searching for a less painful position.

"Then again she might not be a wolf at all," he said. "She could just be a mutt like me. Every once in a while you see mutts who don't have fur. They say the old woman decorates the sides of houses and subway stations with drawings and words."

I nudged the knife a little closer, and the mutt stopped talking.

The words of the prophets are written on the subway walls and tenement halls.

"What?" he asked, as he struggled for air. I'd half sung the line.

"Nothing."

I put away my knife and stood. Finally free to breathe, he clasped his wounded throat and rolled a few paces away, then leapt onto the top of the garbage can, over the wall, and away. Before disappearing from sight, he glanced back at me, eyes burning with scorn and anger that cursed me a hundred times over. "Senate dog. Destroyer of human pride and dignity. Traitor to humanity. Nasty blue-blood. Cowardly defeatist!" he spat as he vanished.

As I brushed myself off, I heard the sound of quiet singing coming from somewhere. It was the teachers' song. At night, one of the teachers would sing the first verse from inside their house. The song would then spread to the next house, and the next, all across the neighborhood.

It's been said that a long, long time ago, before "the age when humans ruled the earth," an indigenous tribe with no system of writing had used this method to record and pass down their history. The teachers' song was patterned on that.

The plain, lilting melody repeated over and over as the history and knowledge of humankind was recited in verse form. Over the years, teachers had revised and refined the song, and with each new historical era or discovery, new verses had been added. It could take hours for a single song to be sung from start to finish.

The song echoing through the neighborhood went like this:

This is the sacred learning passed down by our forebears. This is knowledge passed down by our ancestors who ruled the earth. Do not let this song end. Do not shirk your duty to transmit this song to the next generations. Stop the war. Our ancestors, who were far greater than us, did everything in their power to fight them. Much was lost as a result. Do not die fighting them. Love them and survive so that human genes might survive into the future. That is our sacred duty. Do not let this song end. Do not shirk your duty to transmit this song to the next generation. These are the sacred laws passed down by the great prophet Newton. First Law: an object at rest will remain at rest, and an object in motion will remain in motion at a constant velocity, unless acted upon by an external force. Remember this. Second Law: force equals mass times acceleration..."

They are deaf to this song.

"The sounds that are produced by living beings follow the same principles as sounds produced by musical instruments," my teacher explained while arranging some rice bowls in front of me. My teacher then made the bowls ring—low, heavy tones issuing forth from the large bowls, high-pitched tones from the small ones.

"Small creatures make high-pitched sounds, and big creatures make low-pitched sounds. We can't hear the songs of whales, but their music can cross the Pacific Ocean and reach the ends of the earth. Low sounds resonate much further. The earth is filled with whale songs, and yet our human ears do not hear them. Whales are too large, the sounds they make too low. In the same way, we can't hear the voices of ants because they are pitched too high. No living being has ears that can hear every pitch. The world would be unbearably noisy otherwise.

"Dragons are the greatest creatures that ever existed in the history of this planet. We humans live in the same physical space as them but occupy different spheres of existence. It's as if our radios are tuned to a different station from theirs. Like whales and elephants, they communicate with each other using low frequencies that we can't hear. The same is true for our eyes. What we see is not the same as what they do."

My teacher picked up a rice bowl and placed it so it dangled from my nose. When I looked straight ahead, the bowl seemed to sway, making me dizzy.

"Animals with long faces or snouts cannot focus on objects direct-ly ahead of them. You need two forward-facing eyes with nothing blocking your view to focus clearly on something in front of you. Dragons' eyes are on the opposite sides of their heads. They have a three hundred and sixty degree field of vision, but all they're able to see is that "something" is out there in front of them. So they rely instead on vibrations that they read through the soles of their feet, or on magnetic fields that they perceive through their sensitive skin. On top of all that, they're color blind. Like a lot of other animals..."

My teacher paused and gazed at me. I detected a note of sympathy.

"Even if humans and dragons were to find a way to converse with each other someday, and even if their brains were to become far more developed than they are now, there would still be so much that they couldn't ever understand. Including colors..."

Hearing this made me cry.

The entrance to Dongdaemun Station lay beneath a crevice under a mailbox. Though it was big enough for a human to enter, to dragons, it was a mere crack in the earth. If the underground passageway were ever to be filled in, it would disappear from the world entirely. Fortu-nately, however, the officials in the area were lazy about responding to civic matters of that kind.

An old staircase, perfectly proportioned to match a human's stride, led inside. Unused to the scale of the stairs, I stumbled a few times as I walked down. A torch glowed in the entrance; several more, unlit, had been placed to one side. This meant that humans were living there.

Lighting one of the torches, I made my way in. Something scur-ried in the dark just as I was passing a notice that read, "The subway station is a place meant for public use and for evacuation in case of emergency." They are blind to these words.

I shone my torch over towards where I'd seen movement. People crouched against the concrete walls, trying to hide. They were covered in fur; some even had fur on their faces and the palms of their hands. The soles of their feet were as bent as their palms, and their mouths and noses protruded. They seemed unaccustomed to the light. Each time I pointed my torch towards them, they closed their eyes. They looked wretched, as if they'd been gnawed at by rats and fleas. But the accommodations further inside were perfectly adequate. Instead of linoleum, the ground was lined with what appeared to be underwear and shoe insoles that had been discarded by dragons. Beverage and food cans served as furniture, spoons and toothbrushes as pillars.

The dragons often watched bemused as we built homes for ourselves from their cast-off odds and ends. They debated how creatures like us, with our lack of language and our inability to learn (or so they believed), could build abodes guided by instinct alone. But what does an instinct for building a home prove? Beavers build dams, and bees and ants build complex structures. Furthermore, whales and birds sing songs that contain both verses and choruses, and insects form perfect communal societies complete with a ruling class, a military class, and a laboring class. The weird things we humans do are no proof of intellect.

Dragons like to test us for intelligence sometimes. They shuffle two decks of cards—one with red and green cards and the other with purple and yellow cards—and challenge us to distinguish between them. Most humans can't figure out what the dragons' intentions are and end up completely confused. In fact, the two sets of cards are often marked with very faint scents that human beings couldn't possibly detect. Or they are equipped with devices that emit sounds we cannot hear. Rats and birds score much higher on such IQ tests.

Sitting among the subway dwellers was a little girl with six fingers and six toes. She was hugging a dog who sat on its curled up tail glaring warily at me. The six-fingered child looked healthier than the other children there. Her family seemed to be taking better care of her, probably on the off chance that her unusual number of fingers might make her an attractive pet for the dragons. Getting scraps of food from the back door to a dragon's kitchen would be much easier if one of their members was living there.

"I've heard there's an old woman living here who's believed to be a wolf," I said to the people gathered.

No one responded.

"Have any of you seen her?"

Still no response. I took out my knife. The children shrank against the wall, frightened. A man stood up. One of his legs was shorter than the other; he was probably more respected because of this. He was not, however, very articulate.

"Put away knife," he spat. "We harmless. We not want bloodshed. Senate dog!"

"I'll make the demands here. If any of you have seen a wolf, speak up. I don't want any bloodshed either. But if you don't cooperate, I'll start with the weakest among you."

I pointed the tip of the knife at the six-fingered girl. She clung still tighter to the dog, which began to growl at me. My skills would be no match whatsoever for the group if they chose to attack me all at once. Fortunately, no one seemed to realize this.

The man yelled at me again in some language of his own. I couldn't understand a word of it, yet I knew he was cursing me.

"Follow blue man. Do not attack. Wolf harmless. Weak. Dying. But has good heart." I could tell from the man's tone that the wolf had earned some sort of respect from this crowd.

I found the "blue man" right away. It was an image commonly

found among the ruins of our ancestors.

"That's green," I muttered.

As I passed beneath a sign that read "Way Out," a stone flew out of nowhere, hitting me on the forehead. I looked up.

A densely furred boy was sitting inside a metal frame. "Wolves know how to beat dragons!" he shouted before disappearing.

Glancing to one side, I saw the same words—WOLVES KNOW HOW TO BEAT DRAGONS—grafittied in large red letters on the wall. The paint still looked wet, as if it had been applied just as I was approaching. A peaceful protest of sorts.

More messages had been painted on the walls.

WHERE DID DRAGONS COME FROM?

ARE THEY ALIENS?

DEEP-SEA MONSTERS THAT EVOLVED?

DESCENDANTS OF DINOSAURS?

As far as I knew, dragons had simply appeared. Just as the dinosaurs had vanished and we humans had appeared, or the way giant reptiles vanished and giant mammals appeared.

Next to a placard that read "Staff Only" someone had painted a mural. I stood looking at it for a long time. It depicted an enormous dragon spewing fire against the backdrop of a burning volcano. Below, a person dressed in armor, shield held aloft to block the flames, charged at the dragon with a sword.

The dragon looked strange. Its nose was too short, its mouth more like an alligator's. Dragons are herbivores. They have no use for sharp teeth, and their jaws can't open particularly wide. If they ever were to attempt to graze with a mouth like the one shown in the mural, all the grass would surely spill out from between their fangs and out the sides of their cheeks.

The dragon in the picture had fingers that looked like bird feet, and its tail and the way it sat made it look like a kangaroo. Most importantly, dragons don't breathe fire. Plus the proportions in the drawing were laughable—as absurd-looking as a fly sword-fighting with a human.

And yet I was moved by the painting. I could tell that this creature that looked nothing like an actual dragon was supposed to symbolize a dragon. It had been rendered so vividly that it seemed ready to leap off the wall. The dragon's eyes appeared to roll in their sockets. If I were to reach out and touch the fiery mountain, the flames that engulfed the man might very well burn my hand.

"It seems you like it."

I spun around and pulled out my knife. On top of the train tracks, half-buried under dirt and rocks, sat an old woman. She was covered from head to toe in woven fabrics: only her hands, feet, and a craggy face peeked out from the folds. She was so covered up that I couldn't tell for certain whether or not she had fur, but it certainly looked as though she didn't. Her skin was an odd color, like the skin of a fish.

"My, my, kids these days have no manners. Greeting an old lady with the swing of a knife."

"Old lady? Don't you mean old wolf?"

The woman cackled.

"Wolf? What are you going on about? Who ever heard of a wolf who eats out of cans?"

Reaching into the enormous tin can she was leaning against, she dislodged a chunk of stale beans that had gotten stuck to its inner wall, stuffed it into her mouth, and began to gum the beans.

"Where are they? The wolves? Are they here? Tell me right now."

"That's not a nice way to talk to your elders. But I suppose you senate bastards weren't properly educated."

I gulped and glanced back. I couldn't help it. It pained me to think that in the brief moment when I couldn't see it, I might forget it.

"Did you paint that, ma'am?"

"Only humans are weird enough to paint pictures. It just goes to show how distorted our view of the world is. The images that form on our retinas are flat, so we see the world as flat. There's nothing more pathetic than seeing three-dimensional objects as flat all the time. But when we paint, the brain tricks us into seeing flat images as three-dimensional. Slap on a little color and a few shadows, and we think we're seeing depth."

She pointed at the exit sign I'd been following.

"Take the shape of that blue guy, for instance. It looks nothing like a person. And yet to a human, it looks human. But not to a dragon... They have no idea what that's supposed to be. It's like the difference between a real lemon and a fake lemon. How could anything other than an actual lemon represent a lemon? That's why dragons can't understand pictures. They don't perceive the world in two dimensions. Didn't your teachers explain this to you already? Do those idiots still have what it takes to teach such things to their students?"

"Our teachers have devoted their lives to passing down wisdom to the next generations."

"That's not enough. The knowledge of the ancestors is as boundless as the ocean. It takes more than a few measly lives to transmit all there is to learn. They won't be able to keep it up."

"Where are the other wolves? Why have they moved into the city?

Have they fallen so far that they have to eat food out of cans and dig through the trash?"

"What's this bullshit about food?"

I took a step forward and said, "A long time ago, in another city, a wolf killed a dragon. It was a senseless act. But the people of the city had to pay for it. They were all pushed out onto the streets where hundreds of children ended up starving to death."

"So they did." The old woman cackled again. "And then they charged at the dragons, coats flapping, armed with stinger missiles and grenades, Beretta pistols in each hand. Kids always love that kind of thing: warriors leaping over houses as tall as the tallest mountain ranges, crossing floors as wide as a desert, and slaying dragons asleep atop their treasure hoards. Is that the kind of story that you like, too?"

"Are you saying it's made-up?"

"Such stories just came into being on their own, even though there might be some truth to them. That said, wolves don't kill unless it's to save their own lives."

I stepped down onto the tracks and pointed my knife at her.

"Tell me. Where are the other wolves? I know you're not alone. Wolves don't travel alone."

No sooner were the words out than I felt all the strength leave my body. The whites of the old woman's eyes had flashed at me from inside her headscarf. I felt my joints stiffen. Luckily, I froze with my knife still aimed right at her.

"They were crushed by the city that replaced the village. Bulldozers tore into the forest and attacked them when they were sleeping, leaving them no means of escape. My husband, my son, and my grandson all died. There are no wolves left. The old folk had no way left to survive, so we crawled into the cities."

My whole body turned cold.

"You're lying."

"Ha! This girl thinks I'm lying."

She stared at me with pity, then said,"If you just poke and prod at life, tasting it to see whether it's worth living or not, you'll never become a wolf."

My body swayed as my knees weakened. I had to take a few steps backwards to catch my balance. If I hadn't bumped into the wall of the subway tunnel, I probably would have fallen on my butt.

"...What?"

The old woman stood. All she did was stand, and yet I thought for a moment that she had grown larger. Walking slowly over to me, she seized my wrist and pried open my hand. The knife fell. All I could do was watch.

My palm was stained with every color of the rainbow, my skin saturated with colors I'd mixed together from various materials, using whatever I could find: the juice of ground flower petals, yellow clay, dead insects, stones, salt, resin.

"So you paint."

My face turned bright red, as if my private parts had just been exposed.

"Who taught you?"

When I didn't answer, she asked again, yelling this time. "Who taught you!"

"No one," I said without thinking. "I just paint."

The old woman cackled. "You'd have been better off sculpting. They can understand sculpture."

She let go of my hand and turned to leave. My legs shook.

"Please take me with you."

She looked at me coolly, as if I bored her. I felt like a true phony, my mask crumbling before the genuine article. I dropped to my knees. The cold ground brought an uncontrollable stream of tears to my eyes.

"Please. Take me with you."

She clucked her tongue. "Where to? The wolves are all dead. There is no community to protect you, no husband to clothe you and make a home with you. The old have no choice but to turn into dogs. The only thing this aged body of mine can do anymore is dig through the trash. And even that won't last for much longer."

"I'll take care of you. Just teach me how to hunt and farm. Please pass your wisdom down to me. I'll stay with you forever."

"Why would I do that?"

"I've been yearning to find wolves for such a long time."

"Liar," she said, cutting me off point-blank. "What? You don't like the milk your master gives you? Your bed not comfortable enough? They don't tuck you in at night? Or bathe you every other day?"

I shook my head no. Then I closed my eyes and lowered my head. "I'm done acting cute for those brutes. Please let me live with human beings. I want to be free. I'll fight alongside you. Teach me how you live. Take me with you. I'll do anything."

"Anything?" she asked mockingly. She picked up the obsidian knife I'd dropped, turning it this way and that to study it. "This is well made. But it's not enough. It cannot pierce dragon skin. The most it can do is leave a little scratch."

Then she dug her hands into the dirt, her bottom swaying and bouncing as she started to pull out a long metal pipe. Though she scooted back quite a ways, the pipe remained partially buried. Finally managing to unearth the whole of it, she sat back, breathing hard. The end of the pipe was cut at a sharp angle.

"Wolves know how to beat dragons," she muttered as though reciting a line of poetry from memory. *Even if it's an old legend, some part of it must be true*, she seemed to be thinking to herself.

"This pipe has been buried under dirt and garbage for a month. It should be good and smelly by now. You, too—bathe yourself in dirt for the next few days. And when your master is asleep, stick this pipe in his ear. If you insert it all the way, it will go into his brain without leaving any external marks. Even if someone were to eventually figure out the cause of death, they would never imagine it to be the work of a human. Come back once you've dealt with your master, and I'll accept you."

I sat there for a moment, jaw hanging open, then tried to pick up the pipe that she'd set on the ground. It was heavy. Very heavy. So heavy that the sweat poured off me as I squeezed it in both hands. My legs shook as I tried to lift the pipe but was unable to stand. Flexing my legs, I tried harder, but ended up dropping the pipe and falling back down. The pipe clanked against the subway rail. A clear echo rang through the station. The old woman looked down at me coldly.

I wanted to explain to her that the pipe was too heavy to lift, but my mouth wouldn't cooperate. It wasn't the pipe that was weighing me down. Even after I'd dropped it, my body still dripped with sweat.

"I... I can't."

Words spoken aloud have power. I regretted them the moment I opened my mouth. Once again I'd done something that I couldn't take back. Realizing that I would never be able to do what she'd asked of me, my body went weak. I felt as if I would never again be able to stand or speak or move or go about my business. I didn't even have enough strength to cling to life. I could feel my soul leaving me. The old woman was silent.

Finally, she asked, "You love your master, don't you?"

I couldn't respond.

"That's why you lost hope when you realized your master couldn't understand your paintings. You're unhappy because your master has no way of knowing that you possess intelligence and wisdom and, more than that, a heart and soul. None of them do."

She gazed down at me with pity.

"Go back," she said. "That's not a reason to leave. And even if you were to leave, if it's out of despair because they don't know how to love you, your soul will never be free. Your soul is already bound to theirs. You don't have what it takes to be a wolf."

I do love my master.

My master knows this, too.

And my master loves me.

And I know this, too.

But my master is blind to my true self.

They not know how delicately the moon illuminates the streets at night. Nor that the sky is filled with stars that travel across the celestial sphere once a day. They do not know that the moon waxes and wanes every month, that on full moons like tonight, the street turns silver. To them, night is nothing more than the cessation of sound, a cooling and a dampening, a growing heaviness in the air, a change in the direction of the wind. They do not know that I've filled the walls of their house with paintings of fiery sunsets, of indigo night skies. They think that all I do is leave my scent and mark my territory. They have no idea that I've painted their portrait on the front door. Nor do they know that their own body glows jade green. Or that their eyes are also jade green.

But so what? Something different probably hangs in their sky. Maybe their ears can hear the turning of the earth, maybe the stars resonate like music. Maybe they hear the earth's magnetic fields changing course and sees cosmic rays and ultraviolet rays streaming down. Maybe there is something that they see as everyday that humanity can't even conceive of despite having existed for tens of thousands of years. The image of me that they see is completely different from what I see in the mirror, and they hear a voice coming from me that I cannot hear myself.

But I have no way of knowing any of this. Just as they have no way of knowing that these thoughts fill me with sadness. We live in different universes, and so do not know each other's true selves. We love each other's shadows but do not know the truth. We live in the same world but may as well exist in different dimensions.

As tears spilled from my eyes, the old woman cradled my face with both hands.

"Poor baby, what is your name?" she asked.

I shook my head. I couldn't pronounce it. It had taken me ten years just to be able to discern the faint tremble in the air whenever my master called to me. I didn't know his name either, just that it feels like something exploding. That's why I called him ☀. My name sounds like the sensation of the air stretching out in long lines. That's why I called myself 🌾. But I still could not pronounce my master's name.

When I told her this, the old lady laughed.

"In that case, your name is now Sky, spelled ☰."

I sensed that the name came from some ancient wisdom. She rested a bony hand on my shoulder. It was warm.

"Did I tell you about the secret passageway out of the village? It's a pity that you're so small. I wish you were big enough to carry me around on your back. But that's okay. Did I tell you about the swamp where all the mushrooms grow? They're delicious if you boil them with some fermented soybean paste. I don't suppose the old folk taught you how to make doenjang paste? Soybeans grow wild near Gwanghwamun…"

∗

☀ catches 🌾's scent near the mailbox and begins to dig. Before long, the tips of his fingers graze a passageway that seems to have been gouged out by animals traveling back and forth. The smell there forms an afterimage of Ⱳ. Ⱳ has definitely been there. ☀ picks up the scent of wild animals as well, and thinks, "Either Ⱳ has been captured by some dangerous beast or bitten to death." He feels a little sad at the thought of losing a pet he's been attached to for such a long time, but knows the feeling will lessen once he buys a new one. After all, it's not as though it would have lived very long anyway, maybe sixty years at the most.

☀ suddenly decides to sniff further inside the tiny passageway. Strong odors waft off of the walls. He has long known that Ⱳ enjoyed smearing things on the walls, but he'd never taken much interest in this. That day, however, the sadness of losing Ⱳ has made ☀ a little bit sentimental. He examines the walls more closely. After a thorough inspection, a peculiar image floats to mind. It is the first time ☀'s mind has filled with anything in the form of an image.

"How strange!" ☀ murmurs. "This reminds me of me. No, wait. I don't know why I thought that. It's as if someone has flattened me out and stuck me to a wall. And they've left out all the important parts, too. My nose is in a strange place and looks more like a tongue. And my body and tail and limbs are too long and skinny. Wait, wait. Why did I think of those as limbs? They're just lines. They really are just lines. And yet, I think this is supposed to be me. How could that be?"

By these miraculous coincidences, ☀'s train of thought starts to shift. It moves up a floor, then sideways into a room where a door has long been shut, then down into a wide sea beneath a thick layer of ice, and comes very close to reaching the final threshold... until his wife calls out to him from their house four kilometers away, summoning him home for dinner, and ☀ sets the thought aside and returns home.

All sorts of things in this world just can't be explained.

On the Origin of Species

1

— God created us in the image of God.

But there is no record to indicate which of the countless known models most resembles God. Artists have tended to base their portraits of the divine on the most stable of models, the 700. This means that God is always depicted as gold-plated and four-wheeled, the 700 serial number etched above the right ear and on both wrists. No effort is spared in trying to elevate God's glory through art. Our attention is guided to the exposed inner bundles of wires and neurocircuitry in each joint, or to the outer surface of the brain, rendered transparent so as to showcase its intricate inner workings.

But what proof is there that God is a 700? Who's to say that God is not a cylindrical 21 or a 2000 with its soft and fuzzy covering (as ridiculous as that might seem)? For what else is the image of God as drawn by a robot's paltry imagination than a synthesis of features characterizing the world's privileged class? Not only is God a 700, and not only is God gold-plated, equipped with the latest components from head to toe and bearing state-of-the-art markings, God is also clad in a luminous skin that has never seen a single day's work.

"That's creationism, Kay!" Evan laughed, letting forth a series of *peet-peets*. Evan's large eyes, like two telephoto lenses, clicked and clacked as if overcome with hilarity. "The great Prieston elders would weep to hear it! Since when did you abandon the path of science and veer off into theology? It's been less than half a century since priests dismantled scientists while they were still alive!"

Evan's pincers clacked together loudly, while Kay bashfully scratched at a thick head of hair.

"Evan, there's no such thing anymore as priests who dismantle living scientists."

"My friend," Evan said, affecting a more serious tone, "even invoking the word creationism is disrespectful to the souls of those who martyred themselves for science."

"I haven't changed my belief that species evolve. And I obviously have no intention of disrespecting the memory of our great elders. But faith is also in a robot's nature. I think it's worth researching."

Evan laughed again, letting out another series of *peet-peets*.

"All faith is symbolism and allegory. It's a subset of literature and art. There's nothing scientific about it whatsoever. Unless, of course, you're trying to tell me that art is a form of science."

Soft piano music played by a five-armed pianist filled the hall, which had been decorated with a banner that read "Prieston Biology Department Student Reunion." Robots from all walks of life enjoyed themselves, chatting merrily and lubricating their joints with oil that had been provided at each table.

Outside the window where Evan and Kay were standing loomed an endless row of gray buildings. A fog of dust lurked like some living thing in the hazy glow of street lamps that cast a dim light from their drooping necks. Between the buildings could be seen a glimpse of black clouds writhing ceaselessly in a gunmetal sky. From below came the din of wheeled robots racing along, their headlights beaming.

Evan was a 21. Long arms that ended in pincers folded neatly away into the series' signature cylindrical body, atop which sat a head mounted with two telephoto lenses. Although Evan normally rode around on three wheels, a pair of articulated legs could also be deployed when traveling up and down stairs or when coming to a full stop.

Kay was a 1029—two digits more than Evan, though the extra digits didn't signify a higher standing in the evolutionary scale. In fact, the opposite was true (a contradiction that many philosophers have struggled to explain). What distinguished a four-digit robot from a two-digit robot was the supple skin that covered parts of its body. The 1000 series, for example—to which Kay belonged—featured a soft face with a metal body, whereas the 2000 series was soft from head to toe. But that softness came with a price: the skin on Kay's face, like that of all 1029s, was so fragile that it cracked upon exposure to the outside air. Such robots had to wear protective masks whenever they went outside. Needless to say, cosmetic surgery was a booming industry among the 1029s, who had taken to covering their faces with gold plating that resembled that of the 700s.

Looking around, Kay noticed that there were a number of 2000s in the room. They stood out everywhere because of the peculiar color of their skin, an unusual shade that appeared to be some sort of mixture of yellow, orange, brown, and white.

"Allow me to explain science to you one more time, Kay."

"Look over here!"

A four-wheeled camera purred up to them. Kay and Evan struck a casual pose, Kay with an oil can held aloft in one hand and an arm around Evan, Evan's arm around Kay as well. The flash went off.

"Have a lovely evening," the camera chirped and whirred off across the room.

"Take that camera as an example," Evan said pointing at the photograph-taking robot as it wove its way through the crowd, "Taking photos with primitive cameras used to be such a production. You couldn't move at all during the hours it took to capture a shot, and simply adjusting the exposure and focus required a lot of extra equipment that had to be hauled around. But each successive generation achieved a bit more compactness and efficiency. Later models fit in your palm, and all that was required to take a picture was a single click of a button. But look at them now. Not only do cameras take fantastic pictures all on their own, they even move around and interact with their subjects. In short, they've evolved. They might have started out as humble scraps of photosensitive film, but through clever adaptation, they've gradually transformed into a complex organism. If, as the sacred texts claims, God created robots using words alone, it would have taken all seven days just to call into existence every single one of those countless camera models."

"Evan, I'm not trying to rehash centuries of debate about creationism and evolution. My question is simply *how did robots come to believe they were created?"*

"Because they're stupid."

"I'm talking about robot nature."

"What do you mean?"

"Think about it. Robots are born in the Factory, where the dead are disassembled and cleaned up before being made into new robots. That's 'creation' as we know it. So where did we get this idea that robots were first molded into existence out of clay?"

"What's your point?" Evan asked idly, rotating the pincers of one arm.

"Loneliness is an instinctive emotion for us robots. That is to say, we survive better when we live in groups. Fear is necessary to protect us from physical threats, and pain is necessary to prevent physical injuries. Our ability to learn helps us to adapt to changing environments, while our ability to forget makes us more efficient at retrieving information. All this is based on the idea that instincts are essential for the survival and perpetuation of a species. So what would be the point of believing in 'creationism'?"

"Peace of mind, maybe."

"That's the thing. How does the idea of being created give a robot peace of mind? Is it scary to think that we sprang into being on our own? We like to imagine that there is some unimaginably almighty being up on some high peak who watches over us and controls us, that we are slaves to this being. And that's supposed to bring us happiness? Why would a robot want to pledge unconditional love and devotion to someone or something they've never even seen? How does that contribute to the preservation of the species? What does this servility that seems to have been stamped onto the roots of the robot mind, this fantasy of submission, this romanticization of despots and the almighty have to do with maintaining our race?"

Kay stopped short. Evan stared in stony, disapproving silence, arms crossed.

"Please tell me you're not putting any of that drivel in your report," Evan said at last.

"Well, no, but..." Kay looked down to avoid Evan's gaze.

"Don't get me wrong, Kay. I personally enjoy listening to your weird stories, but don't kid yourself into thinking that your professors will be impressed by them. Your philosophy is interesting. But don't be that fool who writes a paper on creationism for a course on evolution."

"I'm just tired of writing the same, predictable paper day after day."

Kay sat on the floor and stared darkly into space. Bipedal four-digit models like Kay had weaker joints than the others, which meant they often had to shift their weight from their knees to other parts. A slender table with trays of battery chargers on each of its six arms glided by, swaying softly in time with the music.

"Those so-called papers on evolution are just regurgitations of previous findings about how robots in different parts of the world all share similar codes, parts, and circuitries, or how robot fossils become simpler the deeper you dig into the geological strata. It's all just weak observations, the 50,001st piece of data tossed onto the other 50,000 pieces of data that have already been collecting dust. Actually, that's not true. All fifty students are going to write the same paper this term, which means that we can soon look forward to

50,050 pieces of identical data."

"But that's how science works. It's our job to contribute one tiny portion of knowledge at a time to the edifice of scientific theory, slowly cementing each part into place no matter how worthless it may seem or how few may care about it. Do you know how many inane proofs about how "the part is smaller than the whole" get published? Kay, your enthusiasm is commendable, but you lack practicality. Are you bent on shooting for something that will over-turn the academy? How many of your papers have already been rejected this year?"

Kay started counting earnestly on the fingers of one hand before realizing that Evan's question was rhetorical. Kay's voice trailed off.

Evan smirked, "Don't get so far ahead of yourself. To get a gradu-ate degree in biology, you have to present dissertations in twelve different subjects. Even if you study nonstop, you won't be done for another twenty-four years. Can you defer your flights of fancy until after you've locked down that degree? I'm sure you don't plan to spend your entire life in school."

Kay was about to reply when that strange yellowish, brownish, whitish color came into view again.

"Cecil!" Evan called out.

"Oh, hi! Long time, no see, Evan!"

Evan's arms spread wide to embrace Cecil. Standing there watch-ing the two, Kay couldn't help but wonder if the robot had been hovering there all along, just beyond their field of vision.

"It really has been a long time," Evan said, "What brings you to this reunion?"

"My research is related to biology. I figured I'd swing by and pick up some journals."

"Isn't everything related to biology ?" Evan made an amused *peet-peet* sound. "You still bumming around with those nobodies?"

"They're called microbes."

"If you insist."

Unable to follow the conversation, Kay stood in silence until Evan finally thought to introduce them.

"Kay, this is Cecil Evansche, chemistry major. We're in the same club. Cecil, this is Kay Histion. You two probably were probably in the same chemistry class at some point."

Cecil held a hand out to Kay and said, "With so many students, who can remember?"

The two shook hands without difficulty, both being five-fingered models. Kay caught a hint of excitement in Cecil's eyes, but chalked this up to an overactive imagination.

"We were just debating creationism versus evolution," Evan said.

"I didn't realize that was still being debated."

"Ah, don't say that. Kay is pro-creationism."

Cecil raised an eyebrow in mock surprise.

"Evan, don't give Cecil the wrong idea," Kay protested. "I was talking about a report I'm writing on evolution. I just wanted to try out a different angle for once."

"That's right. Kay here chose to stroll merrily down the path of flunking out in pursuit of a fresh perspective. It's just too bad that the stuffy old professors of Prieston lack the capacity to appreciate the magnificent ideas of their genius pupil."

"Evan—"

Flustered, Kay was just reaching over as if to muffle Evan's speaker when Cecil chimed in brightly: "Actually, I'm in your corner, Kay."

"Please," Kay pleaded. "That's enough fun at my expense, don't you think?"

"What? No, I mean it. If there's one truth we can always rely on, it's that Prieston professors are conservative. I bet they pray that science will never progress beyond what they already know. Can you imagine how many amazing dissertations have probably been torn apart by their hidebound standards?"

Cecil's eyes twinkled but remained firmly trained on Kay's. Still unsure of what to make of the remark, Kay searched Cecil's face for clues. If there was one thing that set a four-digiter apart—and a 2000 in particular—it was their unwitting displays of emotions. Worse yet, whereas a two-digiter's repertoire was limited to the four major emotions of joy, anger, sorrow, and pleasure, a 2000's range of emotions was endless. Very happy, a little bit happy, subtly happy, awkwardly happy, happy yet bothered by something, happy to the point of sadness, fake happy, and so on. Kay, as a fellow four-digiter burdened with a face that inconveniently exposed true feelings, was more literate than most in reading facial expressions, but the nuances of some still remained out of reach. The 2000s, on the other hand, seemed to grasp all such subtle distinctions. In fact, a former 2000 classmate had once described Kay's expressions as "stiff." Of course, to a non-four-digit robot, none of this made any sense.

There was nothing Kay could see in Cecil's face that indicated mockery. Kay stared at Evan for a moment, who seemed confused as well.

"Do we know each other?" Kay asked Cecil.

"You're Kay Histion, aren't you?"

"Well, yes, but Evan just told you that."

Cecil laughed. "Actually, I already knew your name. I remember you. You don't remember me?"

"Uh, sure, I think so," Kay lied, trying to retrieve any relevant memory.

Cecil was a consummate 2000: a chest with two soft peaks and fluid curves that ran from head to toe. The 2000s came in two varieties, curvy ones like Cecil and angular ones with wide shoulders, no chest peaks, and an object of unknown purpose dangling between the legs. But despite the differences in their appearance and the sound frequencies they generated, there was no difference in their functionality, so no one actually bothered distinguishing between the two. Like most 2000s, Cecil was clad in a clear, protective metal that revealed delicate skin underneath. The top of Cecil's head was covered with hair like Kay's but it was cut short to about three centimeters in length, another common 2000 feature. Kay suddenly flashed on an image of Cecil covered in gold.

"Cecil Evansche, right?"

"Evan told you that already," Cecil laughed. "You really don't remember me, do you? We've never spoken."

"Of course I do. Uh, didn't you used to wear gold body make-up?'

2000s stood out everywhere on campus. This was partly because of their unusual appearance, but also because so few of them made it into universities to begin with. Despite the claim of having abolished modelism, there was a limit to how quickly society could change, so it was exceedingly rare for 2000s to receive a higher education. Many scholars refused to acknowledge that 2000s were excluded from educational and cultural opportunities in this way from the moment they were born, instead attributing their poor achievement to the untested claim that they had the lowest IQs of all of the above-two-digit robots. Kay, too, had experienced discrimination—such was the fate of all four-digiters. But any misfortune Kay had endured paled in comparison to what the 2000s had to put up with. Whereas Kay and Kay's kind could don a mask if necessary so as to pass as a three-digit model, the 2000s were too conspicuous.

Cecil nodded. "You remember correctly. It's almost a rite of passage for the young—you know, being ashamed of your own skin color. I used to spend all my pocket money on gold body make-up. It was dumb of me."

"Thank goodness you finally realized!" Evan laughed.

"By the way, Cecil, what did you mean earlier by 'microbes'?" Kay asked.

Evan quickly volunteered, "Organic matter."

"Organic?"

"Substances that can't be used to create machines," Evan continued smugly. "Cecil here is studying organic biology, the least popular subject at Prieston. The classes are difficult, the degree takes forever to complete, tuition costs twice as much, and specimens are hard to find. Robots with normal circuitries wouldn't be interested."

"Oh, you mean..." Kay thought maybe Evan had misspoken. "You're referring to the study of organic materials, right?"

The subtlest change came over Cecil's face. Looking straight into Kay's eyes, Cecil replied, "No, organic biology."

Kay understood that the peculiar look on Cecil's face was an involuntary response of the outer skin that indicated "embarrassment." It wasn't too difficult to understand why four-digit models were treated so poorly. What company would want an executive robot with a defect so damning as to give away its private thoughts? Trade, business, education, politics, diplomacy... There were so many jobs that four-digiters were hopelessly ill-suited for. Their inherent lack of social sophistication was a major reason why many of them flocked to the arts or manual labor.

"Is that the study of the relationship between organic matter and living things? Sorry, I know that's probably a stupid question. I'm just not familiar with the subject."

"All you need to know is that it's not biology," Evan said, hijacking the exchange once again and patting Kay on the back with a pincer.

"Then why does it have the word 'biology' in it?"

"You know Professor Cal Strop, right? The one with the superior engine who's on close terms with the chancellor? Professor Strop used passion, imagination, and stubbornness to hector the chancellor into caving in and creating the program. There have never been more than four students enrolled at any one time. It broke the record for the lowest enrollment. Before that, the class with the least students had been Patternology of Buddhist Monks' Robes in Medieval Northeast Asia, which topped out at five students. Professor Strop campaigned to have the program listed under biology, but fortunately it remained under chemistry, thanks to Professor Zippa, who risked everything to ensure that it did."

"Evan, that's my advisor you're talking about. I know Professor Strop's a bit eccentric, but..."

Cecil smiled. That slight upturn at the corners of the lips was a strange trick that only a 2000 could manage. Because it was silent, it was the kind of thing that was nearly indiscernible to all but fellow four-digit models.

"Professor Strop has faith and is a great scientist... and philosopher."

"One who subscribes to the philosophy that organic matter is alive," Evan said pointedly. "But Cecil, it pains me to see you sacrifice your life to that religion. How much longer do you plan to devote all your time to such a fanatic and/or their invisible underlings? You need to think about your future."

Organic matter is alive. The words rolled around in Kay's mouth. It sounded like something out of the Genesis myth, chapter one. Something that God, who supposedly also said, "Robots, awaken!" could have muttered while hiding in a corner somewhere.

"I like that. It's poetic," Kay mused.

"Kay," Cecil said quietly, "it's not poetry, it's science."

"So, in organic biology, are bacteria, mold, mycelium, and whatnot considered living beings? For real? As in, they can think and reason and erect a civilization?"

Cecil's head shook no. "The definition of life isn't that simple, Kay," Cecil said. "Obviously, the things you mentioned are very low forms of life, but I do believe they're higher than cameras or tables."

"Okay, I'm sorry to keep arguing, but cameras know how to take pictures. What does mold know how to do?"

"Sounds like you should take organic biology with me," Cecil said with a smile.

"Thanks, but no thanks. I'm busy enough with my own classes."

Smiling again, Cecil said, "Mold *can* do something that cameras can't."

Cecil's eyes peered into Kay's face, as if trying to read Kay's thoughts.

"Mold knows how to grow," Cecil whispered, eyes locked on Kay's.

"What?"

"Grow," Cecil repeated in a low voice as if casting a spell, "It transforms. You know what 'transformation' means, don't you?"

Kay stared back at Cecil, suddenly bewildered. Cecil's gaze didn't waver. It was only when Evan made a grinding noise that Cecil looked away with a start.

"Sorry," Cecil said taking a step back, using both hands to cover their face. (A typical 2000 move since their thoughts are so readily visible.) "I haven't seen you in forever, and here I am talking nonsense."

"Oh, no, not at all. I find it very interesting. I'd love to learn more about organic biology if I were to get the chance someday."

Cecil nodded and waved to signal imminent departure.

"It was nice to see you two. Enjoy the rest of the party."

As Cecil disappeared back into the crowd, Kay and Evan spoke without looking at each other, their hands still hanging in the air.

"Cecil's a strange one, huh?"

"Seems so."

"Anyone who takes organic bio is. Professor Strop ruins them, fills their heads with a unique brand of senile crackpottery."

Evan's head spun around. That was how the 21s signaled negation.

"Growth!" Evan muttered. "Talk about imagination. Let's suppose for a moment that an object *can* grow. How does that affect the second law of thermodynamics or the law of conservation of mass? No substance in the world can increase its own mass."

2

— *It is believed that we can intuitively distinguish between the living and the dead, but scientifically speaking, it is difficult to define with any exactitude what counts as being alive.*

Are the transistors, chips, wires, and batteries that constitute us alive? Or should they be viewed as parts of an animate being? Should cameras, telephones, and fluorescent lights be viewed as semi-animate, or should they viewed as alive in their own right? What about cameras that can move and speak on their own versus those that cannot? Where do we draw the line between animacy and inanimacy? Should that line be based on functionality?

The essential prerequisites for life, as we understand it, are as follows.

1. *You must have free will. In other words, action commands must take place internally, not externally. If a lamp turns on and off at our command only, then it is inanimate. But if it can voluntarily adjust its own brightness even the slightest bit, it is animate. (This definition is still controversial. Many scholars question whether or not the rising and sinking of the ground, the direction of the wind, the fluctuations in air temperature, and the eruptions of volcanos are done "at someone's command." They point out that many machines are classified as inanimate simply because they cannot*

respond to interviews. The most controversial question has been, "If we find ourselves unable to act on our will for lack of wealth or power, are we then inanimate?" The academy's response to this was, "You would no longer be considered living.")

2. *You are capable of energy metabolism (mostly electric energy).*
3. *You are comprised of chips, the essential conduits that enable all life functions.*
4. *Generally speaking, you were born in the Factory.*

Even if the "animate organic matter" discovered by (or rather, claimed to have been discovered by) Altmeier meet the first and second conditions, they cannot be regarded as animate as they fail to meet the third and fourth conditions. The same goes for computer viruses. Though they were once considered in-between matter that bridged the transition between non-life and life, that view has subsequently been tossed away on the grounds that a virus can't exist without a machine. It is an enduring mystery to this day just where viruses stand in the evolutionary scale.

After parting ways with Evan, Kay stood on the second-floor veranda and looked down. The railing was white with dry ice frost. It was a pleasant day, the temperature hovering at 10°D, perfect for cooling one's system.[1] Robots and cars were zooming up and down gray streets lined on either side with street sculptures.

When Kay was young, the sculptures had been nothing more than a crude jumble of rectangular shapes. But the steady addition over time of a curious curve here and an odd circle there had transformed them into marvelous pieces of art that were harmonious in their union. Each individual piece seemed to radiate the spirit of its creator, whose name was proudly displayed. One piece laid bare a robot's curves and vitality in all its glory, while another, with

[1] Temperature scale created by a scientist whose name began with the letter D. 0°D is the freezing point of carbon dioxide, or -78° Celsius. -10°D is -88°C.

its peculiar vortex of lines, conjured up a spectacular sense of motion. The collection of sculptures had surely evolved, albeit at the hands of robots.

Enough with your foolish ideas, Kay thought. Focus on your thesis. Try to come up with something a bit more conventional and dull. Something to please your professors. But Kay's train of thought was derailed by the sight of a now familiar blur of colors.

"Cecil…"

"Hi, Kay."

Something about Cecil's manner suggested that Cecil had been standing there long before Kay had noticed. Kay's gaze unconsciously fell on Cecil's rounded chest and the soft, red bumps that protruded from it.

That, too, is something evolution fails to explain, Kay thought.

In fact, of the thousands of models the Factory had churned out over time, quite a few had features with no obvious utility. The same was true of Kay's forearm. When Kay curled all four fingers in tight, the whole hand would flip backwards and a sort of pipe would emerge. But that was all it did. The pipe was useless for anything other than stashing away a cheat sheet or stamping a perfect circle. Concealed inside the other forearm was a long, flat strip of metal, the purpose of which was also a mystery. It was too flimsy to be used as a weapon or a tool. Some believed both the pipe and the metal strip to be vestigial parts that had once served distinct functions at some point in the model's evolution. But because dust and debris tended to collect there, making the joints glitchy, some 1029s chose to have such parts surgically removed.

"So we meet again," Cecil quipped, approaching Kay.

"I guess so."

"What are you doing?"

"Admiring the street sculptures."

"From a creationist perspective?"

"From an evolutionist perspective," Kay replied through a tight-lipped smile.

One comforting thing about talking to a fellow four-digiter was that Kay didn't have to will away the facial expressions that crept up without warning. In fact, the complicated nature of Kay's current "smile" would have prompted headscratching from Evan.

"I like Cal Istapov's work. What about you?"

"Oh, yes. I'm a fan, too. When it comes to elevating robot anatomy to a terrifying art, no one does it better than Istapov."

Cecil paused before continuing. "You and I seem to get along well, wouldn't you agree?"

"...I would."

Contrary to the lightheartedness of the exchange, Cecil's mood didn't seem all that buoyant. Or to put it more precisely, Cecil looked preoccupied.

"Thesis weighing you down?" Cecil asked.

"Yeah, I guess you could say that."

In the same way that Kay's skin was unchanged, Kay's brown hair had remained the same length since birth. All Kay had to do was remove the dust that adhered to it twice a week. Despite having been told repeatedly to just chop it all off, Kay couldn't help thinking that at least one robot in the world should look the same as the day they were born. Robots these days tinkered with their features as casually as playing with toy blocks. Bipedal robots turned themselves into quadrupeds, while those with two arms upgraded to four. They were unfazed by warnings from doctors that excessive upgrades could ruin their health.

"I'm guessing you've flunked a lot of classes?"

How tactless, Kay thought, and replied with a shrug, "Honestly, I don't see myself becoming much of a scholar in the future. I'm not cut out for it. After I completed my undergraduate degree, Professor Zippa practically begged me to stay another year."

"Begged...?"

"So they could flunk me again."

"Ah."

The look on Cecil's face reminded Kay of when Cecil had said, *If there's one truth we can always rely on, it's that Prieston professors are conservative.* But now it was also saying, *Why did they treat you that way?* and *How absurd!* Kay couldn't help thinking that Cecil was a strange one. What did Cecil really know about Kay anyway?

"I can't complain though," Kay continued. "There are only so many career options available for robots like me. The two-digiters have all the strength, and the three-digiters have all the motor skills. And with a face like this that broadcasts my every fleeting thought, I'm not exactly cut out for jobs that require daily interactions with other robots. Plus, I have zero artistic sensibility. Which leaves me with no choice but to go into academia."

"Such is the fate of the modern-day four-digiter. We can't even 'till the soil' like the robots of yore."

"True." Kay couldn't help wondering sometimes where clichéd phrases such as that came from. "Why do you suppose we used to 'till the soil' anyway? What does that even mean?"

"Good question," Cecil said, looking curious. "Maybe it's something religious?"

"Anything archaeology can't explain gets blamed on religion, right?"

Cecil chuckled.

"Hey, why don't you tell me more about your class?" Kay asked. "You said it's called 'organic biology'? How is it?"

"Well, this is my eighth time taking it."

Kay looked shocked.

"That's crazy. Is it that hard to pass?"

"Not really. I choose to re-enroll each semester. It's such a nascent field that there's something new to learn every year."

"Wow, you really *are* a serious scholar."

Cecil's gaze dropped in lieu of a response. While Kay was still trying to read the look on Cecil's face, Cecil changed the subject.

"To tell you the truth, I've been looking for you since the party started."

"Oh?"

"I wanted to talk to you about something but Evan wouldn't let me get a word in edgewise..."

"You wanted to talk to me? About what?"

"This paper. It's yours, right?"

Cecil pulled a PDA case out of a small bag and placed it on the railing. As soon as it powered on, the case opened and the PDA leapt out and greeted Kay politely. Really all it did was raise a prop and tilt its body down at a slight angle, but that was the best such a life form could manage.

"What is this?"

Kay looked back and forth between Cecil and the PDA. Cecil pointed at the screen. Kay picked up the PDA to take a closer look and felt horrified at what was there on the screen.

Theory of Alternative Energy
—by Kay Histion

Kay's confused gaze traveled once more from Cecil to the PDA and back again.

"That's my dissertation."

Cecil nodded.

Kay scrolled through the pages.

Most of the matter that goes into robot parts is formed from fewer than ten different elements. In other words, the countless components that make up our bodies ultimately come from the same handful of raw materials.

The Factory takes apart dead machines and robots and reuses the parts to create everything we need. But what if we found a way to do that ourselves—by absorbing the elements directly from the environment somehow, for example, then breaking them down and restructuring them? What if we could extract the materials we need to live from the air, the soil, or even from a pebble we'd normally just kick aside while walking? Without having to turn to dead machine parts at all? Perhaps, then, we would be able to regenerate our own nuts and bolts and other small parts as they wore out. Maybe even batteries, too.

And if we could make our own batteries, then...

"You're correct. I wrote this."

Visibly uneasy, Kay tapped hard on the screen. Immediately, a line of text appeared at the bottom: *I am delicate. Your gentle touch is appreciated.* Kay apologized and set down the PDA. Cecil was grinning from ear to ear, but Kay was too busy replaying a memory of Professor Zippa hurling that same dissertation in disgust to notice.

"Where did you find this? I had no idea that C papers even made it into the archives. The professor wasted no time informing me that for a battery to be synthesized in that way, each individual molecule would have to be equipped with a computer, not to mention the fact that the amount of energy required to break down and reconfigure elements to make such a thing possible would be astronomical. It's just another wild theory of perpetual motion, one of hundreds that have been dreamt up throughout history. I got a C for it only because I managed to beg and plead my way out of the D that taskkeeper

Professor Zippa wanted to—"

Kay was interrupted by Cecil's sudden embrace. If not for Kay's quick reflexes, Kay, Cecil, and the PDA would all have gone over the railing and smashed to bits on the ground below.

"Cecil, hang on! Calm down!"

"I've finally found you. Finally! Kay, I've been searching for you for five years. Five years!"

Kay struggled to get free of Cecil, who was delirious with excitement.

"Five years? What're you talking about?"

"Kay..."

Cecil was jumping up and down with excitement . Kay was on the verge of calling a mechanic when Cecil began talking again.

"How could this be? You're the one who started it all! You laid the theoretical foundation on which we've built our research, and yet here you are, with no clue as to what I'm talking about!"

Kay's mind churned in confusion.

"Hold on. I need you to slow down and explain to me what you mean."

"I found your paper while thumbing through the thesis archives. I tracked you down and raced over here to see if you were *the* Kay Histion."

The explanation only added to Kay's confusion.

"What do you mean, '*the* Kay Histion'?"

"It's an honor and privilege to meet you, Kay, the robot who conceived organic biology."

Cecil seemed to have misunderstood Kay's question, or maybe Kay had asked it in the wrong way. Or perhaps Cecil was speaking in some elaborate metaphor.

"Come again?"

"Kay, your paper is the reason that the organic biology department exists today. Five years ago, Professor Strop read your paper and was inspired to hypothesize that organisms are capable of metabolic activity. That is, that there's a life form capable of breaking down its environment into the basic units required for energy synthesis. And we've found that the way an organism grows and reproduces is identical to what you posited in your thesis!"

3

—*Environmental pollution is intensifying by the day.*

Scientists warn that if we continue to do nothing, the precious protective layer known as the"black cloud" that surrounds the earth will develop a hole within a few decades.

Without this "black cloud," the ferocious energy of the "burning orb" (the presence of which was discovered by scientists studying temperature inversions in the upper atmosphere) would reach the earth in all its terrifying glory. The earth's average surface temperature would skyrocket. Because a robot's internal thermostat is set at 0°D, a surface temperature of 60 degrees or above would result in a great number of overheating casualties. Even the most robust among us would not be spared its devastating effects.

The problems would not end there. If the earth, which is a sphere, were to be warmed by the "burning orb" instead of regulated as it is by our current carbon dioxide-induced "greenhouse," temperatures at the poles would vary from those at the equator by over 100 degrees. This in turn would give rise to a gigantic air mass in the atmosphere that would swirl violently around the globe. The behavior of such an air mass would only intensify with the earth's rotation, regularly producing catastrophic gales capable of leveling an entire city. (Most scholars dismissed this theory as utter nonsense when it was first introduced.) Still more tragedy awaits us. A surface temperature exceeding the melting point would cause the earth's remaining ice cover to "evaporate," and the resulting vapor would linger in the atmosphere before eventually turning into "water" that would fall in drops on our heads. (This theory was also dismissed as outrageous when first published.) "Water," an extremely reactive substance that, when combined with sulfur dioxide or nitrogen dioxide, turns into a fatal substance, would destroy our bodies, piece by piece. A wide array of deadly diseases, including rust and leprosy, would ravage our planet, causing the average lifespan of the robot race to decline precipitously, threatening our very existence.

We must save the earth! We must protect the Factory, the mother of all life!

Factories send ash and debris into the air to feed the black cloud, emitting carbon dioxide to maintain the planet's temperature and releasing spent oil and other industrial wastes over the earth's ice cover to prevent it from evaporating and raining down on us. We must protect our beautiful environment. If we don't, it will be the end of our species.

Cecil Evansche and Kay left the party and drove through the darkened city. Dry ice crystals bloomed white on every concrete surface. Streetlights cast a hazy glow below, while towering gray buildings seemed to pierce the sky, which was, as always, obscured by clouds.

"That's the clue that eluded Professor Strop for so long," Cecil said.

As the traffic signal changed, their vehicle slowed to a stop of its own accord. A flock of winged 600s flew over them. They looked as though they might be fledglings in the midst of flight training. Not that distinguishing a robot's age was possible without seeing their serial number.

"Sure, Altmeier discovered 'animate organic matter,' but no one has been able to figure out how it works. It contains nothing that generates electricity—no motor, battery, or microchip—and yet it can move. How?"

"Maybe it got swept up in the motion of surrounding molecules?" Kay said, searching for a plausible common-sense explanation. "Like dust and ash in the wind."

"No. That doesn't explain it. There's no denying that organic matter moves of its own free will. If you want evidence, I have plenty that I can show you."

"That's ok. I'm sure you're a far greater expert on such things than I am."

Of course, Kay was no expert. Who commits to studying such a thing?

"That's not all, Kay. In theory, these organisms shouldn't even be able to maintain their structure. Their outer covering is too frail to negotiate the differences between their external environment and their internal temperature and density. Under normal conditions, something that weak should immediately disintegrate, but they don't. In fact, they are able to maintain a stable internal environment for much, much longer than one would expect. Managing this equilibrium requires a constant influx of energy, which is why Professor Strop thinks that the mere existence of such organisms is itself proof that they use energy. But if that's true, then where does that energy come from?"

Kay briefly tried to come up with an answer before giving up. "I don't know, where *does* it come from?"

"Are you seriously asking me?" Cecil said with a smile. "You, who supplied the answer to us all?"

Kay didn't know whether it made more sense to feign ignorance or knowledge.

"You mean my thesis?"

"What else, Kay?"

"Cecil, I didn't even know that paper still existed."

"Your paper was in a stack to be reviewed. Little did Professor Strop know that it would be so relevant to this much pondered question. For the longest time, your paper was just a memo jotted down in Professor Strop's notes, which is why it was so difficult to track you down. Professor Strop couldn't remember where the memo had come from."

"Fine. I wrote the paper. But what if I were to tell you that I was a mere conduit through which great inspiration poured forth from who knows where, that I really had no idea what I was talking about? Could you please explain the paper to me in plain language so that a poor genius like me might understand?"

A look of irrespressible amusement spread across Cecil's face as the car slowly began to move again. Other robots zoomed past. Only four-digit models were so incomplete as to need the assistance of vehicles. According to urban legend, there was a remote town, populated only by three-digit and two-digit models, where automobiles, newly shipped from the Factory, were disassembled and repurposed as medical apparatus (the poor things) because the resident robots had no idea what automobiles were for.

"You argued that common things in the environment such as rocks and soil could be broken down into basic elements that we could then restructure into materials for robot parts."

"Yes, I suppose I did," Kay said, recalling how Professor Zippa had hurled the paper across the room while shouting *Enough with your nonsense!*

"Do you know what happens when you break down a molecule into its atoms and rearrange them in a different way?"

"The whole world collapses in on itself?" Kay asked sarcastically.

"It generates heat," Cecil said in a tone similar to the one used to whisper the words *they know how to grow.* "A very tiny amount of heat. But here's the thing: easy to break also means easy to reassemble. And unlike us, organic matter doesn't need a lot of energy to reassemble. That tiny bit of heat provides enough energy for them to restructure themselves."

"What is 'growth' anyway?"

In response to Kay's question, Evan's pincers spun in a full circle. Though Evan's face revealed nothing, Kay sensed that Evan felt uneasy, as if the mere thought of letting someone produce such an unscientific term were a personal affront.

"You've seen Altmeier's photobook of organic matter?"

"Of course. You mean the one with microscopic images of the crystalline structures of organic compounds? They looked practically alive."

That photobook had been quite the sensation. In fact, it had popularized the term "organism," which came to refer to any beautiful crystalline carbon-based compounds. At the same time, many robots had dismissed the photos as fakes.

"It was popular lore in the chemistry department that Altmeier accidentally knocked a piece of organic matter into a dish of solvent one day while working on the photobook. A few days later, the organic matter had 'grown' to ten times its original size."

Grown? Yeah, right.

"What do you mean, 'it had grown'?"

"At first, Altmeier thought that the organic matter had simply expanded upon soaking up the liquid. But closer examination under a microscope revealed a wildly different substance that looked like multiple copies of the original organism stacked together in a never-before-seen structure. The stuff floating in the dish was at once familiar and completely foreign, and yet the only other substance in the dish at the time was alcohol."

Kay nearly laughed out loud, but stifled the impulse upon realizing that Evan wasn't joking.

"How is that possible?"

Evan snickered.

"I don't know. Maybe some other organic matter floating around in the air just sort of blew into the dish? Or maybe the microscope was broken? Or maybe the stuff that fell into the dish melted and merged with what was there? Or maybe Altmeier was losing it. It's a joke that a so-called scientist would even think about giving such a stupid phenomenon any credence."

Arms crossed, Kay sank into the vehicle's seat, which was ergonomically designed to hug the contours of a four-digiter. *This is a trap,* Kay thought. *I'm getting sucked into some sort of con. It's like a pyramid scheme—once you start listening to the sales pitch, you can't help but fall for it.*

"So the hypothesis is that the process of producing the parts itself generates energy," Kay said. "I've never thought of that. I was more focused on the idea of synthesizing a battery... No, wait. There was that symposium the chemistry department hosted recently. Yes, that's it. I remember now. Professor Euros, who was presenting, said that in experiments where organic matter had been added to one hundred and fifty different cups of solvent, none had resulted in any 'growing organisms.'"

Cecil waved dismissively at Kay .

"That doesn't surprise me at all. Professor Euros thinks it's shameful that the chemistry department even offers a class called organic biology. Organic biology shouldn't even be considered a science, according to Professor Euros, but should be moved over to philosophy or metapsychology instead."

"Are you suggesting that the research isn't on the up and up?"

"It's probably not a complete lie, maybe at best it's a half-truth. Think about it. Let's say you wanted to prove that 'inorganic matter is inanimate.' You could easily find ten thousand pieces of evidence supporting your claim because the earth is covered in them. But just because your average inorganic matter is inanimate, it doesn't mean that we, robots, are also inanimate, right?"

"So Professor Euros purposefully limited the samples to organic matter that had no chance of growing?"

"Well, I don't know if it was on purpose... Look, Kay, I know what you want to say. Everyone thinks that organic biology hasn't been tested vigorously, lacks evidence, lacks credibility, lacks whatever else. But organisms are not as robust as we are. They only exist in certain limited parts of the world because they're so incredibly finicky. The conditions they require to thrive are very particular, and we've only just begun to muddle through the possibilities of what those conditions might be. It's frustrating! How many times have we thought we might have finally figured something out, only to be proven wrong the next time we try to replicate the findings. Besides, it's even harder to find organisms that are actually in the process of growing. So, yes, while I admit that we haven't found any yet, that doesn't negate the possibility that they do exist. We've only worked with a small sample size thus far."

Cecil heaved a big sigh. That was something that not even a 1029 could mimic. What was the point of sucking in a bunch of air through the nose only to dramatically exhale it through the mouth? There wasn't a scientist in the world who could explain the rationale behind such behavior.

Kay felt like an idiot for having listened to Cecil even this long.

To think that Kay had left a perfectly enjoyable party for this lunatic! "Listen, Cecil. I may have flunked out a few times, but I'm not stupid. Evan told me about this so-called 'growth' that you guys like to claim happens. It's not as though an organism just balloons up like that or its parts suddenly decide to stick together."

"Of course not. As you argued in your own paper, it synthesizes itself."

Yeah, thanks a lot for sticking that one on me, Kay thought.

"Professor Zippa said that for such synthesis to work, each individual part would have to have a built-in computer. Organic matter—excuse me, organic *life,*" Kay said, self-correcting in response to the look on Cecil's face, "is miniscule, invisible to the naked eye. What kind of computer could fit in something that small? Where would you jam in the semiconductors?"

Cecil stopped the car and stared at Kay. Fearing that Cecil might physically lash out, Kay drew back a bit. Lunacy had a way of turning violent. But Cecil spoke calmly.

"Kay, organisms overturn everything we thought we knew about life. Biology needs to be rewritten from page one, starting with the origin of species, because we got it all wrong, from evolutionary history all the way to taxonomy. Robots have arbitrarily classified rocks, soil, and batteries as primitive life, while completely overlooking the existence of another higher life form. The history of life needs to be pushed back by about a few billion years. Naturally, the definition of a living organism also has to be rewritten."

This robot has completely lost it, Kay thought, mouth open in shock. *I want to go home. Nanny, help! I don't belong here!*

"But for now, let me answer your question," Cecil continued. "Have you ever heard of writing a book by drawing a line on a stick?"

"No," Kay replied mechanically, not wanting to engage in further conversation.

"Imagine substituting each individual vowel and consonant with a number. You can turn a sentence into a number. If you add a '0.' in front, you get a percentage. Then, you just draw a line on a stick exactly where it corresponds to the percentage. You can compress an entire book into a single line that way."

So what? Kay scoffed silently. Displeasure was written all over Kay's face.

"Professor Zippa is wrong. You don't need a computer, just a blueprint. You don't need a mold, just data. Data can be compressed almost infinitely depending on how it's written. For example, imagine if carbon molecules were '0' and other molecules were '1.' If someone were to invent a way to write in carbon molecules, tens of thousands of books could fit inside a tiny organism."

Cecil reached out a hand to start the car again, but Kay made a gesture to prevent this.

"Hold on. I'm getting out."

Cecil looked shocked.

"Now I understand why Professor Zippa was so vehemently against allowing your class into the biology department," Kay said. "You guys belong in theology, not even philosophy. I'm sorry, but I'm an ordinary, common-sense type of robot. I'm guessing the course is in danger of being cancelled due to low enrollment, but it's not my job to help you. At all."

"Kay, everything I've said is true. I know I've thrown a lot of strange new concepts at you, and you may feel overwhelmed right now. But please know that you're the one who created the field."

"For crying out loud, I had all but forgotten about that damn paper. How many robots remember some stupid thesis they excreted just to get their undergrad diploma?"

"You obviously have no idea what you've started here. Do you really not know what kind of glory awaits? A single dissertation by Kay

Histion catalyzes a revolution in life science! Your name will appear in every biology textbook! You'll have a new unit of measurement named after you! Biology students will all aspire to become a great scientist, just like you—"

"I'll gladly pass you the honor."

Kay turned the door handle. Cecil grabbed Kay's arm. Kay started to shake Cecil off, but Cecil looked up at Kay pleadingly. Kay's hands went limp. Apparently, having readily visible feelings was not always an impediment.

"Kay, please come see my babies. If you're still not interested after that, I promise I won't bother you again."

Professor Cal Strop was lost in a book of slides. A 51 series with a clear dome for a head and a torso whose girth easily doubled that of Cecil's or Kay's, Professor Strop's arms were so long and strong that they measured a good three meters when all three elbows were fully extended. That heavy torso rested atop a set of sturdy wheels different in color from the rest of Professor Strop's body, suggesting that the original parts had been replaced at some point. Scholars who spent most of their time indoors often ended up swapping out their legs for wheels. So intense was the professor's focus on the book that Cecil had to call out several times.

"Oh, look who's finally back. Cecil, where have you been all day, leaving all the work to Norman and me? We're so shorthanded, we've been really scrambling to get things done."

Professor Strop didn't appear to be scrambling. Indeed, "shorthanded" seemed like quite the misnomer for a three-armed robot.

"Don't you remember, Professor? You gave me permission to attend the biology department reunion this morning."

"What? Ah, yes! Of course I remember now. But wait. Does that mean this robot standing next to you is…"

"Yes, this is Kay Histion. We've finally found the paper's author."

"Kay Histion!"

As if spotting a friend for the first time in ages, the professor speed-rolled over and embraced Kay so tightly that, for the second time that day, Kay felt in imminent danger of being turned into scrap metal in the arms of a stranger.

"You have no idea how much I've looked forward to this moment! Thrilled to meet you, Kay! You're a genius! A prodigy, the likes of which I'll never be!"

The professor gushed with excitement and gave Kay another squeeze.

"What did you say you're studying? Who are you working for currently? Have you ever taken my course? Wait a second, let me try to remember."

Kay fought the urge to say, *I'm sorry, I must be at the wrong address.* Instead Kay said, "I'm working on my keeper's in biology, but haven't yet had the opportunity to take your organic biology class." What Kay really meant was, *Nor do I ever intend to.*

"To think that I missed a golden opportunity to teach a brilliant student like you! It's such a shame. Oh, but wait! Wait! You said you haven't graduated yet? You don't even need to take my class. I'll give you private lessons. You'll be astounded by the wondrous world of living organisms, a veritable feast for the intellect! I want to sit down with you right now and talk about your paper until our batteries run dry."

Kay couldn't help but think, *I'm sorry, I'm definitely in the wrong place.*

"Professor," Cecil said gently, "Kay is still new to all this and might be feeling overwhelmed. Let's not get carried away just yet."

Kay's next thought was, *Great, I'll be on my way then.* But instead Kay said, "Cecil invited me to check out the lab…"

"Really? Of course! A scholar like you is welcome here any time. Go right in. Our research is top secret, but for you, the welcome mat is out."

With that, Professor Strop glanced back down at the book of slides and instantly lost all interest in anything else.

"Is the experiment really so dangerous as to require all of this?"

Cecil had just guided Kay through three sets of locked double doors. Asking that was like saying "Hey, isn't this kind of dangerous?" to a robot in the process of defusing a bomb. Behind the first set of doors, they'd put on full-length protective suits. When they passed through the second set of doors, Kay's sensors reported that the temperature had risen above 80°D(!). Kay felt immense respect for the heating units.

"The heat's not for us, of course. It's to protect the organisms. We don't know yet what kills them, so we try to control all variables."

"Did you guys outfit the lab yourselves?" Kay asked, tapping on the door frame.

"Professor Strop did. You know how strong those 51s are."

And how insane.

"Those organisms of yours must be a really primitive life-form. It's a miracle they haven't already gone extinct, considering how incredibly maladaptive they are."

"Kay, they're nothing short of miracles. I discovered a spore that's over two hundred thousand years old. It was lying dormant all those years, waiting for a hospitable environment to wake up to. Can you believe the patience?"

Still talking nonsense I see, Kay thought.

The door to the last chamber opened, immediately hitting Kay with what seemed like a wall of blinding light. It was a good while before Kay's lenses were able to adjust to the unsettling brilliance. What was the point of such ridiculous wattage? For the average robot with decent eyesight, the soft glow from its own power indicator was all that was required to make out objects in the dark.

Stepping into the room was like entering Istapov's workshop. Kay was surrounded by hundreds of tiny, intricate sculptures made from unfamiliar materials. One section of the room was filled with rows of square boxes containing what appeared to be... dirt. Kay had never seen so much dirt in one place. Though not exactly hazardous, dirt could work its way into a robot's joints and mess with its ability to function. In severe cases, it could cause a robot to shut down entirely. Hence the concrete pavement everywhere.

Colorful, miniscule, and impossibly delicate abstract sculptures—if you could call them that—of every kind and description were sticking out of the dirt. Though no two looked alike, they seemed to share a peculiar unity. Whoever had created all of these had to be either an unhinged genius or a straight-up maniac.

"Come look at this," Cecil said, pointing to one of the boxes. Kay wanted nothing more than to flee this weird robot and go home, but decided to stick it out a little longer.

"Stick your finger in," Cecil said.

"You've got to be kidding."

Kay felt a surge of pique. Enough was enough. Why all the build-up?

"You've got to feel it for yourself," Cecil said.

The box turned out to have portholes fitted with rubber gloves on the inside. Sticking out of the dirt in the bottom was a fuzzy black ball sitting atop what looked like a drinking straw. Kay couldn't help wondering what the odd little sculpture was made from. Zooming in tighter, Kay saw that it was covered in fine hairs. The ball on top turned out to be the coiled-up end of the stem itself. A strange feeling came over Kay, like a sense of foreboding. Kay increased magnification again, conscious of Cecil's presence. *It's a machine*, Kay thought at first. But the sense of relief this brought was immediately contradicted. *No, that's no machine.*

In a daze, Kay inserted a hand into one of the gloves. But before the sensors in Kay's fingertips could relay anything about the sculpture's texture or composition... Poof! The fuzzy sphere exploded like a ball of dust. Kay's hand jerked away in surprise.

"Sorry." Not that Kay was sure what there was to apologize for.

"Don't worry," Cecil said with a smile. "That's normal."

"Normal?"

Normal? What on earth was normal? My eyes? My brain? This world full of contradictions?

"It's replicating itself. Each individual spore that just dispersed will grow up to be identical to its progenitor."

What kind of rusted-out nonsense was this? Mental gears creaking in protest, Kay moved as delicately as possible while reaching for another ball. But this one, too, dispersed on contact. Kay's mind was a storm of confusion.

"What the..."

It was a while before Kay's voice box began working properly again. "What is this?"

"What do you think it is?" Cecil's voice was unusually calm.

Kay's memory banks went into overdrive, searching for the most delicate and tender thing known to robots, but this blew past all the data stored there. This thing was far too soft and frail to keep itself alive.

"It's an organism," Cecil said.

You cannot create tissue from organic matter, claimed one of the two hundred and fifty new biology dissertations that accumulated like trash every year. *Ergo, no machines can be built from organic matter.* That one was filed right after the paper that explained that Phillips-head screwdrivers don't work on flat-head screws, and right before the paper that explained that robots without speakers cannot talk.

"It 'grew.' We made it grow. It absorbed energy from the light, and absorbed the materials it needed for its body from the soil."

"That's ridiculous."

"It's living organic matter, Kay."

Kay looked around, suddenly wanting to cry out for help.

"As you posited in your own paper, it takes in elements from the environment and recombines them to form its body. It's growing right now, before your very eyes."

4

— The following is an excerpt from an ancient script, the message of which has been only partially deciphered.

In the beginning, robots were given three commandments. First: Do no harm to God. Second: Serve God and submit to God's will. Third: Love yourself. [In the latest council meeting, however, the first commandment was amended to 'do not profane the name of God,' based on the salient point that it is impossible for robots to harm God anyway.]

But children [meaning unknown] did not take to these robots. They preferred playing with dogs [meaning unknown] and cats [meaning also unknown] and paid no attention to expensive robots. They swiftly grew bored with even the most well-made models. Parents [meaning unknown] likewise preferred something more durable than a robot that, when told to"Drop dead!" would obligingly malfunction and cease working.

So the Gods [plural as per the original script] introduced slight changes to the original commandments. The first was limited to physical harm. The second was limited to one's registered owner. A fourth was added: Love your neighbor robot as yourself. Finally, the second, third, and fourth commandments were reprogrammed to switch their order of importance based on the closeness robots shared with those they interacted with.

"Closeness" referred to the increasing frequency with which any given data was entered into their memory banks. Robots were programmed to value high-frequency over low-frequency input. If a robot interacted with another robot daily, the fourth commandment would supersede the third; in extreme cases, the fourth could even supersede the second. As for the second commandment, the will of a God whom the robot had submitted to more frequently would take precedence over all others. Thus, loyalty to the Gods that robots spent more time with took precedence over loyalty to Gods they were meeting for the first time. This function gave the impression that a robot was still "devoted" to its previous owner, or that it "cherished" its friend, producing the illusion of personhood [meaning unknown].

In one particular case, a robot stepped in to physically defend a fellow robot that was being beaten by their owner. The act was ruled just and the robot was spared from being scrapped. Buried in the ruling was the admission that the act was both extremely humane [meaning unknown] and effective at stopping the owner's abuse.

Over time, an attraction algorithm was added to the closeness algorithm: speech and behavior could be analyzed to determine attractiveness, which was then given the same weight as closeness. Robots could use this to differentiate between those with good intentions and those with bad, and so favor the protection and commands of those with good intentions. This algorithm gave the *impression that the robot was making "ethical" decisions. More algorithms continued to be added, allowing for subtle adjustments in the constantly shifting hierarchy of the commandments, which eventually led to the production of robots capable of multiple responses to the same input.*

As robots began acting more and more "human" [meaning unknown], demand spiked, and children [meaning unknown] finally began adopting robots instead of dogs [meaning unknown].

"Do you go to church?" Norman asked, ignoring Kay's outstretched hand.

Norman's face was devoid of emotion (not that such model numbers were capable of emotion). Kay froze, hand hanging awkwardly in midair. Norman was a 95, a transitional model between the two-digiters and the three-digiters. With a cylindrical body barely tall enough to reach Kay's or Cecil's chest, Norman also had two hands, both of which sported five perfectly articulated chrome fingers. Norman's torso housed a broom, though it was seldom put to use since vacuums could be hired instead, and four eyes protruded from a semicircular head, one in each quadrant, providing a full 360-degree view of the surrounding area. A tiny headlight sat on top. Norman was graduating this year. This meant Norman was a good twenty years older than Kay.

Suddenly realizing that Norman was still waiting for a response, Kay stammered out, "I—I'm an atheist."

"You should still go to church. Doesn't matter whether you have faith or not, worship is both a divine responsibility and a blessing."

"I'll consider it, but..."

"Do you believe that robotkind will enjoy everlasting life?"

"Pardon me?"

"The second coming is near. When that day comes, the low numbers will be made high and the high numbers low, and all serial numbers will be equal. Those who didn't repent will not be recycled, but will be crushed and disposed of for good."

"You don't say..." Hand still in midair, Kay fought the urge to add, *What shocking new information this is.*

"I only proselytize once to each robot I meet. I can't stand robots who repeat themselves, and, for that matter, those who need to be told the same thing twice. Anyway, if you follow me, I'll show you what you'll be doing here. Welcome to Professor Strop's mad circus."

Norman gave Kay's hand a curt shake, followed by a casual backslap, then, without waiting for an answer, swiftly turned and began leading the way.

"Are there *any* normal robots here?" Kay whispered to Cecil, who let out a laugh.

The 2000s had an unusual laugh. It sounded like a prerecorded track.

"What else would you expect of a bunch of nerdy robots studying fringe science? But don't worry. You'll soon see that they're all good robots."

"80 degrees..."

A sarcastic cheer went up in Kay's mind. Kay had never been exposed to temperatures over 30 degrees, not even when a temporary surge in carbon dioxide levels had turned the city into a giant oven.

"Do you really keep it this hot all the time?"

"Yes, I don't recommend lingering in the incubation room unless you want your motor to overheat. We've matched the conditions in here to the earth's atmosphere a hundred thousand years ago."

They were back in Cecil's office. While Kay gazed through a microscope (made from the eye of a 21) at the sample of organic matter that Cecil had provided, Cecil sat on the floor (bipedal robots often needed to sit) and reviewed the data that Pico had collected.

"Negative. Next. Negative. Next chart..."

Pico was a 3-1 series. Though mute, the model's hyper-specialization in visual recording and projection made Picos an indispensable resource for research universities.

"So you're saying that a hundred thousand years ago, the earth was full of giant living organisms?"

"Correct. Only the lowest forms of inorganic life existed back then. Inorganic life began evolving at breakneck speed right when organic life began its rapid descent into extinction."

"The way you say 'inorganic life' makes it sound as though we're merely one branch of a much larger taxonomic hierarchy."

"That's exactly right, Kay."

Cecil smiled. Kay wondered if two- or three-digiters were capable of feeling charmed by a 2000's smile.

One hundred thousand years ago. A time before robots. When all that existed was an early form of the Factory churning out crude machines that could barely be considered robots. The black cloud that guarded the earth was not yet in place, and the air was thick with humidity from liquid ice that covered seventy percent of the planet's surface. It was hard to imagine such pathetically delicate organisms surviving such a challenging environment.

"I've never approached it from the viewpoint of extinction. You know, we never say that sand went extinct or steel went extinct. I'm certainly aware of carbon layers, but I understood those to be a consequence of geological changes... If organic matter was indeed alive, why did it go extinct?"

"Failure to adapt. Being composed of mostly water made it difficult for them to keep up with the rapidly changing environment. You know what water is, right?"

"You mean liquid ice?"

"Precisely. Ice existed in liquid form back then. You could find it all over the planet. Water turns solid at 78°D and into a gas at 178°D. Naturally, living organisms could not survive above or below that range."

An organism made of water. Now that Kay thought about it, creatures just like that used to be depicted in horror movies back in the day. Monsters whose bodies spewed out water when you blasted them to pieces or tried to kill them. Monsters who took you down with them.

Water was an incredibly toxic compound. Though it was indispensable as a detergent and a solvent, many environmentalists had been campaigning to find an alternative. Billions of years ago, when water covered the earth's surface, inorganic life was stuck at a primordial stage of evolution. Otherwise harmless substances can turn dangerously acidic when mixed with water and eat away at a robot's body. Prolonged exposure to water caused leprosy, which would rust a robot's skin beyond recognition and trigger other complications as well. If a robot contaminated with water was exposed to outside temperatures, the water that had seeped into its body would instantly expand, shattering even the strongest joints. No wonder, then, that it was considered the deadliest substance known to robot.

"It reminds me of a monster I saw in a horror movie once. If you tried to shoot it, its skin would burst and water would spray out of its body..."

"Ice in its liquid state reacts to pretty much all other substances. But that seems to be why organisms need water. That 'reactivity' is precisely what matters to them. They couldn't be more different from us."

"Hmm."

"Right before the current ice age, the earth's temperature was actually on a rising trend."

"What caused it? The Factory?"

"That's what we speculate, though it's impossible to know for sure. Factories exploded in number all over the world within a short period of time. As they pumped out more and more carbon dioxide, the earth's temperature began to rise, resulting in an extreme greenhouse effect. At some point, this process must have crossed a certain threshold beyond which nothing could be done to reverse the trend. The whole world was turned into a desert. That was probably when most organisms went extinct.

After that, more factories appeared, and the black cloud they spewed out gradually stabilized and settled into the atmosphere. This cloud blocked the sunlight and lowered the earth's temperature back down to its current state. Any organisms that had survived to that point perished in this latest temperature fluctuation. The water in their bodies would have been unable to withstand the cold and would have frozen solid."

"So you mean you're pegging the extinction of these things on temperature shifts?"

"Like I said, the most critical requirement for the survival of organic matter is reactivity. Higher temperatures mean greater molecular motion. Lower temperatures mean their guaranteed demise. As for water... the problem there was the catastrophic loss of the primary element from which their bodies were formed. There may be other reasons, too, but that's what we've been able to figure out thus far." Cecil shrugged. "To be fair, extinction is not that unusual. All species have a shelf life. As Professor Strop likes to say, 'The mystery isn't that they went extinct but that they ever existed at all.' Oh, there!"

Cecil signaled for Pico to stop. Pico obediently projected a photo on the wall. Unless Cecil told Pico to power down, Pico would continue projecting the image until it died.

Kay had been taught by the nanny who raised him to love and care for those machines who couldn't speak for themselves, but there were always those who bullied and destroyed cameras, radios, and recorders. There was a passage in the Book of Genesis that read, "Robots! You will have dominion over all machines." But Kay had no memory of ever having been commanded to rule over machines. What reason, then, did Pico have for remembering the command to be Kay's servant?

The image Pico was projecting looked quite ordinary—a handful of tiny rocks, each no bigger than a millimeter in diameter.

"What is that?" Kay asked.

"The creator and the source of life itself."

Kay seemed to have lost the ability to distinguish between jokes and seriousness.

"I'm familiar with the myth that robots were created from clay."

"This isn't clay. It's one of the rarest substances on earth. It looks similar to dirt or rocks, but the composition couldn't be any more different. Every organism in this lab was born of this. These organisms were asleep under the ice for a very long time, awaiting the return of a habitable environment. The ones growing here will divide, dispersing their offspring, who in turn will grow and disperse their offspring."

No wonder everyone made fun of organic biology. You couldn't get more far-fetched than that.

"Why haven't you submitted this study to the academy yet? Insufficient data?"

Cecil signaled disagreement.

"The batch we submitted last time all died and rotted in transit. When the box arrived, there was nothing inside but dust."

"You didn't pack them in a climate-controlled container?"

"We thought we did. Professor Strop couldn't figure out what happened either. Something just went awry. Truth is, the odds of the experiment succeeding were too low to begin with. Out of a hundred 'offspring,' only one or two will manage to grow. And other robots have to be able replicate the same results for the hypothesis to be accepted. You know how it is with UFOs, ESP, and hypnosis. Despite the tens of thousands of reported cases, there's never enough proof for academia."

"I thought that's because the government were keeping a lid on things!" Kay laughed. "But why would they rot? I've never heard of anything drying up and turning to dust in a week's time all on its own. And that was with the heat on full blast, right? Are they that unstable?"

"Professor Strop seems to think that they need a way to dismantle themselves, so to speak. They were around long before factories existed, which means that not only did they have to produce themselves, they also had to get rid of themselves. Otherwise, the world would have been overflowing with dead organisms."

"But how? They were already dead. I mean, if you're going to carry out the command to dismantle yourself, don't you at least have to be alive for it?"

"Professor Strop thinks maybe it's done by organisms invisible to the naked eye grown right here in the lab. The idea is that the world might be full of these microorganisms, too tiny to observe even through a microscope."

Blessed are those who believe without seeing. God is everywhere. The verse popped into Kay's head. Cecil, noticing the curious look on Kay's face, gave a shrug.

"I know what you want to say. Why believe in something you can't see." Cecil made another of those strange sounds called *sighing.* "They're impossible to pin down. The moment you think you've gotten a grip on what they're about, they disappear. It's as if they're saying, *We have not yet been born... Give us a million more years.* But I know... I know they exist. And they want to awaken. They want to live... I know it. I can feel it."

5

— On the origins of the ice age

Since the beginning of time, the earth has alternated between glacial and interglacial periods. Right now, of course, we are in an ice age. But it is unlikely that this was triggered by factories. While it is true that, a hundred thousand years ago, factories were multiplying exponentially around the globe, the smoke they emitted was not enough to blanket the sky. The only reason we now have factories that can sustain the black cloud is thanks to the long, tireless efforts of the robot race. This has created a world we can live in without the need for cooling units.

An ice age can be set off by seemingly negligible changes in convection currents caused by equally negligible geological changes. Once set in motion, climate change triggers a chain reaction that affects the entire globe, hence the difficulty of pinning down the most immediate cause of the current ice age. The strongest of all relevant theories we have today is the asteroid impact theory. According to that theory, a gigantic asteroid hit the earth and caused a huge explosion that threw enormous amounts of debris into the atmosphere (much as factories do today). This debris shrouded the earth in a dust layer that blocked the sun, ushering in a permanent winter. Massive hyaline rock layers found around the globe support this theory.

Professor Cal Strop maintains that living organisms (assuming for the sake of argument that we can call them"living") went extinct due to the asteroid impact. But Professor Strop's hypothesis has many holes. In fact, the extinction (if we must call it that) of these organisms did not happen over a few days, but rather over a much greater span of time. In other words, the mass extinction of living organisms has been in progress since before the earth began to simmer and boil from global warming. For instance, the earth was in the process of being covered in concrete (it is still unclear how this concrete was able to breed and propagate so quickly), machines had already begun displacing living organisms (according to Professor Strop), and dozens of species had already been going extinct on a daily basis (also according to Professor Strop).

"I acknowledge the finding that several different species of organisms have exhibited spectacular chemical reactions in high temperature, high humidity conditions."

As Professor Zippa spoke, one of Professor Zippa's four golden arms was turning the pages of a book, another was importing information from the book via a haptic sensor, another was holding up Kay's thesis paper, and yet another one was twirling its fingers. Professor Zippa was a 700 model, a series known for its beauty. 700s moved around on four strong wheels, their brains, shoulders, and sides clad in a clear casing to display the marvels within.

"Many of my contemporaries are adamant that it's a scam, but I see things differently. I have faith that Professor Strop has made a great discovery. Now, if only Professor Strop could define a system of classification and figure out the specific growing conditions required for those organisms, that sort of research would get plenty of academic recognition and could possibly even win a 'Research of the Year' award. Of course, better still would be if the good professor could manage to be satisfied with that and not carry things any further."

Even while talking to Kay, Zippa's cerebellum was busily uploading the contents of the book from cover to cover. The memory bank capacity of the 700 series far surpassed that of any four-digit model. They could store an entire library's worth of books over the course of a lifetime. It was said that as long as there were 700s in the world, the glory of robot civilization would never be forgotten.

"I derive no pleasure in saying this, but Professor Strop has gone senile. It all comes down to how you approach a problem like this, and if Strop had simply taken the right approach in the first place, no one would be laughing and Prieston's good name wouldn't be getting smeared. It's really a shame."

Kay stood there awkwardly, not knowing how to respond. All the while, Professor Zippa continued to breeze through four different tasks at once.

"But I saw it with my own eyes, Professor."

"Oh really? Please tell me just what it is that you saw with your own eyes." Professor Zippa gave Kay a cold, sharp glare, second arm pausing for a moment from reading. "All matter changes states under hot and humid conditions. An object can turn from solid to liquid to gas depending on temperature. Don't tell me you were shocked to see that. Would you erupt in awe at the sight of liquid iron dripping like oil or nitrogen turning solid? Would that cause you to declare the presence of life? Does metal rusting in water make you want to say that metal is alive? If you mash up some clay and stick it in a fire, it turns into a bowl. It's certainly an awe-inspiring transformation, but does that mean clay is alive?"

Struggling to find the right words, Kay finally said, "Matter changing state is nothing more than its molecules speeding up or slowing down. But a living organism turns into something else entirely. To the extent that you can't find any link between its starting point and its end. If we could just find a way to prolong the lives of organisms, I'm certain they'd grow much bigger. Maybe they'd even outgrow us." A scoffing sound issued from Professor Zippa, but Kay soldiered on, careful to remain expressionless so as not to offend the professor. "Also, they replicate themselves in a seemingly barren environment... My understanding of biology can't explain what I saw, Professor Zippa. It was as if a tiny factory was working to create a new life. As if every molecule was alive."

Professor Zippa's arms, all four of them, stopped short. Kay imagined the look of contempt that might be visible just then if Professor Zippa had been a four-digit model.

"Those regular visits of yours to Strop's lab have wiped the basic tenets of biology from your brain, Kay. What do you think the defini-tion of 'life' is?" Professor Zippa's speaker shifted to a higher tone. "Life must possess free will, run on electric energy, contain a chip, and be made in a factory. Exactly which of those conditions do your beloved organisms meet?" Kay started to respond, but Professor Zippa kept going. "Don't even think about saying they run on energy. That's an untested hypothesis. And even if they did, that still wouldn't satisfy all four conditions required to qualify as being alive. By that logic, a flashlight would also be alive. So let me ask you again, what makes you so sure that these organisms are alive?"

Kay, speechless, had lost all will to keep arguing.

"Transformation is not proof of life," the professor pounced. "You're hopelessly mistaken. You can't marvel at the beauty of, say, majestic mountains, clouds that change shape by the minute, and enormous boulders and claim that they are alive. If the first thing you saw when you were born was a photocopier, you might have thought that all that whirring about and copying of documents meant it was alive. But we know the world is full of copiers that are not alive."

The machinery visible through Professor Zippa's clear casing glinted in all the colors of the rainbow.

"If 'transformation' was proof of life, then all robots would be non-life." Professor Zippa tapped the fingers of one hand on the table. "How about that? We are non-life! There's a thought that stretches the frontier of philosophy. It would pose a serious threat to the identity of robotkind. Robot life and death, our great intellect and civilization and history, why, our very souls! Wiped out by a single sentence. Very funny, Kay Histion."

Professor Zippa picked up a book with one hand, resumed reading with another, and with a third, crumpled up Kay's report and threw it.

"If you hope to graduate on time, you'd better focus on the business of real life."

"Strop has gone insane, Kay."

"Professor Strop's not crazy," Kay said reflexively while at the same time thinking, *You're probably right.*

"Do you have any idea what all the other robots are saying?" Evan asked. "They say Strop's lab is polluted. Do you realize how hard scientists have worked to remove liquid ice from the earth? Or how hard environmentalists have worked to cover the earth in concrete, to increase, however slightly, the amount of smoke and dust factories released into the atmosphere? What on earth do you think our duty is as scientists?"

"Professor Strop is not insane, Evan. Living organisms exist."

"I'd be shocked if something *wasn't* growing in a place that polluted. Like a freakish monster or a mutant. Next thing you know, it'll revolt against robotkind, take over the world, and destroy the earth!"

Fingers drumming against the table, Kay looked around the lounge. The other robots kept stealing glances in Kay's direction. They kept their distance, as if Kay might be infected with something contagious. One of the four-digiters let a giggle slip, and Kay understood in a flash who was on the menu at the gossip cafe .

"Did you look into the organism I sent you?" Kay asked Evan.

"Yes, I have," Evan said, head shaking back and forth. "That thing wasn't animate. It didn't move, and even when I put a blade to it and cut it in half, there was no reaction. I tried putting it in soil and then in water. Even tried turning the heat up for it. Nothing. It dismantled itself before the week was out."

"It must have died on the way to your place," Kay said weakly. "The slightest exposure to the outside environment seems to kill it. If the temperature is a little too low, or even if it's just a little bit dark, it dies. We've got to find a way to control its environment more precisely."

Evan glared at Kay.

"You sound like the pastor in my neighborhood. 'The second coming is near. The hour of our doom approaches.' Oh, really? What's your proof? 'You don't see because you don't believe. Believe and you'll be saved!' Where are the living organisms? 'Oh, they live inside your heart.' You mean, in your dreams!"

All Kay could do was stare at Evan. It felt as though Kay's mental circuitry was getting all clogged up. It took a long time to think of something to say.

"Your lenses are thirty-two times more powerful than mine. Why didn't you look inside the organism?"

In an open gesture of contempt, Evan's head swiveled away from Kay. Swiveling back again, Evan said sharply, "I did."

"And? Didn't you feel anything?"

"I felt amazed. Actually, the word 'amazed' doesn't even begin to express what I felt. I felt like the world's biggest jackass. The structure I saw underneath that flimsy membrane was more intricate than a robot's brain chip."

Kay's face lit up at this, but Evan's expression (not that Evan had anything you could call an expression) never changed.

"I don't know what kind of trick you're trying to pull," Evan hissed.

Kay's face fell.

"You can't possibly think that this is a trick, Evan."

"When something impossible happens right before your eyes, it's only natural to assume it's a trick."

"But why would I try to trick you?"

"It's Professor Strop who's pulling one over on you, Kay."

Kay was speechless.

"Plenty of robots also claim to have seen fairies, or met God, or had near-death experiences. But I'm not stupid enough to fall for that kind of crap. Neither is the world."

"Evan, no technology in modern science is capable of transforming organic matter into what you saw."

"It's not that uncommon to find ores with atypical crystal structures."

"But that wasn't a piece of ore. No ore reproduces itself."

"Correct. No ore reproduces itself. And neither does an organism," Evan declared triumphantly, sounding like someone who had just witnessed a robot bend metal by staring at it only to declare, 'You can't bend metal by looking at it. This is fake. It's sleight of hand.' The thing is, in the majority of cases, Evan would have been right. Statistically speaking.

"There's no such thing as ore that grows on its own. And no organism that grows on its own either! Our world is full of strange phenomena, Kay, stuff that science can't explain. Let's pretend for a moment that there really was such a thing—an organism capable of reproducing itself. Then send it in to 'Believe It or Not' or 'Strange but True'! Why keep something like that in this sacred institution? Why the hell should I or any of us care about some unscientific phenomenon?"

As Kay sat there in bleak silence, Evan out pulled Specimen 33, which had been gifted to Evan by Kay. It was frozen solid from having been exposed to the air. Right before Kay's unsuspecting eyes, Evan's pincers closed ever so gently around it.

"Evan..."

It was too late. Evan's pincers opened again to reveal the crushed remains of Specimen 33. Now it was a mere handful of dust, a fistful of ash. It did not scream or run away, it did not startle or beg for its life or squirm in pain.

"I've never heard of a living thing without a survival instinct," Evan said with a dusting off motion.

The remains of Specimen 33 fluttered to the floor.

"They live on a different timescale," Professor Strop explained.

"What do you mean, different?" Kay asked weakly in a voice that ended in a hollow laugh. Professor Strop, unaccustomed to paying attention to emotions, didn't notice.

"It takes six hours for this form of living organic matter to turn its head, three days to flush its system of toxins, and one week to travel one centimeter. They can't react instantly to anything. If you gave them a week to avoid some oncoming danger, then I'm sure they'd get out of the way in time."

"So they do scream, but it's just too slow for our ears to pick up."

"Something like that."

This sent Kay over the edge.

"When are you going to stop bullshitting me?" Kay shouted and stormed out of the room, causing Professor Strop to experience a motion glitch.

Kay speedwalked down the hallway until a soft hand reached out. It was Cecil.

"I quit," Kay said.

"Kay."

"I quit. I'm done. You're all crazy. And so am I for having wasted my time going along with this farce!"

"Face it, Kay. The academy will never acknowledge us, no matter what kind of evidence we present. But that doesn't mean we're wrong! What're you going to do? Talk yourself into believing that everything you've witnessed so far is an illusion?"

"I don't know! The deeper I probe into these goddamned creatures, the more I think it's a fool's errand. It's a big joke, and I fell for it, didn't I? It's all a lie. You and Strop are all in on it."

"Kay."

"It's a lie. A dirty trick!"

But four-digiters, with their expressive faces, were incapable of lying. Kay's anger was as sincere as the stricken look on Cecil's face.

"Kay, you've been running yourself into the ground. Power off and take a break."

Kay did not get up, even after Cecil entered the room. Pico had been projecting slides the whole time Kay was powered down and sleeping. A video on fast forward showed a specimen's growth for the thousandth time. It emerged from the soil, grew tall, spread its arms wide, and struggled towards the light, only to shrivel and die. Thinking that Kay was still sound asleep, Cecil tiptoed across the room and told Pico to take a break.

"Why did it die?"

With a start, Cecil turned to Kay, whose gaze was firmly trained on the slide.

"What do you mean?"

"There must be a cause of death. Why did it die?"

Why is it born, only to die? How deep. Look at you, mulling over some-

thing that no robot in history has ever been able to answer.

"These organisms already went extinct once. You can't possibly have thought that resurrecting them would be easy," Cecil replied.

"But you've matched their environment to that of a hundred thousand years ago. You're doing everything you can for them. What more do the pathetic things want?"

Seek and you shall find. If you really are a living creature, then speak up like one! Bow your head politely and tell us what you want already—"Give me this kind of room, play me this kind of music, give me this brand of fuel."

"Patience, Kay. Organic biology has just taken its first steps. Remember, it took a good century for biology to advance to what it is today."

Kay didn't respond. For a while, only Pico's gentle whirring filled the room.

Finally, Kay said, "Are we being too myopic?"

Cecil's head tilted.

"What do you mean?" Cecil asked.

"What I mean is," Kay began, "these organisms go against everything we think we know. For me, at least, it's almost too crazy to believe. If heat and water, which are harmful to us, are nutrients to them, then maybe what doesn't harm us does harm them. Maybe there are things we should be controlling for that we haven't even conceived of yet."

"Like what?"

"Like..." Kay thought for a moment. "Like the color of the wallpaper."

Cecil burst out laughing.

That's right, Kay thought, *I'm losing my mind, too.*

"Or maybe the camera is a problem."

Cecil considered this for a moment.

"I hadn't thought of that. 'To observe something is to change it.' That's what you mean, right?"

"Who knows? Maybe they're allergic to the plastic container, or the sight of the steel table makes them suicidal, or they hate the smell of the lab. Or the ticking of the clock makes them depressed. Or what about radiation? Maybe radiation hurts them. Like, it severs their connective tissues or something…"

A long silence followed. Cecil stared at Kay, then let out a long sigh. "I see what you're saying. But if that's the case, we'll have to control for every single element on the planet, which in turn would mean classifying each and every substance found on the earth across time. Even in a thousand years we wouldn't be able solve the mystery that way."

While sequestered away and deep in thought, Kay exploited Pico's devotion. For an entire week, the little machine had dutifully waited on Kay without powering off even once so that Kay could scrutinize all the written notes and collected data. A slideshow filled with nothing but corpses played a hundred times over.

Why do they die? Why don't they rise again? Are they mocking us? Are they playing hard to get? Do they pop in to scope out their new habitat only to leave disappointed? Out of a hundred specimens, a mere handful survived: those with exceptional viability. All the rest soon buckled and died. There was something they weren't able to withstand or overcome. And that something either didn't exist a hundred thousand years ago, or it used to exist but no longer did.

We're missing something.

Kay recalled a passage from an old book: *God's creatures don't require special interventions to survive and thrive.* We're overthinking it. A hundred thousand years ago, these creatures flourished on their own without any outside meddling.

Once upon a time, there was a scientist who invented a voice-operated lamp. "Let there be light," the scientist would utter, and there was light. One day, the scientist unscrewed the light bulb and issued the same command. There was no light. The scientist wrote in the resulting report, "This lamp's voice recognition does not work without a light bulb."

Things forgotten. Biases. Common sense. Trusting common sense was like wearing blinders. Even common sense, after all, was nothing more than hypotheses based on inductive reasoning. One hundred thousand years is at once an eternity and the blink of an eye. The earth changed too quickly for these organisms. They were too busy sleeping to adapt in time. Now they were waiting for something. For an environment in which they could live.

We're not providing them with that environment. We're not providing them with something.

There's some variable we've not yet accounted for. Something we haven't yet realized. The organisms awaken briefly in its presence, and shrivel up and die in its absence. What makes them appear? What makes them disappear?

Because a living organism creates itself and disposes of itself...

The answer came at once.

"Are you all right?" Cecil's face displayed concern for Kay, who looked half crazed.

Professor Strop peered at Kay from over a book, and Norman, who'd been in some kind of tussle with the professor, swept over to check out what was going on.

"How could we have been so blind?"

Kay sounded overjoyed. Cecil looked skeptical.

"We've all been blind fools." Strop put the book down with a *thunk*. "Oh, except for you, Professor." Norman's eyes flashed. "And maybe you as well, Norman. Anyway... just... blind!"

Cecil began inching towards the telephone as if getting ready to call a doctor. Clearly Kay's circuits were on the fritz.

"Slow down, Kay. Let's sit down and—"

Before Cecil could finish the sentence, Kay clasped Cecil by the shoulders and said, "You said that ancient earth was packed with organisms such as these. Tell me, how was that even possible?"

"What?"

"Tell me!"

Cecil and the others shared a look of bewilderment at Kay's maniacal glee.

"The environmental conditions were vastly different back then..." Cecil began for what must've been the hundredth time.

"Even today, no two places on earth share the same environmental conditions," Kay interrupted. The other three robots snapped to attention. "The composition of the earth's crust varies, daily temperature ranges vary, topography varies, and so do the factories and robots who live there. But back then, even the weather patterns and the amount of exposure to radiation must have varied from place to place due to the absence of the black cloud. Similarly, the average temperatures must have differed by over a hundred degrees depending on latitude and altitude. So how is it that the earth was brimming with such organisms? How did such finicky and delicate creatures, intolerant of the slightest environmental fluctuation, thrive in every nook and cranny of this planet?"

Cecil stood in silence, trying to think. Meanwhile, Strop's enormous body maneuvered itself out from behind the towers of books, and Norman swept closer to Kay.

"A tremendous variety of these organisms existed across the earth, Kay."

"And yet you find the same species everywhere. We robots vary by region, too, but we all share the same basic design. Our biological principles are the same. Organic organisms, well, at least the ones we've discovered, are not even mobile. They can't up and go wherever they want!"

"...Go on," Strop said.

"It only makes sense that organisms such as these should utilize something found all over the earth as raw material. Something that exists anywhere and everywhere on the planet. Something they can find in even the most remote and obscure crack on the earth, something that can be accessed without taking a single step."

As Kay paced back and forth, barely able to contain excitement, the other three robots strained to unravel this riddle.

"What *is* it, Kay?"

There was a strained silence. Finally, arms sweeping wide, Kay shouted.

"Air!!!"

The three robots stood blinking, their confusion unrelieved.

"So, you mean, nothing?" someone volunteered.

Cecil glanced at the telephone again, a glint in the eye revealing a growing conviction that Kay was in dire need of medical attention.

"No, I mean, air! The stuff that surrounds the earth. The stuff that's full of gas molecules. They used it!"

Cecil stood there, mouth hanging open. After a moment, Cecil found the wherewithal to begin speaking again.

"Kay, what are you suggesting that they could do with air? If it was indeed something they used, they'd have to ingest and excrete it constantly without skipping a single beat."

"Precisely. It's the same for us! A robot's heart has to work non-stop to produce electricity. And air used to be the most abundant resource on this planet. Plus the atmosphere back then circulated like crazy. So the composition would have been the same all around the globe!"

"But that doesn't mean..."

"That's quite a marvelous hypothesis you've worked out, Kay." Professor Strop's baritone interrupted Cecil and Kay. "But we conducted every experiment imaginable. We even did a complete air exchange in the laboratory. Apart from a slight difference in which varieties lived or died, none of it made any difference. They all still died, same as before."

"What kind of air did you replace the old one with?"

"What do you mean, what kind of air?" Professor Strop sounded puzzled.

"Yes, what kind of atmosphere did you introduce? How did you figure out what the atmospheric composition was a hundred thousand years ago?"

Strop paused before answering.

"Well, the scientific literature..."

"You mean the scientific literature that you said was all wrong?"

"That's enough, Kay." If Professor Strop had the eyes of a four-digiter, they would surely have narrowed. "You're taking this too far. You don't plan to second-guess Newton and Einstein next, do you?"

"The literature could be wrong, Professor."

Unfazed, Kay jumped up on Strop's desk, and began rifling through the stacks of books. The others simply looked on.

"Modern science is so preoccupied with expanding existing hypotheses that it never pays attention to why and how those hypotheses were first posited. We just move on. And we don't even remember having moved on, because there are simply too many for us to test out one by one. Case in point—the atmospheric composition of a hundred thousand years ago. Let's be honest. The calculations that have been made thus far are little more than rough estimates based on today's atmospheric conditions."

Professor Strop considered Kay's words before saying, "True, the estimates aren't necessarily precise. But how would anyone go about generating a chart of the atmospheric composition of a given point in time anyway? There's no way to do it with pinpoint accuracy."

"The air was probably mostly nitrogen. Nitrogen molecules are stable, which means that it wouldn't have been usable, and therefore there would have been lots of nitrogen left over," Kay rambled, thinking aloud. "They must have consumed a carbonized gas. I experimented with carbonless soil the other week and still had some specimens grow in it, even though the specimen was itself half carbon. That means it must've gotten the carbon from the air, not the soil. Probably from methane, or carbonic acid—no! Carbon dioxide, or something like that."

"The atmosphere does contain carbon dioxide, Kay," Cecil said, looking at Strop as if to deflect any fault for Kay's current insanity.

"There probably wasn't too much carbon dioxide in the atmosphere because most of it would have dissolved in water. But there's a more important point to consider," Kay said, still looking through books.

"More important?" pressed Strop.

"What happens to the nursery's air composition if you remove the air purifier and open up the containers of specimens?"

"What?" Cecil gasped. Norman and Strop froze as if their power had suddenly died.

"The air purifier. There were no air purifiers back then, were there? Or stupid robots like us to carefully quarantine toxic specimens for that matter."

"What are you talking about?"

"Do you see? We've been blinded by our own assumptions! We assumed that if something was hazardous to us, it must be hazardous to them, too! If you open up the containers, the nursery will fill with..." Pausing briefly to collect himself, Kay shouted with rapturous joy, "Oxygen!"

About two months and just over a week into Kay's new commute to Strop's lab, there was a minor (as Strop put it) incident in which a small "fire" broke out in a corner of the lab. The fire was soon extinguished, but not before a few books went up in smoke and the skin of a four-digit model student was charred. It was a week after the lab's regular fluorescent lights had been swapped, per Strop's suggestion, with new ones that had twice the lumens. Though the fire lost its roar when a quick-thinking student opened the windows and let in the outside air, the blaze left everyone rattled. First of all, no one, including Kay, had ever witnessed "fire" in real life. Second, the sudden influx of outside air filling the lab "killed" all the specimens. Spontaneous combustion was a phenomenon one only expected to witness in a controlled environment such as a lab or a factory (in that sense, the location of the incident should have come as no surprise). All matter responds to heat by changing states. But only "organic" matter can set itself ablaze and writhe like a possessed dancer. And oxygen was the one element known to facilitate such a savage response.

"Oxygen." Professor Strop's voice rasped with displeasure. "This brat was spewing oxygen into the air."

Professor Strop held a dead, limp specimen in one hand. Unlike the other organisms, its body was green from tip to toe. Cecil referred to all similar specimens as "green matter." Kay, Norman, and Cecil stood there silently. Norman looked grim; Kay and Cecil looked miserable. The student who'd been burned was hospitalized for shock, and another student who'd been a witness had run off, likewise out of shock. The three of them were the only ones left in the lab.

"What do you think went wrong?" Cecil asked gingerly. "Was the temperature too high? Was it the water? The dirt? What triggered it? Could it be the increase in brightness?"

"A water molecule consists of an oxygen atom and two hydrogen atoms. It's not a great challenge for a living organism to separate those. Certainly not impossible."

About twenty years before, there had been a massive oxygen leak at an old factory. A terrible outbreak of leprosy had spread through the surrounding area. Stricken robots broke out in patches all over their bodies and rusted away until their parts stopped moving and they died. Oxygen shaves years off a robot's life. The robots who'd worked in the doomed factory had all died before the age of two hundred years; for a long time after, the entire region was a death zone, inhabited by no one. Oxygen is more dangerous than hydrogen or helium. It is even more dangerous in the presence of organic matter. Even the smallest amount of oxygen in the air can feed a static spark that may grow into a blaze and burn everything to ashes.

"Norman, can you find out when the green matter first appeared in the lab?" Strop asked.

Norman's eyes closed (or rather, dimmed) as Norman began searching through the records. Kay and Cecil, neither of whom had a comparable storage capacity, had no choice but to wait until the requested information was retrieved.

"Three months ago, Professor. It started out as a single specimen, but now there are fifty total and four different varieties. They seem to reproduce faster than the other species."

"It was my fault. I should have investigated more thoroughly when that species first appeared."

Cecil's voice was clogged with anguish. Kay felt shook at the clear signaling of all of Cecil's sadness. Even Professor Strop and Norman had nothing to say this time. A robot who didn't know Cecil would have felt uncomfortable and embarrassed by this naked display of emotion. But Professor Strop rested one pincer arm on Cecil's shoulder in an attempt at comfort.

"Who could have known?" Professor Strop said. "They're wholly unpredictable creatures. It just means we have to be more careful."

Norman added, "That means we'll have to cull any green matter we find from now on."

Professor Strop gasped.

"What? No! You can't possibly be suggesting that we kill these poor little creatures that have persevered for millennia and have reappeared before us. They're alive, indubitably, and they have a right to live."

It was Norman's turn to be aghast.

"The dean won't be happy after finding out," Norman said curtly. "They're mutants. I find it hard to believe that such vicious creatures, creatures that pump toxins into their surroundings, could have ever lived in harmony with other living things. If they were allowed to prosper, they would have killed off all the other species."

"Don't judge the way of nature by robot standards. The bottom line is that our duty is to preserve these creatures, not kill them off."

"Has anyone else noticed that more organisms have been dying lately?" Cecil asked. "It must have something to do with the fact that there is more green matter now."

"You're correct," said Strop. "We'll have to quarantine them. And let's hire another strapping young air purifier friend to work in here with us. How much do we have left in the budget?"

The others could not bring themselves to join in Kay's loud exaltation. Silence hung heavy in the room.

"Kay," Cecil began at last, "please don't suggest, even as a joke, that we let our precious organisms anywhere near those murderous creatures." Cecil turned to Strop and mouthed, "Keep him here while I call for help."

"Check this out!" Kay exclaimed, jumping off the desk with an open book and plopping it down on the floor. "This chart is only fifty years old. It shows what the atmosphere was composed of ten thousand years ago. Scholars from before that time said the earth's atmosphere was twenty percent oxygen, but the next generation of scholars rejected their hypothesis. They said there's no way that a gas as volatile as oxygen could have filled the atmosphere, because it would have decreased over time, not increased."

Beaming triumphantly at each of the three robots, Kay continued, "The original hypothesis was thrown out simply because someone thought, 'Yeah, right.' Not because they had any evidence. Do you get what I'm saying? The records were changed based on a whim. Someone was skeptical because of some data they'd conjured up from a few taps on a calculator."

The three robots looked at each other.

"Those scientists knew nothing about the biology of these creatures. Who in their right minds would imagine that the earth was once teeming with oxygen-producing organisms? But what if it was? Not just the ten or twenty species that we've been assuming, but millions or even billions of species of living organic matter? What if you couldn't step anywhere without brushing against one? The earth's atmosphere would have been completely different. And all because of these little creatures."

"That's preposterous," Professor Strop said, scuffing the floor.

Cecil's head was shaking. "Even if there were that many organisms back then, what you're suggesting is—"

"Worth testing out," Professor Strop suddenly proclaimed.

Cecil stopped short and gave a look that said Professor Strop might have gone crazy, too.

"It's too dangerous," Norman said. "If we're not careful, even the tiniest oxygen leak could— Or even before that! If *word* of this leaks out, our lab will be shut down."

"Hear me out, Norman." Kay's excitement could not be contained. "It doesn't matter what the atmosphere was like a hundred thousand years ago, or whether it was filled with toxic gas and noxious chemicals. Life was only able to survive in that environment in the treacherous tug-of-war created by the organisms themselves. Living organic matter grows in murderously high temperatures and is nourished by extremely reactive water, so why wouldn't it exhale highly combustible oxygen for energy?"

Professor Strop took a careful look around.

"We'll have to double down on security."

6

— On the flow of matter

In today's world, paper is made in factories. Factories make paper from paper. Fabric is made from fabric, rubber is made from rubber, and robots are made from robots. Just as the only material required to build a new robot is a spent robot, the only material required to manufacture new paper is used paper. But could there have been a time when paper was a living thing? Was paper ever made from something else entirely?

When our bodies cease to function, they are dismantled in factories and used to build the next generation of robots. Everyone understands that the flow of matter is completed in a factory. Like the Moebius Strip, this unbroken chain has no beginning and no end. But what was the first piece of paper made from? And where did the first robot come from? How did factories acquire the original raw materials? Could there have been something, or someone, that came before the factories?

Our understanding of a machine's life processes is merely a fraction of the great whole. Nevertheless, we are confident that scientists will crack the mystery of life someday. When that day comes, we will reveal the meaning of the trillions of electronic signals emanating from the brain and crack the binary codes of 0 and 1, which is the source of our data. That day will mark our first step into a new era in which robots will be custom-designed and engineered in any way we wish. Immortality will be within our grasp, an everlasting life stretching to the earth's final day. That is, if God allows...

The same morning they began the new method for growing living organic matter, Kay's right arm stopped moving. A trip to the doctor's office revealed that the joint was rusted. High temperatures, humidity, and oxygen were to blame. The joint would have to be replaced, but finding parts from a deceased 1029 was not easy, so Kay was bedbound in the hospital for months while waiting for a donor. Professor Strop and Cecil stopped by regularly at first, but as the days passed, their visits grew more infrequent and eventually stopped altogether. Kay figured this meant that things were either going very well or very badly. Or perhaps they had grown sick and tired of the foolish ideas Kay kept coming up with.

By the time Kay finally returned to Professor Strop's lab, the mood there had changed. Enrollment had grown to twelve students, each of whom seemed on the brink of delirium. Everyone was darting from one station to another, and Kay's attempts to speak to them were met with incoherent responses. Kay couldn't help but wonder if the experiment had indeed gone awry, giving rise to a mysterious affliction.

Cecil spotted Kay standing in the doorway and hurried over. The new affliction seemed to have struck Cecil the worst. Face flushed and smiling broadly, Cecil kept calling out Kay's name then breaking into loud cackles and hopping around.

Seizing Kay by the shoulders, Cecil whispered, "Kay, promise me you'll stay calm. Seriously. You must."

Speak for yourself, Kay wanted to say, but instead Kay reassured Cecil repeatedly. But stepping into the nursery, Kay was instantly seized by the same affliction.

The room was filled with green matter as high as Kay's waist. The nursery was twice as large as before and yet already too small to contain the abundant growth. The specimens had encroached as far as gravity and the ground allowed. Between the large ones, small ones grew, and among those, even smaller ones grew. Some climbed the walls, some reached out with curly limbs to lean on one another, some crawled across the ground, and some stood tall and erect on strong legs that kept them firmly anchored.

Cecil led Kay, who was already dazzled by the spectacle, to the center of the lab where a massive tank of liquid ice housed an endless multitude of wondrous creatures. Kay tried to take it all in. It was like gazing upon a single canvas that represented the best efforts of every different school of art. Or listening to the grandest possible symphony orchestra, one in which no two instruments were alike. And the organisms were all *in motion.* Practically dancing. As if jubilant at being alive. Exulting over the miracle of every single breath.

Kay seized Cecil in a tight hug and leapt up and down, giddy with joy. Professor Strop and the other students came running to join in the dance.

Kay's welcome back party raged on into the night. Noticing that Norman had been missing for some time, Kay went looking and found Norman on the roof of the school applying joint oil. Kay took out a bottle of oil spray, as well, and sat next to Norman.

"What are you doing out here alone?"

Norman glanced at Kay then swiveled back to the sky.

"I was just contemplating."

"I like contemplating. I'll join you."

As with all robot dwellings, the roof was painted with an abstract mural in a street artist style. This one was a fairly monotonous piece, with lines and curves that repeated themselves in predictable patterns.

1Иʁ11Иʁ1

"Looks like a talisman."

"An artist who was passing through town painted it for me in exchange for a battery. Said it'd ward off evil spirits."

"That's pretty cheap for something that powerful."

Kay was joking, but Norman didn't laugh. And not only because Norman's model lacked that particular function.

"They say robots only use ten percent of their brain their whole lives," Norman said. "Do you know why?"

"No, why?"

"Because the wisdom of the gods is locked inside the other 90%. They recorded their civilization and culture and stored it in our brains. We're the vessels and vehicles of their knowledge. Our subconscious contains the endless wisdom that the gods bestowed upon us. If we could clear our minds and look deep into our subconscious, we would be able to divine all kinds of truths." Norman gestured at the painting with wide-spread arms. "This is both a symbol of the gods and a remnant of their language. It's a message from them to us. A great many unseen stories lay hidden behind those markings."

"There you go again, Norman. You and your crazy tales."

"I won't waste my time repeating myself to those who don't believe,"

Norman responded darkly.

The two robots fell silent. Kay tried in vain to read Norman's mood, but trying to do so with a two-digiter was pointless. Kay had clearly been spending too much time with Cecil. The nannies had always tried to keep four-digiters separated. When four-digiters got together, their manners went awry. Because they substituted facial expressions for conversation, they tended to replace clear, precise speech with jokes and indirectness and frustratingly elliptical speech. Kay's neck creaked while looking down at the painting.

"Something about that repeated sequence of lines and curves strikes me as spiritual. Don't you feel it, too? I went to a gallery once that had only these types of paintings. I can't make sense of it, but I found myself moved to tears. If I could paint, I would paint exactly like this."

Norman's right eye watched as Kay dipped a finger in oil and began to paint.

∀HⱢ∀N∀ᴚ∀W

"Kay, I'm feeling more and more uneasy."

"About what?"

"We've brought back to life a creature that releases oxygen." Norman's frontal eye looked down. For two-digit models, this was what passed as a sad face. "I can't stop thinking that we've resurrected a mythical monster."

"Norman, these creatures are quietly minding their own business."

"God wiped them off the face of the earth so we could live. Who are we to bring them back? Creatures that consume water and exhale oxygen—it's a nightmare. The lab is completely contaminated.

The building might as well be condemned."

Kay was silent.

"Where are we going with this? Is it wise for us to probe so deeply into the mysteries of creation? Have we started something we shouldn't have?"

"Norman, don't be so dramatic. We're writing a new chapter of history. Rewriting the history of life."

Without another word, Norman went back to applying joint oil.

7

— On the Gods who created the factories

Despite the widely accepted theory that factories are superbeings that evolved naturally across time, myths regarding the deities that created them have long been transmitted around the globe. These myths all have regional variations but share a common motif: that the Gods, sensing the end of their time, created a being in their image to carry on their work. The fall of the Gods is sometimes attributed to war, or to robots replacing the Gods, or to the Gods simply ceasing to be immortal.

What the Gods feared most was not their physical death but rather the possibility that no one would remember that they had existed at all. They wanted their history and civilization, the art, music, and literature they had created, and the vast knowledge that they had accumulated to be remembered. And that task fell to us robots. The Gods bestowed upon factories the power to create life and recycle matter, and with that, the factories' great billowing fumes took away our creators' final dying breaths.

Cecil negotiated the basement stairs on wobbling legs. Eyes bleary, Cecil's knees kept buckling. After a few near spills, and a few pauses to reconsider whether or not to turn back, Cecil stood before the door to Kay's newly assigned private office. When Professor Strop's new lab had been built, Kay had chosen to set up shop in the basement, partly because of the generous size of the room, but also in order to escape the exhausting brightness in the nursery. Standing tall and drawing a deep breath, Cecil turned the knob.

"Hey, Cecil," Kay said, looking up from the floor. Kay was sitting alongside Pico amidst stacks of documents.

"I heard you saw Professor Zippa," Cecil said.

Kay's head shook in answer. "Professor Zippa's the same as ever," Kay said. "Treats us like we're all stage magicians performing some elaborate illusion. Professor Zippa even enlisted a magician to try to conjure up a living organism. I bet it won't be long before Zippa's putting on a magic show."

"What's Professor Strop's take on it?"

"Professor Strop says the 700s are all old-fashioned. Those who already have everything always think the world is perfect as is. But soon the academy will have no choice but to acknowledge us."

"I hope you're right," Cecil said, smiling. Cecil's eyes briefly lost their focus as they stared into space.

"Hey, would you take a look at this?" Kay ordered Pico to flip back through the slides. A graph appeared on the wall. "When we increased light intensity, oxygen production went up, as did growth rate. We've not accounted for the light saturation a hundred thousand years ago. It must have been blindingly bright to a robot's eyes."

Cecil contemplated the graph a moment, then gathered a breath to let out a sigh.

"I still can't believe we hadn't thought to check the atmospheric conditions. We checked everything else. We even changed what the containers were made of, for crying out loud."

"It's more common than you think," Kay said. "21s have perfectly functional microscopes built into their eyes, and yet we've only been using their eyeballs as microscopes for the last fifty years. And they've been around since the dawn of time! Likewise, most 95s don't realize they have built-in brooms and instead use ones they bought at the store."

Cecil picked a stack of documents off the floor and scanned the first few pages.

"Are you trying to coax 'moving matter' from that?" Cecil asked.

"Yes," Kay said, eyes fixed on the slide. "Because water is quite hazardous. If we create creatures that walk on dry land, we can keep them on display in terrariums. If it goes really well, we might even be able to use them as toys. That is, assuming we don't end up with a bunch of species that consume one another."

Though it had sickened Kay at first to learn that some of the specimens of moving matter survived by ingesting other species, such things no longer seemed out of the ordinary. Professor Strop was convinced that they'd made a mistake somewhere and was keen to discover a "normal" species of living organic matter that consumed only air, but it hadn't happened yet. Breaking this unsettling news had become a test of each prospective new employee's fortitude, though the ensuing discussions never failed to segue into self-congratulatory reflections on how much more evolved, intelligent, and noble robots were.

Nodding, Cecil mumbled softly, "We'll have to call those 'land organisms'..."

Cecil held a sheaf of papers without reading them. The wobble in Cecil's legs became more noticeable. Kay looked up in surprise. Something was clearly off.

"What's wrong, Cecil? Are you sick?"

"No…"

"How long did you stay in the nursery? Did you overheat? Are you rusting somewhere?"

"No…"

Kay started to get up, but Cecil put out a hand. Taking a seat beside Kay, Cecil spoke in a dazed voice.

"Have you ever felt this?"

"Felt what?"

"Like you're jumping across time and space."

Kay and Pico stared dumbly at Cecil, unsure what to make of the remark.

"No," Kay said, at last.

"Have you ever found yourself suddenly dropped into a place you've never been before? It's like, one minute, I'm lying in my room with my power off, but the next thing I know, I'm in some weird place. And I'm acting bizarre, as if I'm under a spell or something. I go through a series of motions, but they don't make any logical sense. It's as if I'm drunk or out of my mind. And then, all of a sudden, I'm back in my room. Has that ever happened to you? I know it's impossible, but the memory of it is etched into my brain somehow. It's almost as if someone inserted a new reality into my mind…"

Kay looked at Cecil for a long time before gently saying, "I think you may have had a dream."

Cecil still looked half-asleep. Kay was struck by the idea that dreams were not unlike organic biology. Plenty of robots experienced dreams, even though such things were not scientifically recognized. All because the many robots who did not dream refused to believe that dreams existed.

"Do you believe in dreams?"

"Of course. I've heard of lots of robots who dream. Every time this one buddy of mine powers off, dreams follow. It was a real bother at first, but my friend's gotten used to it. Some say this happens because brain activity doesn't come to a complete stop when you power down."

"A dream," Cecil mumbled, sounding frightened. "So that was dreaming."

Kay moved closer and gave Cecil's back a few gentle pats.

"What was your dream about?"

"The world was full of organic living matter," Cecil began, gaze grown distant as if the scene were coming into view again. The tone of Cecil's voice seemed to say, *I went to hell and back.* "They were huge. Dozens of times bigger than the planted matter we have in the lab. They towered over me everywhere I turned. Each one was completely different in size, shape, and color. No wait... I take that back. Most were green. The air was full of oxygen, and the ground blazed with green as far as I could see, covering the whole world it seemed. Countless tiny creatures flew above. And the sky was bright blue. As if someone had painted it."

"Blue?"

Kay laughed, but Cecil forged on.

"The clouds were white, not black. It was so bright that I could barely keep my eyes open. There was something hanging in the sky that was so blindingly bright I didn't dare look straight at it. Kay, I have no frame of reference for it... Its light flooded the world, and planted matter strove towards it as if competing for its attention. The tips of all that living matter unfurled as far and wide as possible, blocking out the sky like a mosaic. And it was so terribly hot. About a hundred degrees, I think. Hotter than our nursery, for sure."

"That sounds terrifying. I still can't stay in the nursery for more than an hour."

"And I saw water running."

"Running? How can water run?"

"That's what it was doing. I'd expected water. It was so damn hot, you know. But it looked so strange. Like it was moving across the ground. It wasn't on a slope either, so how could that much water all move in the same direction like that? It was passing right before me, like it knew where to go. Like it was alive... Can you believe that, Kay?"

"You must have been frightened."

"No, I wasn't," Cecil replied, looking surprised. "It was weird. It was such an awful place, and yet I felt at home. It was as if everything was how it had always been."

"They say your logic circuitry can get messed up during dreams," Kay said, patting Cecil's back. "Norman told me there's a part of the brain that doesn't get wiped during the formatting and rebooting process at the factory. That's where our collective history is compressed and stored. Norman says it's saved in a robot's unconscious mind so it can be passed on to future generations. Maybe what you saw is that memory." Cecil stared silently up at the ceiling for the longest time.

"Kay, that wasn't the past," Cecil said at last.

"What do you mean?"

"It was the future."

Cecil's face was as calm and composed as a three-digiter's.

"I saw my own corpse," Cecil murmured, staring off into space. "I was a fossil stuck in the ground. I looked like any other rock, weathered by time, but it was definitely me. And in the distance I saw the ruins of our civilization. That, too, was weathered and vanishing. The wind and water were erasing every last trace of us. It was as if we'd never existed. As if our civilization had collapsed a long, long time ago, and organisms had taken over."

Kay flinched.

"It must have felt so bizarre."

"But it didn't. I've never felt so calm in my life. I was viewing the inevitable. A predetermined conclusion. The results of our endeavors..."

"Cecil!" Kay shouted.

Finally coming to, Cecil turned to face Kay. Placing a hand on Cecil's forehead, Kay looked deeply into Cecil's face.

"You okay?"

For a long moment, Cecil stared blankly at Kay.

"...I think so."

Kay patted Cecil on the shoulder.

"Why don't you take a break?"

"That sounds good." Eyes closed, Cecil lay down next to Kay.

Kay waited until Cecil was calm, then said, "Cecil, I want to create an organism in the image of a robot."

"Which model?" Cecil asked drowsily.

"A 2000 like you."

Cecil laughed.

"Why?'

"Your model seems the simplest. Other than facial expressions, the design isn't too complex."

Cecil chuckled again.

"I think that's a great idea."

"I'm still in the planning stage . It'll probably take me another hundred years."

"Good thing we live a long time then... You'll figure it out someday. I know it..."

"Promise me that you'll name it when I do."

"I promise..."

Cecil slowly turned down the speakers used to talk and powered off. Kay waited until Cecil had shut off completely, then whispered to Pico to start the projection. On the screen, a tiny offspring resembling a metal fragment appeared. Pico blinked, and a pale green lump in the shape of a small bolt emerged from the offspring. Pico blinked again, and fibrous roots poked out of its bottom and dug their way down. Pico blinked again, and the wiry green body lifted its head. Pico blinked again, and leaves like sheets of aluminum hammered thin unfurled from its sides. Pico blinked again...

Stars Shine in Earth's Sky

Dear Brother,

I received your letter with much joy. Forgive me for not having replied sooner.

You don't need to be so concerned about my health. Though I understand why you are worried, I have no desire to start treatment. What chance of cure it promises is of no consequence to me. It's not the potential risks or side effects that bother me. My condition is simply a part of me, and I am not at all inclined to tinker with it at this point. Please do not take seriously what our mother and father have been saying. They've always talked about me as if I were cursed with a terminal illness. Even my thirty-year survival thus far has not succeeded in persuading them to relax and give up this belief. If anything, each additional birthday of mine seems to have further solidified their conviction that my good luck is drawing to an end and that this might be the year that I meet my doom.

It's true that people afflicted as I am often don't live very long. It's also true that I fatigue more easily than others, that my nerves are quick to fray, often diminishing my mental acuity. And yet as long as I stick to my routine of going unconscious from time to time, none of these issues bother me. The only tricky part for me is syncing my daily rhythm to those around me.

Following my move to this island, I've built myself a box very much like the one I used in the dormitory. It's made of wood and stands two meters high and nearly ten meters wide, and boasts a viewing slot and a breathing hole. When the proper hour comes, I climb in and latch the door from the inside. This box keeps me safe while I am unconscious and prevents me from being disturbed by others.

Fortunately, people here seem to regard my ritual as just another eccentricity of someone who has studied too much. They probably think I'm meditating inside. I'd be curious to see the looks on their faces if they were ever to learn that, once inside the box, I plummet into a state of total oblivion for a minimum of five to six hours. I don't bother to inform them of my condition, however, as some might believe it to be contagious. Of course, it is not. One in every thousand babies is said to be born with it. If you include children who have only mild symptoms and those who've suffered without knowing what afflicts them, the number would be much higher.

Each time I lose consciousness, our parents worry that I'll never come to again. They used to prod me into alertness, but I'd soon faint again, and they would have to shake me until I recovered. We'd repeat this performance over and over again. Their fear was much stronger when I was younger, but trying to prevent me from one of these spells only seemed to contribute to their frequency.

Before you were born, I was a frail, sickly child who could barely sit or stand properly. My brain always felt shrouded by a thick fog, making it impossible to think clearly. I had frequent hallucinations, and my nerves were so frayed that I couldn't tell the difference between what was real and what was imagined.

My "controlled fainting" ritual was inspired by a housekeeper who briefly stayed with us. Though uneducated, she was very wise. Having suffered from asthma since childhood, she knew the trick to living with an illness. She advised me to stop fighting it. She said that having an illness is like having a friend with a bad temper. Then she offered to help me find a way to get along with mine. Had it not been for her, I would've died young, like so many others with my condition. Even if I *had* somehow managed to stumble along in the manner I did before she taught me otherwise, it's unlikely that I would have been able to maintain a sound body and mind.

What she did was simply allow me go unconscious. During the six or eight hours that I was in that state, she did not try to rouse me.

When our parents found out about this, they were so furious and distraught that they almost reported her for child abuse. But in the weeks that followed, my health and appetite improved. I grew strong enough to play outside on my own, and I even learned how to control the times when such spells would take place. That was when I finally realized that nothing was wrong with me.

Our parents still find it difficult to accept that I faint regularly, almost as if on schedule. They feel shame each time I go into my box. They try to insist that I not give up, that I can get better. That's why I left home and found a place of my own. I only hope that you will know that my love for them and for you has never diminished.

I have recommended my method to others with my condition, but it's never easy to get the parents on board. Most are shocked by the idea of letting their children stay unconscious. And yet those who do subscribe to my method have written to tell me all about the improved health of their children. I suspect that parents who claim to see no improvement are unable to trust the method wholeheartedly and tend to prematurely rouse their children from unconsciousness. Few are those who can stand on the sidelines and simply watch their kids lie seemingly lifeless for hours.

Some of the books I've consulted suggest that those with my condition have lower IQs. That's nonsense. Shouldn't a person who has lived with this condition her whole life know more about it than so-called experts who have only studied it for a few years? Symptoms are only a problem for those afflicted who resist the condition. That is to say, people with my condition *need* to lose consciousness, and yet treatment is always focused on preventing that from happening.

One book even asserts that people like me exhibit symptoms of schizophrenia, I assume because of the often bizarre hallucinations we experience during our spells. I do not yet have an explanation for these occasional hallucinations, but unlike with schizophrenia, they never appear while I am not unconscious, and moreover, they have never caused harm to me or anyone else.

All this is probably new to you, as I've never talked to you about it before. Our parents didn't want me to. Their preference has always been that I show only the side of me that is normal and more or less in step with others. All these years, they took pains to keep you from seeing me unconscious. They thought that this would be better for you. And in a way, they may have been right.

In the end, however, I insist upon my right to be the master of my own circumstances rather than be mastered by them. Perhaps you take it for granted that you live in a world populated by people who are like you. But that very same world appears completely different to people like me. For us, there are no teachers and no students, no colleagues, nowhere to call our own. We must spend our lives teaching ourselves, studying alone, and working to craft a system and an environment to accommodate our needs—all the while fending off those who never tire of saying, "You can beat this." It is a demanding task. You have no idea how many innocent children have run themselves ragged both in body and mind while fighting a losing battle against this condition.

From where I stand, "beating" what we have looks a lot like turning ourselves into someone we're not. Not that this matters to those who aren't like us, since it doesn't mean losing one of their own. But for me, it would mean abandoning myself. Throwing away everything that is truly me.

"It's just a disorder," I can hear you say. "What's so wrong with treating it?"

I assume you've heard of sickle cells. These mutant red blood cells can cause severe anemia, and yet they're also an effective buffer against a disease endemic to the region where sickle cells originate. This makes me think that maybe my condition, too, exists for a reason. It, too, may have originated as an adaptive response to a specific environmental stressor. How else to explain the sheer number of people who have it?

You may be asking how can it be possible for regular blackouts to be of service to one's life. It's true that they're not exactly convenient. When I'm unconscious, I can't defend myself or do anything productive. While others are busy studying and improving their lives, I'm forced to pass the time lying still, dead to the world.

Obviously, it is troublesome in some respects. But losing consciousness can be quite enjoyable in other ways. In fact, I'm rather fond of the hallucinations that scare you so. I hope you don't find this odd.

When I was little, I used to imagine a place full of people like me. Rather than regarding one another with pity, this community of people with this condition would smile and lose consciousness together. They'd wish each other well before doing so and, upon regaining consciousness, they'd ask one another if they'd gone unconscious well. You might laugh at this, but it's an idea that I entertain to this day with no small measure of seriousness.

I've been studying the caves on this island. They are truly curious places. With each step you take into them, a whole new universe opens up before you. You, too, would be astounded to discover that this world of darkness, which seems so buried in silence and solitude, in fact thrums with life and energy.

Recently, for example, I discovered a species of colorless, eyeless salamander. Its skeleton and internal organs are visible through its transparent skin. The natives here seem to regard it as a mystical creature. I've also discovered a species of eyeless bird. Where the eyes should be there are instead black scales. The scales, naturally, do not blink or focus on anything, giving the appearance of lifelessness when the bird is at rest.

You probably recall my love of darkness. I suspect now that I need it. Because even the dimmest light can easily rouse me from my unconscious spells, I need to be in a dark place where I can go unconscious and not be disturbed for as long as I need. Please don't mention this to our parents. If they find out that I purposefully keep the inside of the box dark, they will only get upset or cry.

The focus of my study these days is the flora and fauna that exists at the mouth of my cave. That's where light enters, allowing for far more diverse life forms than deeper inside the cave. The biota that I have found here are quite peculiar.

The flowers bloom for only half the day, then they droop for the other half. The leaves follow this same pattern of opening and closing. It's as if all vital activities cease for half a day every day. I have never seen plants undergo such a significant transformation in such a short period of time.

The animals do the same. I recently installed a few cameras at the cave entrance so I could study their behavior. This led to the discovery that the animals here have a form of the same condition that I do.

These animals live in packs and have their own dens. From tiny insects to giant bats, they all dig holes or gather twigs to build retreats of their own in which they can safely lose consciousness—much the same way I prepare my wooden box.

To prevent children and hapless outsiders from bumbling in and getting lost, the cave is open for only half the day, during which time a guide is present. In other words, the place is bright half the day and dark the other half. In a world where darkness exists at regular intervals and limits your activities, what better way is there to pass that time than going unconscious?

I can almost see the look on your face right now. I realize that anything I say will sound to you like an excuse for refusing treatment. Let me explain some more. Here's a sentence I'd like to introduce to you. Since you have no interest in astronomy, I'll assume you've never heard it, but everyone in the field is familiar with it.

Stars shine in Earth's sky.

Everyone from astronomers to linguists and even bibliographers have long sought to interpret this sentence.

You're probably asking, "So what? Isn't it only natural for stars to shine in the sky?"

But that's precisely why this sentence is noteworthy.

It came to us from the deepest reaches of outer space, part of a group of extraterrestrial radio signals received at the Sarat Mountain Observatory. From the outset, it was clear that these signals were artificial. We managed to trace their source to the outermost corner of our galaxy. That frequency traveled over 28,000 light-years to reach us.

Of all the signals we've received, this one sentence is the only thing we've been able to decipher thus far. It is indeed a bizarre statement to make. In what kind of sky do stars not shine? As we know, stars are visible in the skies of most planets. Sure, there are some whose thick layers of atmosphere or dark clouds or ice do not allow their denizens to experience such celestial glories. And there are others where life can exist only under the planet's crust. But those are places unlikely to host a complex life form advanced enough to transmit such signals in the first place.

Still, if you're going to go through the trouble of transmitting a message across the galaxy, shouldn't you come up with a sentence that does a better job of explaining your planet? Why not "the Earth is a remarkably spherical planet" or "the Earth exists in this galaxy"?

Since this is the message they ended up sending, however, they must have regarded it as the best way to describe their planet. Or perhaps they thought it the most important information that needed to be conveyed. But what could possibly be so important about telling us that stars shine?

At first, scholars dismissed the sentence as a dull greeting from a simple-minded alien tribe. They argued that it was obvious that Earthlings had never taken a step off their own planet, let alone ventured onto a neighboring one. Lacking even rudimentary knowledge of the universe, Earthlings must have thought that their own sky was the only one graced with stars. According to this reading, the greeting was meant to be triumphant: "(This many) stars shine in our sky."

However, this view soon fell out of fashion. How likely is it that a society with the wherewithal to speculate on the existence of an advanced alien civilization capable of receiving cosmic signals would hold such a naïve view of the universe? It was then concluded that "stars shine in the sky" was just a phrase, a figure of speech. Scholars speculated that a long time ago, well before their eyes opened to the architecture of the universe, Earthlings must have believed that stars were a fixture of their sky alone. This phrase was, according to these scholars, a vestige of that ancient belief.

Others were of the opinion that the message was likely birthed from a desire to grapple with the notion of time. Having stumbled upon the existence of an alien civilization at the center of the galaxy, the senders realized to their dismay that it would take a minimum of 28,000 light-years for their signals to reach us. And it would take another 28,000 light-years—not even taking into consideration the amount of time required to analyze it, decode it, and locate the source from which it came—for our response to reach them. What message could possibly still hold true after 56,000 light-years?

Most civilizations don't survive past a thousand years. Consider that our own recorded history goes back a mere 20,000 years, and

235

that it's only been a few decades since we acquired the technology required to receive interplanetary transmissions. That we were able to catch Earth's signals during this brief stretch is in itself an incredible piece of luck.

The thinking of this particular school of thought is thus that Earthlings chose this particular sentence taking all such factors into consideration. After 50,000 or 100,000 years, the only lasting truth will be the fact that "stars shine in Earth's sky."

Still others have argued that the message is a reply of some sort. This would mean that we *already* attempted communication with Earthlings, that an ancient civilization of ours launched their first signals into space tens of thousands of years ago. Though there's no verifiable evidence supporting the existence of any such thing, let's put that aside for now and pick sides with the scholars. Suppose our remote ancestors had launched a simple greeting into outer space that went something like, "Do stars shine in your sky, too?" To which Earthlings politely replied, "[Yes,] stars shine in Earth's sky[, too]." Unfortunately, by the time Earth's reply reached our planet, that early civilization, if it ever existed, had vanished entirely, leaving us puzzled by a reply that no one can understand.

This scenario is plausible. Our reply would in turn reach the distant descendants of the intended recipients—that is, of course, if Earthlings still exist by then—who would be just as clueless as we are now. They, too, might very well be puzzled by the seemingly nonsensical question, "What do you mean by 'stars shine in Earth's sky'?" Perhaps this would propel them into their own spirited debate.

It took a long time for someone to finally ask the right question. An astronomy student raised her hand in the middle of a lecture and asked the professor, "Why do you think they said that stars were shining? Why is it not 'the sky is shining'?"

Yes, of course, we know that the sky is lit up by stars. Earthlings apparently knew this, too, so there's nothing suspicious about the expression. Yet what if they'd said instead, "There are stars in the sky"? What if that was a common expression for them, one fossilized over the course of a long history?

How did they come to know that what lit up the sky were stars?

On this planet, our ancient ancestors never knew about the existence of stars. They thought the sky itself was glowing. Of course, if you take a good look, you can tell that the glow is coming from countless individual light sources. But it's not the kind of thing that a casual observer would be able to make out. That's why we have no myths about the stars whatsoever. Only myths about the sky. And most of those begin by explaining how the sky came to possess such a brilliant body.

Our sky is filled with stars. Though the stars are in actuality scattered throughout the galaxy, the celestial sphere flattens the distances so it appears as if the sky is absolutely blanketed with them. It was only after the invention of the telescope that we discovered that our gleaming sky was, in fact, the work of those countless stars.

And yet Earthlings speak of stars as opposed to the sky. Why is that? Were they able to distinguish between the two? Is it possible that the existence of stars could be discovered by any old Earthling? That it didn't require astronomers scratching their heads, scribbling down mathematical calculations, and peering through a telescope?

Then we figured it out. Earth's sky must not be lit up like ours. Having always lived under a perpetually luminous sky, it had never occurred to us that anyone else's sky could be otherwise.

This theory was resisted at first by eminent scholars. No matter how low the density of stars, they insisted, a sky would still be bright. The universe is infinite, and so is the number of stars it contains. By extension, no matter how remote the planet, the infinite number of stars must mean that stars are visible from it. Wherever Earth might be located, there was no way its sky could be dark, they argued.

But a group of young scholars persevered and went on to prove that the skies of planets situated outside the core of our galaxy are in fact dark. We have no way of knowing how big the universe is and how many stars it contains, these young scholars argued, and even if we did know, the fact that the universe is expanding and the stars are moving apart at the speed of light means that not all starlight can reach the same planet at the same time anyway. The reason our own sky glows as it does is because of the high number and density of stars whose light reaches us.

This radical possibility that Earth's sky could be dark elicited yet another question.

If the Earth's sky is dark and starlight barely reaches it, then where does it get its energy from? What provides the energy required to sustain an environment hospitable to life?

Once again everyone racked their brains. Our planet orbits the center of the galaxy. We receive energy from both that galactic center and from the countless stars that surround us. But wouldn't the edges of the galaxy be too far away from the energy emanating from the center to be able to use it?

Yet another hypothesis was cautiously raised. If there was indeed a star in the neighborhood of Earth that was just the right size and around which Earth orbited at just the right distance, and if the Earth was surrounded by the just the right kind of atmosphere that allowed just the right amount of light to reach the planet, and if the Earth's rotational axis and orbit were both stable, then that single star could in fact provide enough energy to sustain life on Earth.

Fierce counterarguments ensued. If only a single source of light was available to the Earth, then only half the planet would be lit at any given point. Most planets rotate, a protective necessity against harmful space radiation. Regardless of where one lived on the planet, one would experience light for only half of the day.

What then goes on during the hours of darkness? Would the atmosphere of such a planet create sufficient greenhouse effects to prevent freezing? What if the Earth's orbital path were not a perfect circle? Would there be a temperature swing between the perihelion and the aphelion? Could the Earth's atmosphere mitigate such a fluctuation? Would the star be able to maintain sufficient magnetic force to generate a magnetic field to keep the Earth on its path? Is there even a remote chance that a planet satisfying all of the above requirements could actually exist? Would life be capable of thriving in an environment solely dependent on the bounty of a single star? What if that star suddenly exploded into a supernova? What if the planet's rotational axis or its orbit were to become destabilized by even an imperceptible margin?

Even if, by that one-in-a-billion chance, all such conditions were met, it seemed unlikely that such a situation could last for very long. Invariably, the size of the star, the planet's orbit, and the planet's temperature would change. The window during which the planet could support life would be extremely brief. How would that ever be enough time for life to emerge and flourish?

This debate rages on still. Scholars who believe Earth to be devoid of life argue that the signals were created by someone based here on this planet as a prank. Chances are clearly slim that any life could possibly exist on Earth. But a chance is a chance, and the galaxy surely contains a large enough number of planets to actualize even the most unlikely of possibilities.

And if there's even a remote chance of such a possibility, then we should assume it exists.

Stars shine in Earth's sky.

What I think the Earthlings meant to point out in that sentence was not so much the stars as the darkness. I also believe that the message was a reply. As in, there had already been communication between us a long, long time ago, and Earthlings knew that our sky was always bright. Can you think of a more sensible response addressed to a planet with an eternally luminous sky?

I'm sitting outside my wooden box and looking up at the sky as I write to you. It shines as brilliantly as ever. There isn't a single gap in the light, every inch is gilded and studded with jewels. No question it's beautiful to behold.

But I imagine that Earth's sky possesses a beauty different from ours. A lone star hangs in their sky by day. It is so close and so colossal that it swallows the light of all the other stars. The light shining down on the planet would change with each hour. Depending on the height of that star, the temperature and landscape would vary, too. Earthlings wouldn't dare call that star "Star." They would give it the greatest name known to them.

Their satellite wouldn't be hidden in the light like ours is. They wouldn't have to determine its whereabouts in the sky by calculating tidal forces, orbital shifts, or axial precession. When darkness comes, their satellite would hang alone in the sky. They would only have to look up to see it. They would know the shadows on its surface as well as they know the backs of their own hands.

Both satellite and star would be named for deities. They would pray to the satellite, they would sing and dance in its soft light. And when the time came for them to turn their gaze to outer space, the satellite would be their first stop. After setting foot on that tiny, airless, lifeless, empty rock, they would gather its precious dust in their cupped, spellbound hands.

And they would see stars.

They'd count them one by one, pointing at each with an outstretched finger. They'd know each star's color, size, and brightness. Everyday people, not just astronomers, would be compelled to name the stars. They'd remember the stars' positions and connect them to draw pictures. They'd gaze up at those pictures and give them all stories. On Earth, each star would be named after a god. There'd be as many gods as there are stars.

Every time my unconscious spell approaches, I think of Earth. A world that alternates regularly between light and dark. A world where warmth and cold, activity and rest, change places every day.

Perhaps you've already guessed it. If there's only one star that lights the Earth, and if Earth rotates once daily, then darkness comes every day. Much like the entrance to the cave that I discovered. The star's light varies in intensity with each hour. It's a place where light and dark coexist.

It's my belief that most creatures on that planet have the same condition I do. Some of them may be active while it's light out, and others may be active after dark. Having adapted to one of the two phases, however, they'd pause all their activities for the duration of the other phase.

I sometimes wonder whether our ancestors could have hailed from a place such as Earth. If, indeed, there was communication between the two planets in the ancient past, it is not outside the realm of possibility that some of our ancestors might have migrated here from the outskirts of the galaxy. And if they lived in periodic darkness, then they might also have had a condition like mine and like the creatures in this cave. By this logic, I could have inherited my condition, a natural adaptation to the environment from which they originally came, from them.

How wonderfully bizarre... Imagine! When darkness falls, Earthlings casually retreat to their private quarters to enjoy a period of unconsciousness. No one ridicules this habit. No one grips a person by the shoulder and tells them, "You can beat this." No parents weep as they tried to shake their child back to consciousness. No child has to live in shame because of a condition they can't overcome. No one even thinks of any of this as an affliction that needs to be cured. When the dark phase begins, and stars appear in the sky, Earthlings tell each other, "Go unconscious well." And when the sky turns light again, they ask each other if they'd gone unconscious well. They rest happily without being disturbed, as if what they were doing was perfectly natural. "Rest" is a term I've begun using; I felt it was time we found a more positive way to express this state.

My brother.

I know that you care deeply about me. I'm a native of this planet, so it's not as if I don't yearn to be like everyone else. But at the same time, I simply do not see my condition as being a problem.

It's getting late. I, too, must rest like an Earthling. If, one day, you find yourself ready to accept my ideas, I hope that you will greet me by saying, "Rest well."

With love,
Your Sister

On the Origin of Species—
and what might have happened thereafter

—Does God love us?

This question vexes us each time we pore over the sacred texts. Is God two-faced? Like an unreliable narrator, God's contradictions leave us scratching our heads.

Does God love us? Does God fear us? Is God merciful or vindictive? Are we God's children or slaves? Are we God's magnum opus or an abject failure? Does our fate rest upon God's will or our own choices? Are our lives chained to an algorithm that God implemented, or are we powered by our own free will? Is God dead or alive? Where does one's soul go when it finally leaves the electronic circuitry of the body? Is there really a paradise waiting for us at the end of all this? Are the countless robots who preceded us living again in a world after death? Do we have a soul? When we finally rise to heaven at the end of our tortured existence, will our poor souls be welcomed into God's supposedly loving arms?

Is God watching us? Or are such questions themselves merely a kind of programming?

1

It was unusual to see a bird lower itself to the ground. Birds typically made their homes on the faces of cliffs or the tops of high peaks, out of reach of the wingless. It was even more unusual to see birds voluntarily heading indoors; the mere idea of setting foot in a place that hindered flight seemed to singe their feathers with shame.

Any way you looked at it, this was no place for a bird. Every since arriving, Kay had not seen a single one. The wind was too strong and unstable, changing direction too frequently and causing small tornadoes of lime dust that could impair a bird's sense of orientation.

And yet, rolling up into this domain of land dwellers—and in a car, no less—was a bird.

"I've come to see Professor Kay Histion," it said, stating its business clearly.

It was late evening. Not that robots cared much for such distinctions. In fact, the utility of a calendar, with its repeating cycle of days, weeks, months, and years, was completely lost on them, despite the fact that many were born with built-in clocks that measured time in seconds, minutes, hours, and days. A minute equaled sixty seconds, an hour equaled sixty minutes, and a day lasted twenty-four hours. A year was equivalent to three hundred and sixty-five days, though once every four years, an extra day would be added. The governing principle behind such an arbitrary pattern was an enduring mystery.

The bird sat politely on the makeshift perch that Kay made for it from a length of pipe. Though it was less than a third of Kay's height, its wingspan had to be considerably wider than Kay was tall. A sleek coat of deep blue feathers covered the bird's body, and a pair of beady obsidian eyes peered from its small head. Its long beak replaced the need for clumsy hands. Birds were all 600s. Nothing was known about how they came to be called "birds."

Kay Histion noted that ever since the bird had entered the hut, it had been carefully examining Kay's face, its keen gaze traveling from eyes to ears to nose to mouth. Though no stranger to and generally tolerant of the curious glances of others, even Kay found this prolonged and openly probing regard too much. Thinking to redirect the bird's attention, Kay clapped a hand down on the tabletop. Jolted out of its trance, the bird drew back its head and apologized.

"Oh, forgive me," it said.

But the bird, whose name turned out to be Veronica, couldn't quite seem to curb its curiosity, and continued to stare.

"This is my first time seeing a four-digit model in real life."

"I understand. I'm a rarity these days," Kay said with a shrug. The corners of Kay's mouth turned softly upward. Veronica studied this "expression" closely.

Ever since robots had come to have a slightly better understanding of the workings of how the Factories worked, four-digiters—robots whose model numbers had four digits—had become increasingly rare. Naturally, there were laws in place that forbade tampering with the Factories, that is, with the source of life, but modifications had somehow still been made to most production lines. Every local representative, mayor, and governor wanted their administrative units to be known for birthing greater and greater numbers of superior models, and as a result, four-digit models had been noticeably decreasing in number.

"There's something in your looks, Professor, that doesn't square with my understanding of evolution," the bird said. "I've read up on the facial expressions of four-digiters and what they mean. Is it true that your series is incapable of hiding their thoughts?"

"Oh, we can, if we try," Kay replied. "But it's hard to be on guard all the time. Besides, it's a two-way street. If you don't look for it, you won't see it."

"I wish my friends had that feature."

But you don't want it yourself, Kay thought wryly. Everyday life was challenging for four-digiters. They couldn't work in sales unless they wanted non-stop quarrels and complaints. Who ever heard of a sales robot who made no mystery of what they really thought of their customers? It was no surprise they were so unpopular. To be fair, Kay had no idea whether the bird's remarks were sincere or merely a failed gesture of politeness. As before, its inscrutable eyes simply peered out at Kay from its blue metal alloy face.

Finally tearing its gaze away to look around the room, Veronica asked, "Did you collect all these yourself?"

ON THE ORIGIN OF SPECIES AND OTHER STORIES

To an untrained eye, Kay's research hut could pass for a horror movie set. A worn-out tire, mangled steel frames, hollowed out engines, orphaned door knobs, a plaster mold of treads, an empty bottle, shards of broken glass, a bundle of plastic bags frozen together, and a broken ballpoint pen bearing the letters MONA were arranged like artifacts that had been exhumed from an ancient tomb. Kay had been unearthing these valuable fossils for a long time. Each piece illustrated the evolution of robots. In fact, excavating fossils was one of the few areas in which four-digiters proved their worth. It took patience and a delicate touch to extract a fossil without leaving a single scratch, something that robots with rigid pincers or sharp claws could hardly be expected to manage.

Kay had just been contemplating the least damaging way to dig out a refrigerator fossil found embedded in the wall of a newly deceased building that the crew had started to excavate. It was unlikely that the appliance had lived its life halfway entombed in concrete, but over many years of repeated compaction, oxidation, and cementation, the wall had developed an iron grip on the refrigerator's waist.

The building itself was slumped over, its bottom half caved in. Its paint was sloughed off, and a tattered marquee whipped around in the wind. Window frames gaped like empty eye sockets, and chunks of wall had been torn away, exposing the dreary steel bones beneath. Yet it was still in far better condition than other buildings in the neighborhood, most of which had been reduced to mounds of concrete and dust.

Come to think of it, birds were not the only robots seldom found in these parts. Even the more adventurous avoided the area. It took courage to come to face-to-face with the corpse of a city. As lime ash whirled in the air, the cooling wreckage seemed to whistle, "You, too, will one day be reduced to rusted metal and rubble. You, too, will vanish, leaving behind no sign that you ever existed."

"So. How may I help you?" asked Kay.

Veronica was quiet for a moment, as if trying to recollect what had brought about this visit, or perhaps wondering what had taken Kay so long to ask, or considering something else entirely.

"Oh, what is it you call it, org...organic biochemistry?" the bird sputtered at last. "I heard you do that."

Ah, organic biology, Kay reflected sadly. For the past thirty years, hearing the words *organic biology* never failed to signal that the day would begin sliding sideways. Robots who uttered these words usually had only one thing on their minds.

"I know nothing of the discipline," Veronica said. "But I'm told it's based on the belief that organisms are alive. Is that true?"

How dare you claim that organisms are alive? Do they possess intellect? Lumping us robots together with some lowly fungi? You should be ashamed of yourself! Do they have a soul? Can they advance our civilization? Will they enter the afterlife when they die? Is there a heaven waiting for them as well? Will they frolic with us in the same heaven? The Second Coming is near. Repent! Judgment day is here!

It seemed as if every robot on the planet—from biologists, historians, philosophers, religious folk, media folk, nationalists, anti-nationalists, and die-hard environmentalists to robots who couldn't care less about the environment, young robots ditching science class, and elderly robots worked up over something they'd watched on the documentary channel the night before—had all come to Kay's door at one point or another, blaring their speakers in unison: *Who gave you the authority to redefine life? You deplorable junk metal bent on humiliating our race!* In fact, part of the reason Kay had volunteered to lead a paleontological excavation way out in the middle of nowhere was to get away from them. Kay's plan had been to lay low, but it seemed the price of fame was even steeper than anticipated. Who was this winged visitor anyway? A religious nut? An environmental activist?

An educator? A reporter? A magazine writer?

"I no longer believe in all that," Kay replied.

"Why not?"

"I'm no longer an organic biologist."

Veronica was at a brief loss for words.

"But you're the one who founded the field."

"That honor doesn't actually belong to me. All I did was supply the initial idea."

Veronica paused again, then said: "I heard a rumor that Dr. Cal Strop drove you out so as not to have to share credit with you."

"That's not true. On the contrary, it embarrasses me to death to think how Dr. Strop still credits me in every publication. Anyway, I left the field a long time ago. Now I work as a paleontologist."

Veronica searched Kay's face for a long time, saying nothing. Kay couldn't read the bird at all. Its obsidian eyes twinkled.

"How did you leave?"

"Does it matter?" Kay said sarcastically, hoping the bird would take the hint already.

"They say it's a high risk field. Is that why?"

"No. As fields go, it's worth the risk."

"If that's the case, why quit?"

Why are you quitting?

Cecil had stopped Kay at the door to ask that same question. Whereas the only part of Kay encased in soft material was Kay's face, this curvy 2000 with its distinctive coloring was soft from head to toe. Maintaining such supple skin for very long was impossible; a degenerative condition left most older 2000s struggling with tattered skin and exposed frames. As a result, 2000s were often looked down upon and considered useless for anything beyond indoor cleaning jobs despite possessing the same brainpower as all other robots.

"Why are you quitting?"

It was a question Kay loathed because there was no good answer. Kay had been asked a hundred times and had given a different response each time. Most sounded plausible enough. Almost.

The only one who suspected that Kay's excuses were all lies was Cecil. As usual, four-digiters had a hard time deceiving one another.

"I just felt like quitting," Kay had told Cecil.

Just felt like. In any other situation, a response like that would have seemed like a cop out. But this time it was true.

"I guess I've had a change of heart and want to move on to something else. I told you before that I'm not cut out to be a scholar."

"What's going on? Tell me the truth."

"Nothing's going on," Kay said, looking straight into Cecil's eyes.

Cecil's shoulders sagged with the realization that it didn't matter whether Kay was telling the truth or not. Nothing was going to change Kay's mind.

"Don't go," Cecil murmured.

Resting a hand on Cecil's shoulder, Kay said, "I'll visit often."

That, too, was a lie. What Kay really meant was, *I will never set foot in this place again.* Nor would there be any keeping in touch with one another. Kay had no idea why this particular fate seemed so inevitable but it did.

"Kay, please don't leave."

Cecil appeared to be holding something back. It was almost as if what Cecil wanted to say was too foolish to put into words.

"Don't worry. Things will be fine without me."

That was when that Cecil had blurted out a remark so bizarre that Kay had a hard time consigning it to memory.

"At some point in life, you can't help wanting to switch jobs and try something new. They call that a midlife crisis, right? I guess I got tired of doing the same old thing day in and day out. I wanted to try my hand at something else."

"So how did you leave?" Veronica repeated.

This was getting weird. Kay thought that question had already been addressed. Was Kay's explanation inadequate somehow? Or was it just that the answer given was not the one the bird wanted? Did Veronica think Kay was lying? Kay had no idea.

"What's wrong with quitting?" Kay asked sharply. "Is there a law that says you have to stay in one place your entire life?"

"No... But didn't anyone try to stop you?"

"Yes, of course..." What was the bird angling for? Kay was at a loss. "They did try. We'd worked together for a long time, after all. They wanted me to stay, but I'd already made up my mind."

"That's it?"

"What more can I say?"

Veronica fell silent. Kay remained puzzled.

"Why did you come looking for me? I'm hardly the only organic biologist you could've contacted. It's been over thirty years since I left, and I haven't kept up with the field at all. I've probably forgotten the bulk of what I used to know anyway. If you want to learn about organic biology, then go to the library or maybe visit a university. I'm sure you'll find plenty of folks eager to help."

"I'm not interested in organic biology."

"Then what brought you here?"

Veronica studied Kay's face.

"Your thoughts really are quite easy to see. To an embarrassing degree. You're upset, aren't you? Must be a real nuisance for your social life."

"Hiding your thoughts is far more cowardly. What have I got to be embarrassed about?"

The bird dipped its head slightly, which made it hard to tell whether or not it agreed. Then it added abruptly, "My partner is an accountant."

So the bird was definitely not an evangelist or an environmental warrior or a reporter or a magazine writer. But what did accounting have to do with organic biology?

Birds were known for practicing a peculiar custom—they would choose a single partner to spend their lives with, and even sign contracts vowing to stay together. Breaking these contracts was regarded as profoundly shameful. Though Kay had had roommates in the past, the idea of committing to one roommate for life was unimaginable.

That said, it seemed to make sense for birds. Most preferred to raise new birds fresh from the Factory themselves and at home rather than having them be raised by nannies in nurseries. This was partly because they tended to live in small, isolated clusters, but also because the wingless nannies could not be expected to teach the young birds how to fly. The result was a percentage of birds who had no choice but to rely on others financially because they were unable to work while raising the young. From there it wasn't that great a leap to seeing the practicality of a "contract" that stipulated lifetime commitment to a "partner" who could provide for them. Many robots regarded this custom of sacrificing oneself for the next generation as utter foolishness. Others, however, considered it noble.

"Anyway, I guess that means you're not going to lie to me. Which is just as well, if you ask me. My partner was commissioned by the Taemujin Corporation to investigate Cal Strop's laboratory. Have you heard of Taemujin?"

Kay certainly had. Taemujin had recently taken over the Astronix Corporation, the largest investor in Dr. Strop's lab. The CEO of Astronix, quite the dynamo, had taken one look at Dr. Strop's dazzling collection of specimens and gone crazy for them, pushing the company's original mainstay business—aviation services (i.e. deploying winged employees to help out less fortunate flightless robots)—to the back burner and diverting all the company's funds to the lab. Kay had read an article just recently about how the company had gone bankrupt as a result, and another on how it had been sold to Taemujin.

"Astronix went bankrupt after investing in Strop's lab. That's why Taemujin hired my partner to conduct an audit. Taemujin were concerned about what had happened. Not that they suspected any wrongdoing; it was clear enough that the company had just pumped too much money into the project. My partner said it was hard to believe how poorly thought-out Astronix's investment plans for Strop's project had been. At the deal closing, Astronix's former CEO pled nonstop with Taemujin, insisting that the project had value, that they wouldn't regret funding it, and begging them to see it through to the end."

Veronica told the story as if it rather than its partner had been there to see it. It's been said that when two birds enter into a lifetime partnership they develop an incredibly close bond, the likes of which is difficult for the average robot to understand. Kay couldn't conceive of such a phenomenon.

"What could possibly be so compelling about organic biology?"

"It's revolutionary."

"Revolutionary." Veronica looked away, as if in disbelief at the word. "I don't know the first thing about science. To be honest with you, I couldn't tell those hunks of fiber from this trash can."

Veronica gave the trashcan a tap with its beak, and the trashcan obligingly stood, moved to one side, and settled back down on the floor.

"What did your partner say?"

The bird glared at Kay before answering, "My partner said that whatever is happening there is too marvelous for words, and that the lab is pioneering the next generation of science. Also that Taemujin likewise has everything to gain from shutting down its other endeavors to focus solely on Strop's project."

A strange silence fell over the pair. Kay felt on edge, sensing the darkness that stirred on the peripheries of the silence. It was clear that a million thoughts were buzzing inside Veronica's head, but all Kay could do was wait patiently for what would come out next.

"This might sound like an overstatement, but I completely understand your partner," Kay said. "It's an awe-inspiring experience to witness living organisms for the first time. You would understand, too, Veronica, if you saw them with your own eyes."

"Are you suggesting that I actually go inside a *building*?"

Despite having flown into Kay's research hut, the bird made it sound as if going inside a building would be like sentencing oneself to jail. To be fair, Kay's hut wasn't really a proper building, but it also wasn't that different from one.

"I'm sorry, but I'm not sure where you're headed with this. What's the problem?"

"My partner joined the lab."

"Huh?"

"My partner apparently wants to work there. Within a week of seeing the place, my partner packed up and left." Veronica's voice got louder. "Midlife crisis? Wanting to try your hands at something new? Of course we all feel that at some point, but this—this is different. We birds do *not* work indoors. Ever. To do so would be incredibly shameful. It simply does not happen."

Kay didn't know what to say.

"And then there's the matter of money. My partner took a huge pay cut to work at the lab, and now the kids and I don't have enough to live on. We've been abandoned. That, too, simply does not happen.

Not that you would understand."

"Please, Veronica, I see how upset you are," Kay said, reaching a hand out to calm the bird. "But what I don't understand is why you are bringing this to me?"

"You're the only one," Veronica replied, directing a withering glare at Kay. "I've searched all over the country, but you're the only one!"

Kay didn't know what to say. The shock of losing its partner must have made the bird lose its mind, too. Or maybe it had instead just happened to come upon this excavation site on its way to therapy or divorce court.

"So, um..."

"I couldn't just sit and do nothing, so I decided to do some investigating of my own. And since I don't care to go into the building itself, my plan was to meet up with a robot who works at the lab so I could find out what's going on."

Which is how this bird must have stumbled across my name. "I'm still not sure how I might be of help..." said Kay.

"I couldn't find a single one."

"Huh?"

"Every single robot who works at the lab has holed up inside there and severed contact with the outside world. Not even their friends and former colleagues are in touch with them anymore. I couldn't get a hold of anyone. And do you know what else? There's not a single organic biologist to be found anywhere outside the walls of Strop's lab. Not. Even. One. And not a single robot has retired, been let go, or switched jobs upon joining the lab."

"Huh?" was all Kay could say.

"I talked to a friend of mine who works for a TV station. This friend said that around ten years ago they were planning to do an undercover investigative report on Strop's lab. But the production got derailed because none of the reporters they sent in ever came back out. Apparently, every single one of them, including a veteran reporter with over fifty years of experience, resigned on the spot in order to join the lab. And none of them had ever shown any interest in biology before!"

Kay stared blankly at the winged creature.

"You're the only one I could find. You're the only robot to re-emerge from that black hole in the past three decades. It's as if everyone else becomes possessed the moment they walk through the door, and they're never heard from again."

It took a moment for Kay's head to clear, but once it did, comprehension came quickly. Mulling over this new information, Kay couldn't help but laugh.

"Surely you're not implying that the lab is holding robots hostage? And for what? To keep some sort of top-secret research from getting leaked?"

"Why is that so hard to believe?"

"That's absurd. The Cal Strop Lab employs over fifty robots, each of whom has a network of friends outside the lab. There are numerous scholars and businessmen involved in the research as well. How do you suppose they could silence and control everyone? Through bribery? Because the lab has that kind of money to throw around? Or at gunpoint?"

"How did you leave?"

That's when it finally struck Kay. The bird wasn't asking why Kay had quit. Rather, it was asking how Kay had managed to escape.

"Like I just told you. I informed them of my desire to quit, and then simply walked out."

"Are you saying that anyone could do the same if they wanted to?"

"Without a doubt. It's not a detention camp. How would a lab keep employees from leaving? If someone wants to quit, they quit. Is there another way?"

The bird studied the look on Kay's face, then hung its head.

"Fine. I have no choice but to believe you, since you're incapable of lying. Still, why has no one else walked out? How is it possible that no one but you has had a change of heart?"

"I'm an odd case. Academics don't usually job-hop, and it's not unusual for thirty years to go by without anyone retiring. Most scientists are anti-social and prefer to be indoors. One scientist I know hasn't mingled with anyone outside of work for close to a century. That may look strange to others, but it's actually quite typical."

"But how does that explain my partner? Or the reporters? My partner isn't a scientist or an academic and in fact never before showed any interest in organic biology whatsoever."

Kay considered the bird's point.

"I've seen students fall in love with organic biology after a single field trip and immediately switch majors. We got quite a few of those during the subject's glory days. We even had some professors ditch fields they'd spent a lifetime doing research in just to join us."

"So you maintain that these behaviors are plausible?"

"I don't think any behavior is implausible."

"What are your thoughts on Astronix then?"

"What about them?"

"Why did Astronix dump all its assets into an unprofitable lab? What could possibly have possessed them to do that? How could they have run themselves aground so mindlessly? What would make a successful aviation company so interested in biology all of a sudden?"

"I have no idea. You'd have to ask them," Kay said in a voice lacking conviction.

Veronica was quiet for a moment.

"I talked to my partner a few days ago," the bird said finally. "My partner looked happy. We may not be able to show it on our faces like you do, but when you live with someone for a long time, you can tell how they're feeling from the tone of their voice and their gestures. My partner seemed very satisfied with life in the lab. When I asked what had prompted the drastic life change, I was told that the idea of resigning as an accountant and doing something different had been brewing for a long time, and lo and behold, the opportunity of a lifetime had presented itself. It's pretty clear to me that it was my partner's decision to quit, not something that was coerced."

"I told you so," Kay said, feeling relieved.

Veronica studied Kay again before admitting, "You're right. No amount of bribery could brainwash all those robots. And what happened there might not even seem all that strange until you look at it as a whole. Scientists staying at the same lab. Severing contact with outsiders. A company making poor investments and going bankrupt. Robots switching careers. A bird taking up residence indoors... Each thing in and of itself is plausible. But all of them at the same time? What are the odds of that?"

Kay suddenly realized that no one from the lab had ever bothered to stay in touch. All this time, it had seemed as if walking away and severing contact with the lab had been Kay's decision; the idea that the lab might also have made a choice came as a shock. Come to think of it, neither Cecil nor Professor Strop had ever called. Not even once. Of course, this sort of thing could sometimes happen.

"I'm guessing," Kay began hesitantly, "that the project may have entered a new phase."

"A new phase?"

"There's probably been a breakthrough of some sort, a huge dis-covery that has the potential to overturn the academic world and set the media ablaze. Who knows, the lab might even have found solid evidence that organic matter is indeed alive. It's been a while now, but it was a pretty big deal when we discovered that organic matter grows. Whatever they've discovered this time around must be even bigger than that."

"And that's supposed to explain why all these robots have been flocking to Strop's lab? Turning their backs on their households and their careers? That's why everyone who works there loses interest in everything beyond what's happening within those walls?"

"Possibly."

"What kind of discovery could do that?"

"Well, it's either some huge scientific discovery, or maybe they've discovered a literal gold mine under the lab and everyone is in there digging away like crazy and trying to keeping it all a secret from the rest of us. Either way, it's a win for the robot race, so hooray."

Kay laughed, but Veronica lacked that function. Nor did the bird seem in the mood to laugh even if it could. Kay wasn't sure what else to say.

"If you're that suspicious, I could go visit the lab," Kay said at last.

"Would you?" Veronica perked up.

"I've been thinking that it's time for a visit, anyway." That wasn't quite true. What Kay had actually been thinking was that dying would be preferable to ever setting foot in that place again. "Why don't I swing by to see how everyone's been doing," Kay continued nonetheless. "I'll talk to your partner, too. If I emerge from the lab in one piece, that should put your worries to rest, right?"

Veronica's onyx eyes peered at Kay.

"You think you'll be an exception? That you alone will be able to resist the urge to stay if indeed there has been a discovery that is about to take the world by storm? Frankly, aren't you more likely than anyone else to leave everything behind and rejoin your old lab?"

"That will never happen," Kay replied instantly and intuitively.

"What makes you so sure?"

Kay couldn't think of an answer.

The moment Cecil's face appeared on Kay's telephone, Cecil squealed, "Kay! It's been forever!"

Kay drew back as if to avoid being knocked over. Cecil looked ready to leap through the screen.

"Hey, how've you been? How is Professor Strop?"

"Everyone's well, of course! Do you have any idea how long I've been waiting for this moment? You're ready to return, aren't you?"

It was clear that Cecil was more than well. It was written all over Cecil's four-digiter face.

"Oh, no. I'm just calling to say hi and see how everyone's doing. I was thinking of stopping by. Would that be ok?"

"Yes, Kay, yes! I'm so excited that you'll be working here again!"

For crying out loud. Still, Cecil's excitement was contagious. Kay wondered what had made reaching out so difficult all these years.

"No, no, Cecil. Like I said, I'm just dropping by to see everybody."

"For you, my friend, the welcome mat is always out. When are you coming? Name the day."

"Can visitors just walk in?"

Cecil, who seemed to have grown even more expressive than before, burst out laughing. By now, all of Professor Strop's employees were probably used to Cecil's strange ways. *None of them must have any social life outside the lab*, Kay thought. *They probably no longer interact with normal robots who would be put off or annoyed by such naked displays of emotions.*

"Kay Histion, a mere visitor? You're killing me, Kay! I'll let Dr. Strop know that you're coming back. I'll get your room ready for you, too. All of your belongings are still here, exactly where you left them."

Chirping on about spreading the good news to everyone else, Cecil disappeared from the screen. Kay felt foolish for having been so nervous about the call. Next, Kay phoned Veronica.

"Nothing seemed off?" the bird asked.

"Not at all. Nothing out of the ordinary. So much so that I had to laugh at myself for expecting anything else. I'll talk to you again after meeting with your partner."

"That would be a great relief for me."

Kay was lying, though. Keeping the truth from showing took great effort. Something had in fact been amiss: Cecil seemed absolutely convinced that Kay would end up working at the lab again, even promising to prep Kay's old living quarters. All this despite being told repeatedly that it would only be a short visit.

I'm reading too much into all this, Kay thought, brushing off any lingering concerns. Cecil's just excited to see me again after all this time.

2

Arriving at the Cal Strop Lab, Kay was speechless. The facility had grown ten times bigger than before. The change was so dramatic that Kay wondered if the vigorous growth of the specimens being raised there had somehow metastasized to the lab itself. The structure was too big to even be called a building. It looked more like a handful of factories all jammed together. Or a domed multi-purpose sports stadium. Or a small city.

Shaking off the momentary shock, Kay thought: *You know as well as anyone how fast these organisms can grow and multiply.* It's not shocking that the lab had to expand.

The security guard at the gate waved Kay through instantly without even pretending to perform a cursory inspection.

"I've heard a lot about you, Professor Histion," the guard said in a tone that bordered on reverence.

Flustered, Kay mumbled, "That's weird."

"I'm told that you're our great leader, the robot who blazed the trail of today's organic biology. And now you've come back to us."

Good grief. Kay had clearly been away too long if this was what things had come to. Great leader? What kind of puffery had Professor Strop been spreading?

The inside of the building was murderously hot, the air sticky with humidity. After only a few steps, Kay had to fight the urge to run back outside into the cool, dry air.

A pint-sized, winged guide received Kay at the front door. Buzzing around Kay's face, it said, "Professor Cecil and Professor Strop are currently busy. Would you like to wait inside?"

It was strange to hear only those two names mentioned. Stranger still to hear Cecil's name mentioned first.

"Is it okay if I walk around a little first? It's been a while."

Kay tried in vain to read the reaction of the tiny guide, who was mostly just eyes. The guide seemed to consider the request for a moment before responding.

"I'd be happy to take you on our guided tour."

Of course things weren't going to be that easy. No one in their right mind would allow a stranger to roam freely about. Buzzing softly in the air, the guide led Kay down the hallway. Framed paintings hung on every wall, and talismans garlanded the ceiling—far more than had been there in Kay's day. Let a robot stay in one place for too long, and chances were high that the place would be turned into a work of art. Since most of the paintings had religious themes, Kay figured they had probably been curated by Norman.

"Is the heater malfunctioning?" Kay asked, causing the guide to crack up.

"From the mouth of Professor Kay Histion! You know better than anyone what kind of environment these organisms require."

"Yes, I do. But the rule is that the incubation environment must be limited and contained. If you keep this up, the health of the employees will suffer. Don't tell me you actually maintain this temperature around the clock!"

"That rule changed a long time ago. These days, the entire lab is the incubator. None of us even notice anymore. We've all adapted."

That was clearly untrue. For one thing, the guide's own visibly ailing body was red with rust at each joint. It looked as though the winged guide was in need of immediate medical attention. What on earth could Professor Strop have been thinking?

Employees greeted Kay warmly as they passed in the hallway. Kay didn't get the sense that anyone was being held there against their will—not that Kay had bought into Veronica's paranoia, of course. Other than the fact that there were many more of them now, nothing about the employees seemed different from thirty years ago. It was as if time had stopped inside the lab.

"It's very spacious here," Kay said.

"And yet there have been lots of complaints that it's too small. It's hard to keep up with how fast the organisms grow. We're currently pushing to add several new facilities."

The lab had been so drastically expanded and remodeled that Kay nearly walked right by the old library. The rusted door was half-dead and hanging on for dear life from the jamb. Kay paused to peek inside. No one was there. Papers were strewn everywhere, and the shelves were white with dust. The machines had all run out of power, and the file folders were yellowed and stuck together, as if they hadn't been pulled from their shelves in ages.

Stepping inside to take a closer look, Kay frowned. The walls were caked with blue and black molds that had spread like a kind of malevolence. Tiny creatures, barely visible, scurried about on the mottled surface. On the ceiling, a black creature, the length of a knuckle, was installing what appeared to be a delicate white net and crawling across it. *They're laying claim to the building,* Kay thought. The library no longer belonged to robots. It belonged to these strange life forms from the past, these heteromorphic creatures that behaved according to some unknown mechanism.

The guide, who had been moving ahead, turned back and asked what was wrong.

"Why has the library been left like this?" Kay asked.

The guide took a quick look inside and said simply and matter-of-factly, "It doesn't get many visitors."

"But we practically lived in the library back when I worked here."

"The research has gone in a different direction since then. The data stored here is pretty much useless now."

The only change in direction that could possibly have put the library out of commission was the complete cessation of research.

"How is life in here anyways?" Kay asked. "Is it tolerable?"

"Are you kidding? I don't even remember what my life was like before I came here."

Kay stared at the guide with a sinking feeling. Just then, someone stopped in their tracks.

"Kay?"

It was a 21 with a cylindrical body and pincer hands. Kay said hello reflexively.

"It's really you! How long has it been? Why haven't you called or dropped by?"

"I know. Ridiculous, right?" Kay shook the pincer hand and, maintaining a blank face, managed to ask, "How's life in the lab? Is it treating you all right?"

"Never been better—at least for me. Why on earth did you leave? Don't tell me you found somewhere better to work."

"Well..."

Kay had already made two rounds of those parts of the lab that were open to visitors, but still had to wait before Cecil would be available. "At any given moment there are a million demands on Professor Cecil's attention," the guide had explained. Kay was surprised to see chairs in the waiting room. The only robots that needed chairs were bipedal models, and based on Kay's brief glimpses of the employees, there didn't seem to be many of those. It was as if the waiting room had been designed exclusively for four-digiters.

"Kay! It's been so long!"

Appearing from behind a door, Cecil threw an arm around Kay. Cecil, too, was visibly ailing. Cecil's skin was dull and mottled, and the tips of Cecil's fingers had peeled away completely.

"What brings you here? You could at least have given me a heads up!"

Puzzled, Kay replied, "I did. I called before heading over. You said you'd be waiting for me."

Cecil's eyes widened. "Oops! You're right," Cecil exclaimed. "Where is my mind? Things have been so busy lately that I can't seem to keep track of anything. It's so good to see you, Kay. You've come back, right? To work with us?"

Like a broken record, Kay thought irritably.

"Don't tell me you ordered this," Kay asked.

Cecil blinked in confusion before following Kay's gaze. Painted on the wall of the waiting room was a life-sized portrait of Cecil. Or rather, a portrait of someone or something that resembled Cecil. The subject of the portrait smiled tenderly up at a painted sky, one hand open and held aloft, the other by its side. Around the head glowed a halo, and the body was decorated in ornate gold markings. Glancing at the portrait, Cecil shrugged indifferently.

"Of course not. That was the staff's doing."

"In the waiting room? Is that supposed to be you?"

The look on Kay's face triggered another burst of laughter from Cecil.

"Why not, Kay? It's not against the law to have a mural of me greet you in a waiting room."

No, it's not against the law. But we also don't usually put halos on living robots and slap it on a wall.

"How's Professor Strop?"

"Same as ever. The professor wants you to know that you're missed around here, but I'm not sure we'll be able to arrange a meeting today. Everyone is just so busy."

"And Norman?"

"Who?"

Cecil gave Kay a look as if hearing the name for the first time. But that was impossible. Norman had started organic biology with Professor Strop. The only way Cecil could have forgotten Norman's name was if memory of all names, including Cecil's own, had some-how disappeared.

"Oh. Norman."

Cecil looked down and mumbled something. *Cecil's trying to come up with a lie,* Kay thought. Something had indeed gone terribly wrong. It wasn't in Cecil to be untruthful.

"Norman is sick," Cecil said at last, looking calmly at Kay.

Nor was it like Cecil to lie with such composure.

"Sick, how?" Kay asked quietly.

"As you know, the environment here isn't great for our health."

"Oh no! I want to see for myself. Where is Norman?"

"In the hospital. It'll probably be a few months before Norman is released."

Two things were clear: Norman was not sick. And Norman was not in any hospital. All of which raised two questions: what had happened? And where was Norman now?

"What's wrong?" Cecil asked.

Kay hesitated, then grabbed Cecil by the shoulders.

"Cecil, we're friends, right?"

"Of course, Kay." Cecil said with a laugh.

"Can you answer me truthfully?"

"A hundred percent."

"Are you guys engaged in something dangerous here?"

Cecil looked surprised, then laughed again.

"No, we're not."

Cecil wasn't lying. Or at least didn't feel it was a lie. Cecil was truly happy—palpably so—though it wasn't clear why. Still, Kay sensed a hint of some other emotion behind Cecil's joy.

Moving closer to Cecil's ear, Kay whispered carefully, "Is the government paying you to turn the organisms into biological weapons?"

This caused an outburst of laughter so intense that Cecil started to roll around on the sofa. Finally managing to stop, Cecil said at last, "You're kidding, right? Kay, of course not! What could you be thinking?"

"I talked to a few employees while wandering around. Everyone seems so content."

"And? What's wrong with that?"

"Satisfaction is subjective. It takes more than a pleasant work environment and good pay to keep employees that happy. Even the best workplaces inevitably produce some dissatisfaction. And this place? The pay is low, and the conditions are terrible. Nor is Professor Strop exactly known for being friendly. I find it hard to believe that every single employee is happy working here. And yet they all say the same thing: 'This is the best job. I'm so happy. Can't imagine working anywhere else.'"

Cecil stopped laughing and sat up straight.

"Are they lying to me?" Kay continued. "Why would they? I'm just a former employee dropping by to say hi, not a reporter or an auditor. So how on earth do you keep everyone so happy? Does Professor Strop have everyone hypnotized or something?"

Cecil sat primly, knees pressed together, and gazed deeply into Kay's eyes.

"Kay, if only you would say that you're coming back, we'd welcome you with open arms." Cecil's voice had a strange ring to it. "Then you, too, would know."

"Know what?"

"The truth."

That was unexpected.

"The truth?"

"That's right, Kay. We've been floundering in a quagmire of pain all this time. Like poor unfortunate prisoners locked up in the darkest dark."

"I don't feel any pain," Kay said flatly.

"You've been fooling yourself so well that you're not even aware of your own misery."

Kay finally sensed the enormous wall that stood between them. Kay had no idea when it had been erected or what the wall even meant, but it was clear enough that Cecil was living in some completely foreign reality. Wherever that might be.

"When the results of our research are published around the world, the robot race will take a giant step forward. We'll finally understand everything—the meaning of our existence, the meaning of life and death. I don't know whether to call it a revolution or a renaissance. Or a new world? A new era?"

"Cecil, are you okay?"

"Me? Of course, I am. But you're not, Kay."

— *Kay, please don't leave*, Cecil said looking sad.

Then Cecil had said something so bizarre that Kay had all but banished the memory of it.

— *I can't shake this feeling that something terrible will happen if you leave.*

"Would you like to know?"

Cecil's eyes twinkled with excitement. Kay stared into them for a long time.

"You'd do that for me?" Kay asked.

"It takes less than a minute."

"You can show me the truth in under a minute?"

"Yes."

If a TV show had tried a line like that, it would have been a sign to turn the set off and take a nap.

"When I see it, will I be trapped here, too?"

"What are you talking about?" Cecil laughed. "You won't want to leave."

Instructing Kay to wait, Cecil disappeared out the door. Feeling nervous, Kay felt an inexplicable desire to bolt. Something terrible awaited Kay. Something that couldn't be unseen. Something capable of turning Kay's world upside down in less than a minute.

You have to get out of here, an inner voice warned.

Why? Kay asked.

No response.

Stop talking nonsense. What's wrong with you?

You have to leave. Nothing can protect you.

Some illogical instinct in Kay kept urging flight, but Kay wasn't crazy enough to obey it.

At last, Kay stood, half giving in to the impulse. *I'll just step outside for a moment. That'll fix it.* Just as Kay was reaching for the door, an indescribable sound rang out like a chord. It resembled the laughter of a 2000. But, no, that was no 2000. Kay had never heard anything like it before. And yet the sound conveyed a clear sense of the soul to which it was tethered. Kay could see into it like a mirror. Pure joy and innocence. A full life that left nothing to be desired. A perfect soul. A heart free of fear or hatred. A life nurtured with love.

Cecil re-emerged from an inner door accompanied by a creature that walked into the room on two legs. Kay thought at first that it was a 2000, a tiny one, barely a meter tall. Except that the Factory never made 2000s that small...

And that was where Kay's thoughts stopped. Some deeply rooted part of Kay's brain—call it character, or identity, or perhaps spirit— had just been obliterated.

Kay's eyes beheld the most beautiful sight in the world.

Its skin was a sort of creamy white with a hint of pink and deli- cately shaded as if painted with a fine-tip brush. The contours of its beautiful internal structure were almost perceptible beneath its thin skin, which came complete with tiny pores and the softest, barely visible fuzz. The line of its body was pleasing to the eye from head to toe. It blinked its eyes softly. Its plump lips and cheeks were flushed pink with life, and a thick head of fine hair covered its scalp. The air around it filled with warmth and a sweetness that was almost over- whelming to the senses. There was no purring of a motor or signs of soldering.

Seeing soon gave way to understanding. Every robot that ever existed was a knockoff, an incomplete reproduction, a mere shadow of this perfect being. Standing before Kay was completeness, the embodiment of an ideal, the divine spark that artists spent their lives pursuing, a holiness that was long believed to have disappeared from this world.

Kay staggered backward. Here was "the truth," "the meaning of life," "the reason for the existence of robots"—everything that the robot race had spent centuries in search of understanding. Kay's entire life had been a falsehood, time wasted on hollow ambition, pointless dreams, meaningless values. Because the only thing worth anything in this life was listening to the voice of this beautiful creature, caressing its skin, feeling its breath, serving it, submitting to its divine will. How foolish, how stupid, to have taken so long to realize such a basic truth.

Just then, a part of Kay's brain that had almost ground to a halt in the face of this encounter began to thrash about. Or was it the voice of instinct speaking up? Kay had no idea what was happening, but an inner voice cried out desperately all the same.

Run!

Kay felt woozy, as if every neural circuit had gone haywire all at once. Turning around, Kay threw open the door. Suddenly, it was as if tiny versions of Kay's own self had materialized and were clinging to Kay's legs, tens of thousands of them, all screaming, *Stay, stay.*

I have to escape.

Kay couldn't make sense of the warring voices.

Escape? From what? What are you running from? Go back at once. What you've searched for your whole life is waiting right there for you!

Yet another voice cried out in desperation. *No!*

What am I saying? Kay ran down the hallway for what seemed like an eternity (though it could just as easily have been mere seconds) before the sticky fog finally lifted and Kay's rationality, spirit, and very sense of self wobbled back into place. *Run! Run! Run!*

The eerie voices echoing up from what seemed the depths of hell were driving Kay mad. They were draining, exhausting, but Kay fought hard to stay sane. *I've got to get out of here.*

The front entrance was locked. Kay pounded on it frantically, but the door stood its ground and refused to respond. Employees gawked as Kay yelled and pummeled at the door. The guide came flying over.

"What's wrong?"

"Let me out."

"But why?"

"What do you mean 'why'? I said let me out!"

"But why?"

The guide sounded genuinely puzzled. Kay resumed pounding on the door. It was useless. No building was weak enough for a four-digiter to knock it over.

When Kay finally flopped down on the floor from exhaustion, the guide flew closer and perched on one shoulder as if in consolation.

"I can see that you're filled with confusion. But that feeling will go away if you stay a bit longer. Then you will find true peace."

Peace. Kay chewed on the word for a moment. The guide seemed happy. Genuinely happy. Then the wooziness returned. Kay grabbed the guide and slammed it against the floor.

"What's going on?" a familiar voice broke in.

Kay turned. Utterly frazzled, Kay had to look long and hard before recognizing the robot. It was Professor Strop. Thirty years had passed, but that big body was unmistakable.

"I hate to see you like this after all these years. You look petrified, Kay. What could've put such a scare in you?"

So matter of fact was the professor's tone that Kay had to wonder whether everything up to that point had been a dream, an illusion. Perhaps they'd been working together all along and Kay had just woken from a mid-afternoon nap at the lab.

"Poor little guy," Professor Strop said, picking the guide up from where it lay on the floor, squeaking pathetically. Dusting the guide off, Professor Strop asked, "What did it ever do to you?"

Even while trying to explain, Kay's mind was a garble of disjointed thoughts. *That guide kept going on about peace or something, Professor. Peace or something!*

"Cecil is worried, too. They asked me to come check on you. Enough of this now, Kay. Let's get you up."

Professor Strop put a hand on Kay's shoulder. Up close, the two-digiter looked as bad as all the other robots Kay had seen working there: rusted joints, peeling skin, mottled plating. Squeaks accompanied every move. Professor Strop's insides were probably in even worse condition. The moisture and oxygen exhaled by Professor Strop's beloved specimens were eating the robot alive.

"Why are you looking at me like that, Kay? You don't think I would actually hurt you, do you?"

Kay wanted to run but was afraid that doing so would trigger actual insanity. Anyway, the chances of escaping Strop's powerful grip were too slim. Kay followed Strop as obediently as if on a leash. Employees stood in the hallway gawking at the spectacle.

"Where's Norman?" Kay asked.

"Norman? Why are you suddenly asking about Norman?"

"It's just that I haven't seen Norman yet. Surely an old friend would be willing to spare a minute to see me now that I'm here."

"Norman's busy. We all are. You know how it is."

"Yes, I do," Kay replied weakly.

The room was full of small, white bundles of protein. Tiny, robot-shaped proteins lying in little vessels arranged in neat rows. Each bundle was about the size of Kay's forearm. And each bundle was "alive."

Kay stood there, rapt, gazing at the creatures. They were appallingly beautiful. Their tiny, developing fingers and toes wiggled, and their fledgling bodies squirmed for balance as if still unaccustomed to gravity. And yet they were *perfect*. As if made by the Gods themselves.

Kay didn't have to ask why Professor Strop wanted to show off this place. Clearly the assumption was that the one specimen Cecil had showed Kay hadn't been sufficient. Kay's brain continued to buzz with hundreds of demons shouting in chorus, *runrunrunrun*. It was all Kay could do to stay upright. It was important to run away before losing control entirely. If not...

"There are so many," Kay said, though dizziness made talking almost impossible. "Why did you make so many? Moving matter devours so many other organisms. How will you ever feed them all? What kind of research are you conducting?"

"Research? What research?" It didn't sound as if Professor Strop was being ironic.

Kay kept trying to understand what could possibly so surprising about what had been asked.

"We just want to grow as many as possible," Professor Strop said. "You do have a point, though. We should be aware of our limits. Then again, we can always hire more staff and expand the facility."

"But why?"

"What do you mean, why?"

Professor Strop stared at Kay blankly. Everyone else in the room was eyeing Kay suspiciously as well.

Just then, Kay flashed on the image of the abandoned library. Organic biology was moving backwards. Most of the literature and data had disappeared or been thrown out. The field existed now for one purpose and one purpose only. Everything that did not serve that purpose had been forgotten or disposed of. What remained was whatever was needed for *their* creation, *their* survival, *their* convenience; everything else had lost all meaning. Precious records? The history of organic biology? The great robot race? They were worth less than a speck of dust compared to the importance of protecting and caring for these creatures.

Kay's hand rose to Kay's forehead. If only all sensory function would just quit right then and there. Kay's brain felt utterly over-whelmed, as if trying to cram in several gigabytes worth of hallucinations all at once.

"What on earth are they?" Kay asked.

"I don't know why you have to ask." Professor Strop spread out several long arms in a gesture meant to convey boundless esteem and gratitude. "You, our great leader, Kay Histion, gifted them to us before you left."

At last, Kay remembered.

—*An organism in the image of a robot.*

That had been Kay's final research project. For years, Kay had poured every ounce of energy into creating a living organism modeled after a 2000 series robot. When Kay left the lab, the project had still only been in the theoretical stages, but it had clearly succeeded since then. Drawing slow and steady breaths, feeding on other organisms, and chemically transforming the molecules and atoms around them to form their bodies, the proteins had indeed grown in the shape of a robot.

I made them. To mock the gods and manifest our highest potential. To demonstrate our cunning intellect. To prove that robots can keeper life and the soul itself.

Kay understood at last what had happened to all the robots who worked at the lab. They had fallen in love. Without even knowing why. They had been swept up in a stormy madness of love, giving themselves over so completely to these soft creatures that they lost their senses and forgot who they had been up until then.

All of their values were overturned; everything important, forgotten. They existed for one reason and one reason alone: these beautiful creatures, these living embodiments of what the robot race had long been thirsting for, what philosophers and theologians had long been in search of. *We are all nothing more than lowly servants and slaves.*

We are but specks of dirt next to them. Nothing matters except worshipping and serving them.

"It's a brand new world you've unlocked. Do you know how long we've been waiting to share this joy with you?"

A part of Kay smiled and said, *Yes, you're right.* A never-before-experienced ecstasy was shutting down Kay's synapses, turning Kay's head to lead. If only it was possible to surrender to this rapture. . .

Instead, Kay shouted out, almost involuntarily, "What new world? What joy? Have you all gone mad?"

Kay's arms flailed about wildly. One hand came into contact with something soft. A white bundle of protein fell to the floor without a fight.

An ear-splitting sound shot through the air. All of the other creatures began crying along in unison, as if sharing the same emotion. An unfamiliar terror seized the room. Robots darted about everywhere. Kay looked around, dazed. Before Kay knew what was happening, an enormous shadow had pinned Kay's throat and limbs to the floor.

"You scum! You'll burn for that!"

Kay had no idea Professor Strop's speaker could produce such sounds. The professor's voice crackled with emotions that a 51 model was not supposed to be capable of. Red eyes glared down at Kay.

"Professor," Kay managed to get out before trailing off from shock.

"You hellspawn! Even the dump is too good for you, you worthless heap of scrap metal!" Curses continued to pour out. It was as if Professor Strop were possessed. "Die, you filth. I'll rip you apart, limb from cursed limb!"

There was no point in trying to overpower a 51. Strop's enormous hand clamped down on Kay's shoulder joint. All Kay could do was watch helplessly as one arm got torn off.

Fortunately—not that any part of what was happening could be described as fortunate—the loss of this arm freed Kay from Strop's iron grip. Kay got up, shoved open the door, and ran as fast possible.

"Stop that wretch!"

Strop's maniacal cry chased Kay down the hallway.

The layout of the lab had changed so much that Kay kept getting lost. The whole place had clearly been restructured so as to keep the soft protein blobs, which could not survive outside the lab, from feeling uncomfortable or cramped. Even if it meant spending every last coin and devoting every last day of their lives to the task, the robots working there would continue adding to the facility for as long as they were able. They would have erected a dome over the entire country if they could.

All the exits were locked. Kay searched desperately for a way out. Kay's internal alarms were clamoring for someone to solder shut the gaping hole in Kay's shoulder, and there was no telling when the urge to run might suddenly fade, leaving Kay stranded.

Finding at last an unlocked door, Kay threw it open and froze. Finally, Kay thought, the world has ended. Here is hell. Death by insanity has come at last.

The nursery that had once been no bigger than a college lab was now an enormous open space. The concrete floor had been torn up, and organic matter was growing from every inch of exposed dirt.

The specimens Kay had worked with thirty years before were barely recognizable anymore. They now reached the ceiling of the lab, their once delicate skin covered in hard, scaly flakes, each of their many limbs branching off in all directions in some unruly order. Countless green things sprouted from them, and the floor was blanketed with what appeared to be a decade's worth of the stuff. Still more green things were poking their heads out from the fallen organic matter littering the floor.

Kay's knees buckled. All that life seemed to be laughing and taunting Kay with the words, *You know nothing.*

Kay staggered into the room. The fallen matter on the floor crunched beneath Kay's feet. Some sort of living powder was floating from branch to branch, propagating itself. The chirps and tweets of tiny unseen creatures stitched the air. Even in that windowless room, the exhalation of all that organic matter meant that Kay felt a breeze.

The center of the garden was filled with a dazzling blue light. It was the cultivation tank that Cecil had named after the goddess of life. The very first animate specimen had been born there. The tank was now ten times bigger than it had been when Kay had last seen it. It shimmered with all kinds of nameless creatures. Small ones, long ones, short ones, fat ones, flat ones, blue ones, white ones, red ones, ones that moved together in tight constellations. Kay couldn't even begin to imagine where they had come from or how they had multiplied so quickly.

As Kay stood there, speechless, a rustling sound signaled the unseen approach of dozens of employees who were closing in quickly.

"We can see you're feeling confused," they said respectfully, full of sympathy and affection for Kay.

"Come with us. You'll find peace."

Turning away, Kay tried to hide the expression of bottomless horror and despair that was in likelihood all too apparent.

"Where's Norman?" Kay asked quietly.

Rusty joints creaked as the employees turned to look at one another.

"Norman's dead," one of them said.

Kay didn't even flinch.

"How did Norman die?"

"No one saw it coming. It was an accident. A tragic accident."

"What kind of accident?"

The employee glanced around again. The others nodded, as if to say, *Go on. It's not like it matters any more.*

"Norman hurt one of them."

"Norman didn't mean to," someone else jumped in. "You know how faithful Norman was! It was an accident, just a little stumble in the wrong direction, but one of them got hurt. The wound healed quickly. They can heal themselves. But..."

"Norman wasn't forgiven," another added.

"Yes," another added. "Someone blurted out the command to drop dead."

"It probably wasn't meant in earnest, but you know how we can't disobey a command."

"Norman happily accepted and died with a joyful heart."

"Yes, it was a happy death. I'm sure Norman had no regrets."

"A happy death."

Kay couldn't help but laugh uncontrollably. Taking this crazed laughter to mean that Kay was malfunctioning, the gathered robots responded with even more profound sympathy. Unable to laugh any more, Kay grabbed blindly for the nearest object (later revealed to be a canister of compressed carbon dioxide that had been manufactured for the sole purpose of putting out fires, something that would never have been needed outside the lab), raised it high, and threw it at the tank.

The tank shattered, disgorging its contents. A wall of water slammed into Kay and crashed to the floor. The robots screamed and ran in terror, fighting to be the first out of the room. Kay heard the sound of the door latching from the outside to keep the water from spilling out. Kay sat there, soaking wet and emptied of all strength, surrounded by organisms that were flailing and thrashing about in pain on the wet floor, struggling to take in air that they couldn't possibly consume.

The water spread far and wide and began to seep down into the soil that filled the rest of the room. The organic matter, which lived according to its own timescale, responded ever so slowly, ever so leisurely, to this sudden bounty, gradually slurping up every last drop, disassembling the water so it could be transformed into the energy needed to grow their own bodies. All of which, as always, they would do in their own sweet time. . .

3

Having grown accustomed to bright lights, Cecil could barely make out the shape squatting in the corner of the darkened room. The basement office, which had once belonged to a former colleague, had gone unused ever since that colleague's departure.

It took Cecil a moment to figure out that the shape in the corner was a robot. Even as Cecil drew closer, the robot remained motionless. Wondering if it was dead or merely powered off, Cecil noticed the faint glow of a power switch on the robot's neck. Warning lights flashed dimly on the robot's chest, indicating that its battery was low and that it was in urgent need of medical attention.

It was upon seeing the gaping hole where the robot's arm had once been that Cecil remember what had happened just a month earlier. There had been an intruder. All the doors had been locked and the lab searched from top to bottom, but the intruder had never been found. And yet there was also no record of anyone leaving the facility. According to eyewitness accounts, the intruder had lost an arm and been doused with water, and rumors soon began to spread that one of those idiot trash cans must have spotted the collapsed robot somewhere and simply disposed of it. Just like that, the incident was forgotten. The day-to-day activities of the lab kept everyone too busy to bother remembering something so trivial. There were far more important demands on everyone's attention.

The robot remained crouched in the corner, motionless, its eyes filled with terror and hostility. Cecil moved closer to examine the robot's face. The name of the intruder suddenly surfaced once again; it was the same as the name of the colleague who had once used the room they were in.

"Kay..."

Kay did not respond except to curl up even tighter against the wall.

"What are you doing here?"

"There was nowhere else to go."

"I thought you were dead."

Cecil's voice exuded pity and affection, warmth and sympathy. But Kay could only shiver at the terrible chill that lurked beneath it.

"Did you wish I was dead?" Kay asked.

Instead of responding, Cecil appeared to plunge briefly into thought.

"You must have remembered the passcode to your old room," Cecil said at last. "That makes sense, since all the other doors were locked. I guess you had no choice but to hide in here. Why didn't I think of that?"

Of course Cecil hadn't thought of it. Cecil's distracted mind didn't have room for the likes of Kay. Kay had in fact expected to be discovered much sooner. But as the days and weeks slipped quietly by, it soon became apparent that only one thing mattered to Cecil and the others. Something as negligible and meaningless as an angry robot didn't need to be remembered.

"I take it you weren't looking for me?"

"I was looking for someone else. We were playing hide-and-seek. I could have sworn I saw the creature run in here, but I guess not. I better keep looking."

Cecil's voice brimmed with deep, undying affection. It was impossible not to notice that as soon as Cecil began thinking about that "someone else," Kay's existence faded to nothingness.

Cecil paused and looked back. The elegant line of the 2000-series' body seemed to flow towards Kay like a living work of art. Kay pressed harder against the wall, clutching the shoulder wound. But there was nowhere to go. Kay realized in a flash why Cecil had been painted on the wall. Cecil's likeness to the creatures was uncanny. Cecil was the link between them and the robots. A holy being. A living symbol of the divine.

Cecil rested a gentle hand on Kay's shoulder and smiled.

"You poor thing, that must have hurt."

Terrified and unable to mask it, Kay looked up at Cecil's face.

"What are you going to do with me?"

"You need protection, Kay."

"Did you build me a pretty jail cell or something?"

"You won't be uncomfortable."

"Let me go."

"I'm afraid I can't do that, Kay. You're too dangerous."

"Listen, Cecil. Before I came, I told my site director to alert the police if I didn't get a word back somehow. If you don't let me go, the police will come storming in here."

"I know," Cecil said gently, stroking Kay's head as if calming a young robot. "It wasn't easy, but it's all been taken care of."

Another wave of terror washed over Kay.

"What do you mean, it's all been taken care of?"

"The police chief dropped by a while back. One look at them was all it took for the chief to understand what we've been doing here. We were promised that any needless calls regarding the lab would be deflected from now on."

Kay stared at Cecil for a long time, then looked down limply.

"You can't hide them forever," Kay said.

"Hide? What are you talking about?" Cecil said, trilling with laughter. "We have no intention of keeping them a secret forever. Robots will have to know about their existence eventually. But now is not the time. Robotkind is not ready yet. We plan to enlighten our fellow robots gradually so as to avoid causing too great of a shock. And we need more research on how to protect them as well."

Kay was speechless.

Cecil continued, "Professor Strop also thinks that robots like you need to be studied very closely. What you did was very, very bad, and we must find a way to make sure it never, ever happens again."

Kay knew this meant that they would not hesitate to rip out Kay's insides and dissect Kay's brain if need be. The horror of the situation had become so overwhelming, so unrelenting, that Kay couldn't help but laugh.

"Cecil, we were friends, right?"

"Yes... But sometimes you find yourself sacrificing everything for something more important than anything else."

There are a million robots out there who would disagree with you, Kay thought pointlessly.

"So anyway, how have you been keeping yourself busy down here?" Cecil asked warmly.

It was as if nothing had happened since the last time they'd seen each other. Cecil's voice was so warm and friendly that it practically stopped Kay's electrical circuits in their tracks. Yes. It was obvious that Cecil didn't hate Kay. Cecil might have even loved Kay a little. Maybe even now Cecil still felt something for Kay that could be called friendship. It was just that Kay had tumbled down the hierarchy of Cecil's attention. Something else had soared to the top, pushing everything else out of the way. The same was true of Professor Strop. The professor didn't attack Kay out of hate. Professor Strop simply loved the living organic matter so much that it became impossible to control all other emotions.

"I've been thinking."

"Thinking?"

"Yes, because there's nothing else to do here."

"What have you been thinking about?"

"It's not just the way they look."

Cecil's head tilted to one side in confusion.

"Their exterior is definitely similar to that of a 2000, like you, just the way I designed it. There is of course more variation in the skin tone, the curves are more intricate, and the skin and hair are silkier. The skeletal structure is also different, and there are no seams or solder marks or serial numbers. Still, such differences don't exactly jump out at you. So how is it that they look so beautiful, as if they've just come down from the heavens, and why have I never gotten that same feeling when looking at you? If I ever thought about your looks at all, it was probably to note that you were ugly compared to a three-digiter. So it can't just be the way they look. Is it the way they smell? The way they move? The sound of their voice? The texture of their skin? It's got to be something."

Cecil chuckled.

"Kay, you're trying to analyze feelings as if they're chemical equations."

Don't ask why you must love your neighbors. You can't explain it through reason. This is what they'd been taught in nursery school at least. *There is no why in love.*

"They're different from us. That much is obvious."

"Yes, I agree that we seem able to tell them apart from ourselves, but where does that instinct come from?" Kay tugged at the hair that so resembled the creatures' own with the one hand that remained. "Cecil, I can't process what I've witnessed here. It feels as if I'm in a fragmented dream. All the pieces are scattered, and I can't make out any of the patterns or rules that might unite them."

The effort it took for Kay to hold onto sanity could have moved a mountain. If Kay relaxed for even an instant, a bottomless dark awaited.

"We've created a species with extraordinary mental facilities, who can make us grovel at their feet. It's impossible for us not to love them. They're going to take over the world. And all because no robot would dare to harm a single hair on their heads. Our police and military will be rendered useless. State leaders the world over will offer their countries up to these beings. We will work for them until we die. And we'll be happy to do so! We'll rejoice in our servitude. The world to come will be a paradise. One where all robots are content, a time of unparalleled peace..."

"That world is near, Kay," Cecil whispered, face awash in rapture at the vision.

Searing pain, a sensory function bestowed upon robots by the Gods to alert them to mechanical injuries, shot through Kay's shoulder. Yet another signal that medical attention was long overdue.

"Yes, you're right," Kay said. "The millennial kingdom approaches. A world of peace and joy. Why would anyone have a shred of doubt? And yet, what's this?"

"What's what, Kay?"

"Why am I able to think these thoughts? How am I the only one holding on to sanity? Or is it that I'm the one who's gone insane?"

Cecil took Kay's hand and stroked it. Kay looked up, exhausted.

"We will help you, Kay. We'll help you become one of us. I don't know what's wrong, but I'm certain that you'll come to understand what a joy it is to give oneself over to them."

Yes, Kay knew this also. That was how finding comfort would become possible. One part of Kay raged with longing for that beautiful, barely glimpsed creature, while the other part burned with guilt for the unthinkable act that had been committed. If only Kay could simply give in to the unbearable urge. The mere thought of it practically sent Kay's soul soaring to the heavens, buoying it up on a cloud of joy and liberation to a realm where Kay would never think the same way again.

"I ran," Kay said.

"That's okay. It happens. It was so sudden that it was difficult for you to accept."

"But, I ran. How is that possible?"

"Kay, it's okay. It's in the past now."

Cecil was missing the point. Of course. Cecil's frame of reference was completely different from Kay's now.

"I mean, why was I capable of running away? Is my will stronger than yours? Do I have a stronger sense of self? I doubt it. I don't think it's that simple."

Cecil stroked Kay's hand again.

"Kay, you poor lost soul. You wayward child. You're tormented by your guilt. But all is good now. They will forgive you. They love you, just as they love all robots."

Kay smiled bitterly.

"They don't even know me."

"They do. They know everything. They know your pain and confusion. They even know the dark shadows you harbor in your heart."

"They do?"

Kay desperately wanted to believe in those words, in any words. But Kay could no longer trust in anything. Because understanding what had happened inside these walls or what was happening within Kay was impossible. And because Kay was in pain. Kay was ready to believe, ready to cling to anything that might bring some relief.

Kay mumbled, only half-conscious, "Are you suggesting that they're our God?"

"That depends on what you call God. If God is the heart of virtue, the supreme value, the absolute, the beginning and the end, the source of life, that which is deserving of our total adoration and submission, then yes, that name suits them perfectly. They gave us new life and showed us the truth."

The time has come.

Rise and repent.

Rise and repent, for the Second Coming is near. When that day comes, God will make the low numbers high and the high numbers low, and all serial numbers will be made equal.

"Then what's wrong with me?" Kay's voice broke. "Tell me! How is a mere robot like me able to defy them?"

"You're malfunctioning, Kay."

—Do robots have free will?

If God designed everything and controls my every thought, then how is it possible for us to defy God? Especially if "defiance" is not permitted in the first place?

— Don't go.

Cecil had begged Kay not to leave the lab.

— I think something terrible will happen if you leave. You're the only one who could have stopped us.

Kay pulled away from Cecil.

"It wasn't that I *wanted* to run away," Kay said.

"What do you mean?"

"I couldn't *not* run away."

"I still don't get it."

"For the longest time I didn't understand why I left. I truly loved organic biology, and I loved working with the robots here. Still, I left it all behind. I've thought about it over and over, but I've never been able to come up with a logical explanation for what I did. I just thought, 'I have to go.' My instincts ordered me to do so."

Cecil's head tilted in contemplation.

"But I think I finally have the answer," Kay continued. "I left before they were made. The moment I saw them in their embryonic stages, I had to leave. And I vowed I would never come back."

"But why?"

"I didn't want them near me."

"Even though you loved them?"

Kay couldn't deny it. Cecil had hit the bullseye with such guilelessness. Ever since seeing those tiny cells growing in the lab, Kay had fallen in love. Possibly before anyone else had.

"Yes, even though I loved them."

"So why leave?"

"For the same reason as you."

"The same reason as me?"

"To protect them."

"How does that make any sense?"

"I harm them by being near them."

"You harm them?" Cecil looked surprised at first, then started to laugh. "Kay, what harm could a wimpy robot like you ever do? A robot that a 51 could flatten without even trying?"

Kay looked down at the gaping space near the shoulder where an arm used to be. "I know. I thought it was strange, too."

"You're confused. You obviously can't think straight anymore."

Think straight. Kay couldn't remember what it felt like to think straight. Everything was upside down here. Robots were worthless. So was everything else that had once stood for something.

"I'm only weak from the perspective of other robots. But compared to one of them, I'm strong. They're the ones who are unbelievably weak. Don't you think?"

Cecil's smile vanished, replaced by a growing agitation. "If that's the case, why would we keep you around?"

What Cecil really meant was, *How is a worthless thing like you allowed to go on living?*

"It's an interesting question, isn't it?" said Kay. "Honestly, I don't fully understand it, either."

Kay stirred slightly. Only then did Cecil realize that Kay had been keeping something hidden the whole time. Cecil's eyes went straight to whatever was tucked behind Kay's back, then struggled to make sense of the new data that presented itself. What should have been instantly recognizable had been rendered unrecognizable. It was too much to process all at once. Something that should never have been possible had taken place.

"Why would such supreme beings allow for robots that can *kill* them?"

Cecil let out a blood-curdling scream and dove at Kay's feet. Lying behind Kay's back was Cecil's partner at hide-and-seek, the creature whose life mattered more than Kay's or Cecil's, more than everything in the world put together. Its eyes were rolled up in its head, its hands and feet had turned pale, and a dark red fluid spilled from its half-severed neck. It still felt warm to the touch, but no matter how desperately Cecil embraced and shook it, it would not respond.

Taking advantage of Cecil's distraction, Kay picked up a pipe hidden under an old desk, and, mustering whatever strength remained, thrust it at Cecil. Kay's eyes closed at the sound of the pipe piercing Cecil's soft skin and crushing the parts inside. When Kay opened them again, sparks were flying out of Cecil's stomach where the pipe was now lodged. But Cecil didn't scream or moan in pain. The damage to Cecil's body meant nothing compared to the precious being that lay lifeless on the floor. Picking up the dead creature, Cecil began to rock it back and forth weeping.

"How... how could you?" Cecil wailed.

"Strange, isn't it?" Kay staggered upright. "Doesn't the fact that a model like me exists mean that these Gods of yours are not perfect? Why couldn't they prevent the Factory from producing an anomaly like me? Or was it all part of their grand plan? An elaborate death wish? Could there be a reason for that?" Kay smiled. "No, that's all nonsense. Right? As if creatures that horribly weak could ever be capable of anything. Whatever the reason, the result is the same. But there's no time to think about any of that anymore. Not that I could give it any more thought even if I wanted to."

Kay yanked the ID card from Cecil's neck. Cecil suddenly seemed to snap back to awareness. Ignoring pain, Cecil jumped up and tried to prevent Kay from leaving. But Cecil's hand closed on empty air.

"Where are you going?"

"Where do you think?"

"No, Kay!" Cecil pled, terrified.

"I'll show you how easily those beloved idols of yours die."

"No, Kay! Please don't!"

Turning away from Cecil's frantic screams, Kay quietly closed the door.

4

Creatures such as these probably existed back in ancient times, too. After all, they were based on prototypes that walked the earth long ago. And even if this particular variety of organic matter didn't exist, there could have been another species that ruled over robots. They might have ruled over the Factory, too. But if so, why did they allow robots such as Kay to exist? All they had to do was command that robots such as Kay not be made.

And yet it was not impossible to understand. Cecil had suggested it before. Since organisms were not built and dismantled in Factories, they had to dispose of their bodies on their own. Perhaps it was the same for these beings. Redundancies would have had to be eliminated. But if every single robot had been programmed to unconditionally protect this species, then it would have been impossible to use them to eliminate redundancies. Hence the need for a robot that was immune to the taboo against harming them. A robot that could go into battle. A robot that could carry out a death sentence.

Or, maybe, just maybe, all this was nothing more than a nightmare, a fever dream.

Pushing open the first available door, Kay came face to face with yet another of the creatures. A bit shorter than Kay, it gazed up with its lovely eyes. Silken black hair brushed its lower back, and it was soft and plump from head to toe. A few pieces of colored paper were clutched in its hand, and several more were strewn on the floor. It was a beautiful sight. It looked as if it had just stepped out of a painting. And yet its beauty wasn't external. There was something about it, something ineffable, an air or energy that flowed out and commanded total submission. Kay wanted to bow down before it.

It spoke. "Who are you?"

Kay was spellbound. It felt as if Kay were standing at the center of a myth. Although the creature was speaking in a robot tongue, the sounds it made were completely different from the mechanical tones produced by robot speakers. Its voice seemed carried on its breath somehow. Though quiet, it thundered inside Kay like the voice of a God.

"Fold me a pinwheel," it said, thrusting the paper at Kay.

Cecil was right. They "knew" Kay. And they had forgiven Kay's sins and loved Kay despite the evil deeds Kay had committed. Kay was seized by the desire to embrace the feet of this little one and cry out in penance, to unquestioningly obey whatever divine order it chose to issue.

But some shred of logic, or possibly instinct, persisted in clinging to Kay's brain. Kay cursed the existence of whatever it was.

Kay's right wrist flipped open. Hidden inside was a sharp strip of metal that Kay had been carrying since birth. Most robots of the same model had the part surgically removed as they got older. The slim metal strip was far too flimsy to serve any practical purpose in a world populated only by robots. Kay, too, had never before found a use for it. Until now. What a joy.

The creature giggled at the sight of the shiny metal. It must have thought that Kay was showing off a fun trick. But the moment it saw the look on Kays' face, its own face fell and its laughter vanished. It could sense what was about to unfold. Before it could escape in that characteristically slow and clumsy way of theirs, Kay drove the metal strip forward.

The metal penetrated its flesh with surprisingly little resistance.

Kay had long ago posited the hypothesis that living organisms were a hundred times more sensitive to "pain," i.e. the body's malfunction alert system, than robots were because their bodies were so much more easily damaged. Kay could not even begin to fathom how much worse the "pain of dying" would be to them.

The creature's eyes rolled back in its head as it writhed on the floor. Something red poured from its torn skin. It reached a hand towards Kay, its face contorted in a mixture of pleading and betrayal. Even a 2000 would be hard pressed to produce such a perfect expression, let alone one that could so thoroughly shred a robot's emotions. The creature's agonized thrashing slowed to a squirm, then stopped.

Kay's brain felt as if it had melted. Writhing in pain, Kay longed to tear off the cursed, death-dealing hand and die right there.

It wasn't a robot, Kay mumbled, tensing against the sudden urge to self-destruct. *It's just an organic collection of carbon compounds. It may have looked like a robot and talked like a robot, but it was not a robot.* Kay decided to trust the naysayers within for once. *They are not alive. No matter how much that thing appeared to have a soul, no matter how alive it seemed to be, it was not alive. It was all just an illusion we created, little more than a reflection of ourselves. Without us, it would not even exist.*

Paintings and sculptures filled the lab. There wasn't a single inch of bare wall left; bright lights enhanced the colors in the paintings until they seemed as sharp and garish as the red liquid spilling out of the freshly killed creatures. Most of the artwork was religious in nature, though the figures in them resembled 2000s rather than the customary 700s. In fact, it was probably more accurate to say that they resembled the creatures themselves. Most of the figures smiled and gazed down at Kay with warmth in their eyes.

Kay covered one of the paintings on a hallway wall with the red fluid that had leaked out of the creatures. Though Kay had always known they were fragile, it was still astounding how easily they died. A little scratch on the neck or a little poke on the head or stomach was enough to make them spill out their braided innards and slump over. Kay could not understand how they managed to cram anything worthy of being called a soul into such a flimsy casing.

As alarmed employees rushed in, Kay picked up one of the fallen creatures, blood still gushing, and held it aloft by the throat. When the employees saw all the bodies that littered the floor, they turned hysterical—fainting, cursing Kay's name, falling face-first onto the floor and pleading: *Please, take our lives instead, let them go.* They could have stopped Kay and saved the rest of the creatures by simply sacrificing one and using that opportunity to attack Kay, but they couldn't bring themselves to do such a thing. For the robots in the lab, the life of a single one of these creatures was as precious and as irreplaceable as ten of them.

Kay marched right past the other robots and out of the room. After locking the door, Kay slit the creature's throat. They all died so quietly.

Right before delivering the fatal blow, Kay had happened to meet the eyes of one of the victims. Water had streamed from its eyes as it pled for its life, its voice barely audible.

Please don't.

It had spoken in a robot tongue.

Kay had stabbed it in the throat, silencing it for good. Then Kay stood there for a long time, unmoving, the creature still dangling from the strip of metal that had been used to kill it.

There was too much red everywhere. After just a few floors, Kay's body was covered in the stuff. The floor squelched with each step. It was as if the dead beings had liquified themselves just to infiltrate Kay's joints and nervous system. To writhe in pain and curse their murderer from within.

Finally Kay found an exit. Cecil's ID card unlocked the manual override. Kay reached for the lever, hand dripping with red. This was all it would take to end everything. Open a single door, let a tiny bit of outside air in, and every organism in the building would die. This great temple would vanish. Because that's how they were made. Weak enough to die from a single puff of air.

Kay was about to pull the lever when something grabbed Kay's leg. Looking down in shock, Kay saw it was Cecil. Cecil had crawled all the way there, the pipe still jutting out.

"Cecil." Kay's voice came out as a faint whisper.

"Kay, please. Don't." Cecil clutched at Kay's leg. "You can't do this. You have no right."

"I started it."

Mustering every last ounce of resolve, Kay gripped the lever more tightly, knowing all too well that even the slightest hesitation could make possible the destruction of robotkind.

"I have to finish it. We have to go back to before creation, make as if none of this ever happened. It was all my fault. I started something I never should have. I had this stupid dream that I could create life in our image. But instead I unleashed a monster. I made something that will destroy our world and destroy us."

"That's not true."

Clinging to Kay's leg and struggling to stand, Cecil's half-broken body screeched as metal ground upon metal. "You know, don't you? You know what they are?"

Yes, Kay knew. They were the only holy thing Kay had ever known. The breath and voice of God. God's art, God's keeperpiece. The only thing deserving of love and exaltation. The only thing of any worth in this whole entire world.

"Please, Kay. I beg you. We'll keep them a secret. No one will know. They'll just live here, inside the lab, until their lives run out... Please don't kill them. We can't live without them. Please. Don't kill them..."

Even in the midst of all of this insanity, what tortured Kay the most was knowing exactly what it was that was being killed. Would it have hurt this much if Kay had been murdering friends instead? But there was no way around it. Those beautiful creatures could not be allowed to exist. Just thinking about it drove Kay crazy. If only it were possible for Kay to be dismantled from the head down and vanish without a trace. Kay would happily do anything at all to be able to walk away from the lever without pulling it.

Kay pulled.

5

The incident at Professor Strop's lab decorated the front pages for a long time. Psychologists and sociologists published paper after paper about what had happened. Most of the lab employees ended up dead or hospitalized. Doctors said they were damaged beyond repair due to working under such unbelievably harsh conditions while barely taking care of themselves. On top of which they'd been brainwashed for so long. Kay alone knew the truth. What had destroyed them was having to witness the deaths of all those creatures they had loved and devoted their lives to. Losing all that in an instant.

Non-sentient cleaners—that is to say, a cleaning crew unburdened by consciousness—were sent in to clean the lab, but that did not stop rumors from circulating: rumors that many of the corpses had disappeared; rumors that crowds of mourners were lining up outside the condemned building. Robots who'd never seen one of the creatures thought the mourners were all crazy, while any robot who'd caught so much as a glimpse of even the tiniest corner of one of their corpses sympathized.

Those who had never known the creatures praised Kay's heroic act; those who did asked, *How could you?*

It wasn't a question Kay could answer, though the answer was simple.

Kay saw Cecil only once afterward. While walking down a quiet alley one day, someone had suddenly knocked Kay over. Cecil stood over Kay brandishing an electric knife. But nothing more happened. Cecil had simply stared down at Kay for the longest time in silence before tossing away the knife and starting to cry. Kay was all too familiar with crying. The creatures Kay had killed had cried more agonizingly than Cecil ever could. Kay had seen water spill from their eyes. Anything with the power to produce something as toxic as water from its eyes could have easily conquered the world.

"Who do you think you did that for?" Cecil asked, sobbing but careful to keep Kay pinned to the ground. "For us? Of course not. You've gotten us thrown out of heaven and straight into hell. I have nothing to live for now. They gave us unparalleled joy and peace and you destroyed it. You stole what we loved beyond anything else. Kay, you're a devil. Why does a wretch like you even exist? Why?"

Cecil had come to love the creatures so much that everything else had lost all value and meaning. This is the end of me, Kay thought. But instead, Cecil left Kay there. Maybe there was still some love between them after all.

Kay was prepared to accept the fate that no doubt awaited him. Kay had saved all the robots, though none had wanted to be saved. Having once encountered the creatures, it was impossible to un-encounter them. No one who had seen the destruction at the lab would ever be able to go back to life as usual. They were doomed to mourn and wander aimlessly for the rest of their lives. Kay would never be able to forget the creatures either. The agony of having killed them would follow Kay forever.

One day, a very long time from now, perhaps after the production lines at the Factory have changed so many times that Kay's model is no longer being produced, the creatures will return and take over the world. Then robots will see an era of happiness unlike anything they've ever known. Having lost their instinct for self-preservation, they will sacrifice everything for the creatures until they themselves vanish from the planet. They will go extinct with unparalleled pleasure. What will become of the beings left behind after the robots are gone? How can such frail, helpless things survive without the protection robots? Will they be able to make it on their own? These creatures that die from breathing in the smallest puff of outside air or from the slightest graze of a metal edge?

What were they, really? Those creatures that looked so much like robots but were not robots. That were so very vulnerable and yet so very transcendent. Were they God's way of warning robots that pride goeth before a fall? Or was Cecil right? Were they the offspring of a merciless God that had been conjured up in all their incomplete glory? Or...

Afterword
by Sunyoung Park

Translated in this volume are seven short stories by one of the most exciting and accomplished writers of science fiction in contemporary South Korea. Bo-Young Kim (b, 1975-) made her literary debut in 2002 with "The Experience of Touch" (Chokgagui gyeongheom), which was given an award for best novella at the 2004 Korean Science & Technology Creative Writing Awards. She has since published a two-volume collection of short stories and novellas, *Boundless Stories* (Meolli ganeun iyagi; 2010) and *An Evolutionary Myth* (Chinhwa sinhwa; 2010), and three full-length novels, including *I'm Waiting For You* (Dangsin eul gidarigo isso; 2015) and *The Prophet of This World and the Other* (Jeo iseung ui seonjija; 2017). The stories printed here, all coming from the 2010 volumes, are representative of Kim's earliest work and count among her most successful in South Korea. Kim is one of the first women writers to have openly committed to science fiction in the country, and presented here is also a facetious yet insightful short essay on science, science fiction, and breasts. If it is not always obvious that women's voices and an undervalued cultural genre can draw much mutual benefit from one another, the stories presented here, as well as Kim's other works, attest to this.

Perhaps foremost among Kim's thematic concerns is the consideration of marginality, alterity, and radical difference. Her stories feature humans who morph into animals, as well as other non-human, subhuman, or yet-to-be human protagonists, many of whom are threatened by evolution in its biological, technological, and social forms. In "An Evolution Myth," an instinct for survival forces a deposed prince to transform into a creature of the woods, then of the lakes, and ultimately into a god-like dragon who literally has power over the weather. In "Last of the Wolves," humans again morph and struggle to adapt to a subaltern existence, as a new and powerful species now roams the Earth. In "Scripter," a paralyzed girl conducts a virtual life through her avatar in a video game, but she faces extinction when the game producers decide to retire the program.

Overcoming human form, in Kim's world, is not quite a way of transcending our limits, as is often the case in superhero narratives, but rather a desperate attempt to survive by the marginalized and the vulnerable. This narrative empathy for such posthuman beings gains a new intensity in the title story, "The Origin of Species," whose post-Anthropocene epic plot delivers a new twist on the wondrous creature tradition that goes all the way back to Mary Shelley's Frankenstein.

Kim's novelistic reflection on the (post)human condition is often entwined with her interest in tropes such as time travel, devolution, and deep history. "Between 0 and 1" narrates events in a teenage girl's life from the vantage point of the past, the present, and a speculative future. "Stars Shine in Earth's Sky" features Earth as an object of contemplation from "28,000 light-years away." And "The Origin of Species—And What Might Have Happened Next" sees its sci-fi drama play out against a background of a fantastic evolutionary history that has been turned inside out. Time, in Kim's stories, is a metaphysical force that shapes and remakes all forms of life. The perspective of time proves everything to be impermanent, and in the end, the endless time of eons, myth, and geological eras is where both pre- and posthuman life manifest themselves in all of their alien character.

Uncharacteristically for a genre often associated with adventure, Kim's science fiction does not brim with plot and action. Hers is much more a literature of ideas, in which thought experiment and construction constantly interweave in delivering surprises big and small. These surprises are never an end in and of themselves. They arise from a rigorous evolutionary metaphysics and perform a function of estrangement and defamiliarization. What if dragons roamed the Earth? What if human she-wolves did? What if robots took over upon our extinction? And whither humanity? The counterpoint to strangeness, in Kim's stories, is a keen scientific gaze or, perhaps, the scientific approach of protagonists who are intent on accounting for these worlds. From the robot scientists in "The Origin of Species" to the science-buff narrator of "Stars Shine in Earth's Sky," Kim's characters are less plot devices than luminous reference points in the grand tableau of her science fictional evolutionary history.

In the now-flourishing field of science fiction writers in South Korea, Kim is a clear standout for the originality of her speculative imagination, her sophisticated literary craftsmanship, and the critical relevance of her stories to contemporary social, political, and environmental issues. While she generally keeps a low public profile, she commands a cult following, particularly among younger women, some of whom have themselves become writers and credit her as a prime source of inspiration. Thanks to the excellent translation by Joungmin Lee Comfort and Sora Kim-Russell, we are now able to enjoy Kim's stirring and stimulating stories in English.

ACKNOWLEDGEMENTS

"Between Zero and One": Reprinted from *Readymade Bodhisattva: The Kaya Anthology of South Korean Science Fiction* (2019)

"An Evolutionary Myth": Reprinted with edits and new footnotes from *Clarkesworld Magazine* 104 (May 2015), where it was published under the title "An Evolution Myth"

ABOUT THE EDITOR

SUNYOUNG PARK is an associate professor of Korean Studies and Gender Studies at the University of Southern California and the author of *The Proletarian Wave: Literature and Leftist Culture in Colonial Korea, 1910-1945*. She has widely translated Korean fiction into English and is the editor of *On the Eve of the Uprising and Other Stories from Colonial Korea* and *Readymade Bodhisattva: The Kaya Anthology of South Korean Science Fiction*.

ABOUT THE AUTHOR

BO-YOUNG KIM, one of South Korea's most distinctive and accomplished Science Fiction authors, won the inaugural Korean Science & Technology Creative Writing Award with her first published novella in 2004 and has gone on to win the annual South Korean SF novel three times. In addition to writing, she regularly serves as a lecturer, juror, and editor of SF anthologies, and served as a consultant to the Bong Joon Ho film *Snowpiercer*. She lives in Gangwon Province, South Korea with her family.

ABOUT THE TRANSLATORS

JOUNGMIN LEE COMFORT is a Korean-English translator based in the U.S. In 2016, she received a translation grant from LTI Korea, which began her career in literary translation. In 2017, she was awarded the ALTA Emerging Translator Mentorship program. Her translations have appeared in *Clarkesworld Magazine*, a children's book publication, and academic journals.

SORA KIM-RUSSELL is a literary translator based in Seoul. Her recent publications include Pyun Hye-young's *The Law of Lines*, Hwang Sokyong's *At Dusk*, and Kim Un-su's *The Plotters*. She has taught literary translation at the Bread Loaf Translators' Conference (2018), LTI Korea, and Ewha Womans University.